'You have a name. It's Anne.'

'Anne,' she said. 'It's a pretty name. But it doesn't somehow sound quite right…'

'It will do for the moment,' James said firmly.

'There's something else, Lord Aldhurst…'

'What is it?'

'You said…you told that doctor that he might be in danger if he took me in. What did you mean?'

'I didn't want an argument about where you should stay, that's all.'

She shook her head. 'Please be honest with me! What *are* these marks on my wrist? I *have* been tied up, haven't I?'

'It looks like it.'

'So there *is* danger… I knew it. I have this feeling…of some kind of threat… But I don't know what it is!' She held her head in her hands. After a few moments she looked up again. 'Why can't I remember?'

James heard the beginning of panic in her voice and said, 'Stop! It won't do you any good, Anne. And you can forget about danger. I told you last night—you're perfectly safe here. Or…do you not trust me?'

'Of course I trust you. I have to. There's no one else.'

Sylvia Andrew has an Honours Degree in Modern Languages from University College, London, and before ending up as Vice-Principal of a large comprehensive sixth form college taught English for foreigners in Switzerland, Cambridge and in Compton Park, an international finishing school for young ladies, which was housed in a beautiful country mansion leased from the Devonshire family. The house and grounds have provided inspiration for several settings in her novels. She and her husband Simon now live in a small market town in the west of England, which is full of the Georgian architecture they both love. And just a few miles from their home is the marvellous Dorset Jurassic Coast World Heritage Site. In 2000 Sylvia wrote a historical celebration of the town's splendid fifteenth-century parish church in a millennium *son et lumière*, which was a great success.

She and Simon belong to the Georgian Group, the National Trust and English Heritage, all of which help them to satisfy their love of historic houses and wonderful landscapes. Simon lectures all over the place on architecture and wild orchids, while Sylvia tries to do nothing, and usually fails, since she is heavily involved in the local museum. She just can't keep away from old maps, newspapers, photographs and census returns! Her other passion is theatre performances of Shakespeare. She and Simon have one married daughter, whom they visit quite often, and a very precious grandson called Joe.

Novels by Sylvia Andrew:

LORD CALTHORPE'S PROMISE
LORD TRENCHARD'S CHOICE
COLONEL ANCROFT'S LOVE
A VERY UNUSUAL GOVERNESS
THE BRIDEGROOM'S BARGAIN
MISS WINBOLT AND THE FORTUNE HUNTER

And in the Regency series *The Steepwood Scandal*:

AN UNREASONABLE MATCH
AN INESCAPABLE MATCH

REAWAKENING MISS CALVERLEY

Sylvia Andrew

First published in Great Britain 2010
Large Print edition 2011
Harlequin Mills & Boon Limited,
Eton House, 18-24 Paradise Road, Richmond, Surrey TW9 1SR

© Sylvia Andrew 2010

ISBN: 978 0 263 21851 0

Harlequin Mills & Boon policy is to use papers that are natural, renewable and recyclable products and made from wood grown in sustainable forests. The logging and manufacturing process conform to the legal environmental regulations of the country of origin.

Printed and bound in Great Britain
by CPI Antony Rowe, Chippenham, Wiltshire

REAWAKENING
MISS CALVERLEY

Chapter One

A sudden gust of wind blew a spatter of rain into James Aldhurst's face. He pulled up the collar of his greatcoat and rode on, cursing in turn the weather and his own stupidity. If he had had a grain of common sense he would now have been sitting before a roaring fire in Norris's inn on the Portsmouth Road, a glass of the landlord's famous punch in his hands, and every prospect of a good dinner for himself and Sam Trott. And a comfortable bed to follow. Instead, for the last hour or more he and Sam had been battling against wind and rain, picking their way through mud and stones loosened by the storm, as they rode along the narrow lane leading to Hatherton. He should have paid more heed to Norris's warnings. This was no night to be out. Behind him he could hear his groom grumbling under his breath, no doubt saying much the same to himself. Why on earth had he allowed his grandmother to send him here at this time of year? Here he was, riding through probably the worst storm for years, and wishing with all his heart that he had ignored her and waited for better weather.

After a few minutes he noticed with relief that they were passing the crossroads that lay only a mile or so before the entrance to Hatherton. Before long this nightmare journey would be over and he would be enjoying the usual warm welcome from his grandmother's household, people who had known him all his life. His gloom lifted for a moment as a shaft of moonlight broke through the clouds. It could be a sign that the storm was at last easing. They quickened their pace, and it wasn't long before they were encouraged by the sight of a familiar drive leading off to the right. 'Cheer up, Sam!' James shouted as they turned into it. 'Another ten minutes and we'll be home and dry.'

The groom was not mollified. 'Home, mebbe. It'll take more 'n that to get me and the horses dry, Master James. Soaked through we are.'

The clouds were clearing more rapidly as they rode on along the avenue of trees, and the wind and rain eased. Visibility improved, and it was just as well. The horses had to pick their way through a mass of debris brought down by the storm. In places the drive was almost blocked by broken branches. They rode on slowly, concentrating on negotiating their way through, but when they were not more than a few hundred yards from the house James saw an obstruction on the road ahead, which was clearly not a branch. In fact, it looked like nothing so much as a heap of sodden rags. What was it, and what the devil was it doing on the drive? He pulled up his horse, jumped down and walked on a few paces. Sam joined him, and after an amazed glance at each other they bent down to look more closely. It was a body, and though it was lying face down in a bundle of wet clothes, it could be seen that it was the body of a woman.

'Dead, is she?' asked Sam.

'Dead, or unconscious. Let's see.'

James bent down, gently turned the woman over, and smoothed back the tangled locks of hair covering her face. He caught his breath. In the cold white light of the moon the face could have been carved in marble, its exquisite purity marred by a dark line running down from her temple.

'I think she's still alive,' he said slowly. 'But it's too damned dark to be certain. We'll have to take her up to the house.'

'She's had a nasty bang on the head,' said Sam.

'Yes, we'll have to handle her carefully, but we must move her—she can't stay here. I'll carry her. You bring the horses.'

Not without difficulty, for her wet clothes were heavy and cumbersome, James took the woman up into his arms and set off for the house, now just a short walk away.

An elderly housekeeper met them at the door. 'There you are, my lord! I didn't hardly expect to see you in this weather. Come in, come in. I've got a nice fire going in the—' She stopped abruptly. 'Gracious me, Master James, who is that? Mercy on us, don't tell me you've had an accident. Whatever has happened?'

'Never mind that for the moment, Cully! Where did you say the fire was? In here?' He nodded to Sam, who hurried over to open the door on the right of the hall. A huge fire was burning in the hearth, a large damask-covered sofa on either side. James put his burden down gently on one of them. Mrs Culver gave a cry and bustled forwards, exclaiming, 'Whatever are you thinking of, sir? That sofa will be ruined! Just look at the mud on the woman's boots—and her clothes are soaking wet!'

James ignored the comment. He took off his overcoat and handed it to the groom, then brought a lamp over and put it on a table by the sofa. 'She's just a girl! Sam, get one of the other grooms to see to the horses. You go to fetch Dr Liston. Mrs Culver, have a fire lit in one of the bedrooms, if you please, and tell the maids to make up the bed. And put out one of Lady Aldhurst's nightgowns.'

'But, sir—'

'Don't waste time, Cully!' James said, carefully removing the girl's heavy boots and rubbing her feet. 'She needs warmth and attention. Come back here after you've told the maids what to do. Bring one of them with you to help. Wait! You'd better bring some blankets with you, too.'

The housekeeper drew a breath, saw further protest was useless, and left the room stiff with disapproval, still shaking her head and grumbling. After she had gone, James fetched a shawl which was draped over the other sofa, put it over the girl and knelt down beside her. She was lying motionless, barely breathing. The sooner she was in a warm bed the better, but he was reluctant to disturb her more than he had to before the surgeon had seen her. Liston lived not far away—he should be here shortly.

He studied the girl's face, starkly white against the rich fabric of the sofa, her eyelashes a dark fringe against her cheeks. He was concerned to see that the wound on her temple was still oozing blood, and fetched a napkin from the side-table to wipe it carefully away. She groaned and stirred restlessly, and he held his breath. Then her eyes flew open, large eyes, widely spaced, startlingly, vividly blue, twin pools of colour in that white face. She looked at him apprehensively, then, after several attempts to speak, she whispered, 'Who…who are you?'

His deep voice was calm. 'My name is James Aldhurst. This is my grandmother's house. We found you lying unconscious outside in the rain, and I gathered you up and brought you in here.' She seemed to be looking for reassurance and he added, 'Don't worry. You're quite safe.'

She shut her eyes and said, 'My head hurts. I think I fell… I was running… I couldn't get up the bank...' Her eyes flew open again and this time they were filled with panic. She struggled to move, but gave up with a cry of despair. 'I can't... My head! Oh, my head! But I have to...' Clawing at his arm, she said, 'Help me! Please help me! Don't let them catch me! Please!'

The desperation in her voice startled him. He took hold of her hand. 'I told you. You're safe here. I shan't let them find you. Lie still. The surgeon will be here very soon to look at you, and if he says you can be moved we shall make you more comfortable. But you must stay still for the moment.' The blue eyes stared into his, then she gave a small nod, winced and closed her eyes again. Her hand fell away from his.

James looked at her anxiously. The hand had been icy. Where was Liston? And why was Mrs Culver taking so long? He went to take the girl's hand again to warm it, but was shocked into an exclamation when he saw a band of rubbed skin, red and sore, encircling the slender wrist. He picked up the other hand and it was the same. He replaced them both carefully under the shawl and frowned. This girl had evidently been tied up till quite recently, and her bonds had been cruelly tight. What had been going on? Who was she? How had she come to be lying in the middle of his grandmother's drive at eight o'clock on a storm-driven night? He shook his head and got up impatiently. The answers to those questions must wait. What was needed at the moment was help for the poor wretch! Where the devil *was* Mrs Culver? He went into the hall and shouted.

Mrs Culver came down the stairs followed by a maidservant struggling with a quantity of blankets. Almost in the same moment the house door opened, and Sam appeared, accompanied by Dr Liston.

'Thank God! Come this way, Liston. We need you too, Mrs Culver. Thank you, Sam. You'd better go and change out of those wet clothes.'

The surgeon followed James into the room and they went over to the sofa. But, after telling the maid to stay with the surgeon while he examined his patient, Mrs Culver drew James to one side and spoke to him firmly in a low voice. 'Your lordship, I've known you since you were a boy and witnessed a good many of your pranks. I've even saved you once or twice from their consequences. I'll be frank with you, sir. Your grandmother trusts me to look after this house when she's away. I'm not sure she'd approve of what's going on here tonight. This young woman—who is she?'

'I don't know, Cully. Sam and I found her lying on the drive not far from the house. What would you have had me do? Leave her there?'

'You didn't need to bring a beggar woman like her into your grandmother's sitting room! She might even be a gipsy! I don't like to think what Lady Aldhurst would say. And here you are, ruining her furniture with that girl's wet clothes and muddy boots, putting her in one of the best bedrooms, giving her your grandmother's clothes to wear, calling Dr Liston out at this time of night to see to her... What has come over you?'

'She's no beggar, Cully. She's in some kind of trouble, but she's no beggar. There's a mystery here and I intend to get to the bottom of it, but before that we must keep her alive. Is the bedroom ready? If Liston gives the word, I'd like to take her upstairs.' He turned back to the sofa, and Dr Liston straightened up, looking grave.

'As far as I can tell there's no serious damage apart from that bang on the head—but it was a hefty one.' He gave James a strange look. 'Her wrists...'

'I've seen them.'

The surgeon nodded. 'Sam tells me you found her lying on the drive, and from the look of her I'd say she had been there for some time.' He shook his head. 'I don't know, Lord Aldhurst. I don't know. I can't do any more for her tonight, but I'll come back tomorrow morning. For now she needs a warm bed with hot bricks and blankets, and complete rest. It's quite likely she'll develop a fever. I'll send my man over with a paregoric draught, and if she is restless you could try giving her some of that. But my best advice would be to give her water, nothing more. And keep her well wrapped up.' He shook his head. 'We shall have to see.'

James nodded. 'There's a bed ready for her. Mrs Culver?'

The housekeeper had been looking at the girl, who was now lying white and still, a vivid bruise on her temple. 'She looks very ill, it's true, the poor thing. We'll put her to bed. I'll have one of the men carry her upstairs.'

'I'll carry her up,' said James. 'She needs gentle handling.'

Mrs Culver pursed her lips, but said nothing, and, signing to the maidservant to follow her, she set off up the broad staircase. 'We've put your…

guest in the green bedroom, my lord,' she said, at her most formal. Mrs Culver had not yet been won over, and wished him to know it, but she would keep her opinions to herself in front of the younger servants. 'If your lordship would put her on the bed, Rose and I will see to the rest.' And, before he could say anything, she went on, 'We will handle her as gently as we can, my lord, never fear.' She waited till James had put the girl down, then firmly ushered him out of the room. 'I shall let you know when we have finished,' she said as she shut the door.

James went along to his own bedchamber where one of the servants was waiting with dry clothing, but he hardly noticed what the man was doing. His mind was full of the girl he had just rescued. During that brief moment of consciousness she had appealed to him so desperately, had clung to him as if he was her only hope. Why was she so afraid?

He waited impatiently for word from Mrs Culver, and when it came he wasted no time but went along straight away to the green bedroom. They had bathed the girl's face and hands and put her in one of his grandmother's lace-trimmed nightgowns. Her wrists were neatly bandaged and lay on top of the covers, which were otherwise pulled up around her. She was quite still, her eyes closed.

'She shouldn't be left alone,' said Mrs Culver. 'I'll have one of the maids sit with her tonight.'

'It's all right, Cully. I'll stay.'

'You can't do that, my lord! It's not fitting—'

'Cully, you might as well save your breath,' James said impatiently. 'You've known me long enough to know when I've made up my mind. I'm going to sit with that girl tonight. She might recover consciousness at any time, and I must be there when she does. Mine is the only face here she might recognise.'

'How would she do that, my lord?'

'She was conscious for a moment or two while you were upstairs, and I spoke to her. She was frightened out of her life. She is obviously in some danger—you must have seen her wrists before you bound them up. Now don't argue with me. Just inform all the servants that they are not to talk about our visitor to anyone—anyone at all. Until we know more of the circumstances her presence here must be kept secret. Understood?'

When James spoke in that particular tone, Mrs

Culver knew better than to argue. 'Very well, my lord, I'll make sure they hold their tongues. I'll send a maid to you in a while to see if there's anything you need.' She went out, closing the door softly behind her.

James adjusted the lamp so that its light did not fall on the figure on the bed, and sat for a while, studying the girl's face in the dim light. Not conventionally pretty. A short, straight nose, a generous mouth, beautifully modelled cheekbones... The chin was a little too determined for prettiness. She lay so still—what would animation do to that face? Would she simper at him as much as most of the girls he met nowadays? He rather thought not. There was intelligence in the brow and firmness in the line of her jaw. If anything, she might be a touch too independent for most men...

He shook his head and got up impatiently. What nonsense! How could he possibly judge any girl's character, just from the sculpted lines of a face as white and as motionless as the pillow behind? When she recovered she would probably prove to be no different from all the rest... He stood for a moment, looking down at her.

The movement of the covers was almost imperceptible, but there was enough to reassure him. She was breathing.

He walked over to the window. The storm was now quite over, and the fields and hedges were silvered with moonlight. Nothing stirred. He wondered what his grandmother would say if she knew he was standing here in the middle of the night keeping watch over a sick girl, a perfect stranger? Something trenchant, no doubt. She had been annoyed enough with him before he left. Those damned newspapers! He stared at the scene outside with unseeing eyes, even forgot the girl in the bed behind him. He was back in London in his grandmother's room in London. She was sitting as always in her chair by the window looking out over Brook Street...

The Dowager Lady Aldhurst was an upright figure with a silver-topped cane in her right hand. Tiny as she was, she dominated the room. She was wearing black as usual, but her dress was trimmed with a collar of Alençon lace, and a very pretty cap of the same lace covered her beautifully arranged frosted-black hair. A cashmere shawl was draped over her arms. On a small table next to her chair was a glass of Madeira, together with a plate of small biscuits and a pile of papers, on top of which was a copy of the *Gazette*.

When James came in she greeted him with no particular warmth, but her expression softened as he walked towards her with his characteristic easy stride. Tall, broad shouldered, with dark grey eyes and black hair, he was the image of the man she had loved and married more than fifty years before, and he had always held a special place in her affections. As James bent to kiss her cheek he smiled appreciatively as he caught a delicate trace of perfume.

'I see you're wearing the cap I gave you, ma'am,' he said as he sat down. 'It suits you. I swear you look younger every day!'

His grandmother was not to be mollified. 'No thanks to you, sir!' she snapped.

He smiled ruefully. 'What have I done this time, Grandmama?'

'It's what you *haven't* done!' She picked up the copy of the *Gazette*. 'Between the social announcements and the gossip I have never read the *Gazette* and the rest with so little pleasure. Read that, if you please!'

James took the paper and read, '"Lord Paston

has announced his daughter's engagement to the Honourable Christopher Dalloway..."' He raised an eyebrow and, handing the paper back to her, said with a puzzled frown, 'I wish the happy couple every joy, but I am not sure what it is supposed to mean to me, nor why it should cause you such displeasure...'

His grandmother glared and took the paper back from him. 'That isn't all,' she said angrily. 'Read down the page, sir! Look at the other announcements! Sarah Carteret is to marry someone I've never heard of—her mother won't be pleased about that! And next month Mary Abernauld will marry Francis Chantry—'

This time his tone was more cynical. 'So Mary is to be a Countess? I hope her father knows what he is doing. Chantry gambled away his first wife's inheritance in pretty much record time— let's hope he doesn't lose his new one's fortune as quickly.'

'Arthur Abernauld is no fool, James,' said his grandmother. 'He'll have seen to it that he won't!' Then she snapped, 'Don't try to change the subject! I haven't asked you in to talk about the Abernaulds!'

'I'm relieved to hear you say so. They're a tedious

lot. What *did* you want to see me about—apart, of course, from the pleasure of my company?'

She tapped the paper with her finger. 'It's this. Did Barbara Furness tell you she was going to Scotland? According to the *Gazette*, her parents are taking her for a prolonged stay at Rothmuir Castle. Does this mean she has given up waiting for you to make her an offer and intends to accept the Marquess after all?'

James leaned back in his chair with a lazy smile. 'That is something you would have to ask the lady.' When Lady Aldhurst simply held his eye and waited in silence he added, 'Surely I don't need to tell *you*, of all people, that Lady Barbara has never expected an offer from me. What is more, I don't believe she would have accepted me if I had made one.'

His grandmother looked grave. 'That's not the impression you were giving the world, James.' She poked her stick at the sheets still lying on the table. 'And it's not what the scandal sheets are saying, either. According to them, she has left London with a broken heart. Is that true?'

'Let me see.' James picked up the offending newspaper, but after a quick glance he murmured,

'Barbara has been busy! So this to be my punishment!'

'Is it true?'

James got up and said impatiently, 'Of course it isn't! Barbara is simply playing one of her tricks. She was furious when I told her she was behaving badly to a friend of mine, and thinks she can pay me back through this piece of nonsense. Lady Furness insisted on taking her daughter to Scotland, but I'll be amazed if Barbara isn't back in London before the month is out, heart whole and perfectly free of any engagement. Why on earth do you read such unedifying rubbish?' He looked at his grandmother, and said, surprised, 'You surely don't believe it?'

'I no longer know what to believe, James. And you can stop towering over me like that. Sit down, sir! Sit down and look at me!'

His jaw tightened and for a moment it looked as if he would refuse. Then their eyes met and he shrugged his shoulders and sat down. His grandmother thought for a moment and then said slowly, 'I can see you're annoyed with me. You think I'm an interfering old woman, and I suppose you're right. But I care about you, and I care even more for the good name of the Aldhursts.

It's an old name and a highly respected one, and I am not prepared to see it bandied about in newspapers such as these.'

'Why the devil does the world have to take such an interest in my affairs?'

'Oh, come, James! You must know that you've been regarded as one of London's most eligible bachelors ever since you were old enough to enter society. Lady Barbara is only one of a large number of girls whose names have been linked with yours in the past year or two. Three others are also in that newspaper—Mary Abernauld, Sarah Carteret *and* the Paston chit. You are acquiring a reputation, James.'

'Really, ma'am, I thought you had better sense. You more than anyone must know what it is like. I have only to dance once with a girl, or happen to be more than once in the same room with her, or even raise my hat to her in the street, for the gossips' tongues to start wagging. I hardly knew the Carteret girl. Our so-called affair was only ever in the girl's imagination, fed by her mother's ambition. I never remotely considered asking her to marry me.'

She shook her head. 'You have never to my knowledge remotely considered asking anyone to marry you.' She put the *Gazette* back on the table with a sigh. 'Three of London's most desirable young women—four with the Paston girl—all well born, all well bred and all passably good-looking. And now they are all about to marry someone else.' She gave a frustrated tap on the floor with her stick. 'You've known Barbara Furness a long time. I had such high hopes of her.'

'She was John's friend, not mine.'

'But John is dead and you are alive. You could well have made a match of it. Now you've lost her to Rothmuir, who must be fifty if he's a day! What stopped you? Is there some truth in what they are all saying? That you think no woman is good enough for you?'

James was offended. He said curtly, 'You must know me better than that! Of course that's not true!' He turned away from her and gazed out of the window.

Lady Aldhurst said more gently, 'Then what is it, James?'

He shook his head. 'I've been introduced to innumerable girls since I came out of the army. They all seem such polished articles. They've been trained to smile, but not too much, to converse, but not too wittily, to play an instrument, but not too brilliantly. They have been to the best dressmakers, the best milliners, and they have without exception been taught every trick of proper deportment. So much effort in pursuit of a suitable match...'

He paused and turned round to look at her. 'The trouble is, ma'am, there is so little to distinguish one from another.' He corrected himself. 'No, Barbara Furness is different. She is a minx, but she at least makes me laugh.... John loved her, and since he died I have very occasionally wondered whether she and I could tolerate one another enough to make a marriage work.'

'Well then—why not Lady Barbara?'

'The feeling didn't last. She is beautiful enough, and she amuses me, but I want more than that from a wife. I'd rather not marry at all than feel nothing more than amusement or a somewhat lukewarm regard for the woman I intend to share the rest of my life with.'

'But you *must* marry, James! You owe it to the family. You're the last of us now that John has gone. You *must* have some sons. Or do you intend to let the line die out altogether?'

There was a long silence during which James

continued to watch the carriages and horses, the vendors and servants passing in a constant stream up and down Brook Street. At last he said with a touch of bitterness, 'You're right, of course. I owe it to the family. When John died I "owed it to the family" to give up the Army career I loved. After my father died I "owed it to the family" to spend months rescuing our estates—Charterton, Aldhurst, Baldock and the rest—after he had neglected them for years.'

'You haven't mentioned the most important. You haven't mentioned Roade.'

'I haven't been to Roade. I dislike the place,' he said curtly.

'Your grandfather and I loved it, James.'

After another pause he turned round and said grimly, 'And now I suppose you think I owe it to the family to secure its survival.'

'Quite right! You've waited far too long as it is. You need to marry.'

'You know, ma'am, I was fool enough to hope that one day I would find someone special—the sort of woman who would mean as much to me as you meant to my grandfather. But I'm beginning to think she doesn't exist.'

For a moment Lady Aldhurst looked her age.

But before James could utter another word she had pulled herself together, and was at her most astringent as she said, 'That is, of course, a pity, and I am sorry for it. But I've waited long enough to see you settled. It's time you found someone to marry even if she isn't your ideal. The Season will be on us in a month. There's bound to be a suitable bride among this year's crop of débutantes. You must make up your mind to choose one!'

He smiled ruefully. 'They are all so...so young, ma'am.'

'Most debutantes are, James,' said his grandmother drily. She regarded him for a moment, then said in a softened tone, 'There's always a chance that one of them will suit you better than you think. Here's one who might be different.' She picked the paper up again, and read out, '"Sir Henry Calverley, one of the government's most senior diplomats, is returning shortly to London in order to take part in this year's London Season. It is understood that he wishes to present his daughter, Miss Antonia Calverley, at the Court of St James. Miss Calverley should prove an interesting addition to London society. She left England when she was a child and has since then been her father's constant companion, helping him in his work and mixing with some of the most distinguished families in Europe." Now there's a girl who could interest you. You cannot say she will be your average debutante.'

'No,' he said moodily. 'She's probably full of stories about life in the highest circles. And, if she is so used to managing matters for her father, she will probably expect to manage a husband as well. That doesn't sound like the one for me!'

Lady Aldhurst looked at her grandson thoughtfully for a moment, then seemed to make up her mind. 'I can see how open-minded you are in your search for a wife, James,' she said drily, 'but before you start, I think you should pay a visit to Hatherton. You haven't been there for ages, and Mrs Culver and the rest of the servants would be very happy to see you. And you can take a look at Roade House while you are there. Talk to your people. It wouldn't do any harm to you or your reputation to get out of London for a week or two—a month even. There would still be time for you to be back here before the Season gets fully under way.'

'I suppose you think I really ought to stay at Roade.'

'I would not dream of suggesting anything of the sort! The place has been shut up for so many years that it would take an army to make it fit for anyone to spend even a night there, let alone a week or two. No, you must stay at Hatherton. And, while Mrs Culver and the rest are making their usual fuss of you, you can visit Roade and see what needs to be done to it. It is, after all, your chief place of residence, and when you do marry I hope you and your wife and children will live there.'

She shook her head at him, and then put out her hand. 'Go, James. A visit to Hatherton and Roade might give you a purpose in life, help you to see your future in a more positive light.'

Chapter Two

James had hesitated. Then he had recalled the many happy times he had enjoyed at Hatherton Grange. It was a relatively unpretentious country house, but Aldhursts had lived in it for three hundred years before his great-grandfather had built Roade House on higher ground a mile or so away. After his grandfather had died his grandmother had left Roade to move down to Hatherton and had made it her own. Its servants and tenants were all fiercely loyal to her, and many of them were old friends of James, too. He and his brother John had been brought to live with her there after she had discovered that her two small grandchildren had been left behind at Roade, while their parents travelled abroad.

At Hatherton he and John had learned to ride and shoot under the strict supervision of Tom Gage, his grandmother's gamekeeper and chief groom. Mrs Culver, her housekeeper, had bound up their injuries, looked after them during childhood illnesses, and scolded them after their many escapades. And his grandmother had given them the love his parents had denied them. Hatherton had always held a special place in his affections. It should be a good place to come to terms with the life ahead of him.

So he had looked at his grandmother and nodded. 'Very well,' he had said. 'I'll go.'

But when he had set out from London that day he hadn't expected to be sharing the house with a mysterious stranger, let alone a young woman! Where had she come from? The road to his grandmother's house was an unfrequented lane; their nearest neighbours were four miles away, and the Portsmouth Road was several miles to the west. And how had she come by that ugly bruise on her head? The rope burns on her wrists?

He turned to look at her and saw that her eyes were open. 'You're still here.' Her voice was a thread of sound. He came over to the bed and sat down.

'Are you warm?'

She frowned. 'Too warm. Water? Please?'

Mrs Culver had left a pitcher on the chest by the bed. He poured a little water into the glass beside it, raised her slightly and held it to her lips. But she had taken no more than a sip when her eyes closed.

'Who are you?' he asked softly.

He thought that she hadn't heard him, but then, 'I'm An...' she began. She stopped and a small frown wrinkled her brow. After a moment she tried again. 'I'm An...' There was another pause, longer this time. 'I know who *you* are,' she said at last. 'You said I was safe here.' He nodded and she gave a small sigh. 'I'm An...'

'Anne who?'

Her head moved restlessly on the pillow. 'I don't...'

'It doesn't matter.' He put his hand reassuringly over hers. 'You can tell me later. And you *are* safe here, I promise.'

'I know. Your name is James Aldhurst. This is your grandmother's house.' Her eyes opened. 'Where is she?'

'She isn't here. She's in London.'

She closed her eyes again and seemed to fall asleep. Thankfully, he tucked the covers round her and relaxed. After a while one of the maids came in to see if he needed anything. She offered to sit with the girl for a while too, but James refused. The frantic appeal in the girl's eyes, the way she had clung to him, had touched him, and he intended to be there when she woke again.

The girl slept quietly for an hour or two, but after a while began to mutter and turn her head restlessly on the pillow again. James had to replace the covers as she tried to push them from her, but she protested,

'No, don't! I'm too…hot. Too hot. Thirsty…'

When he lifted her again and gave her a sip of water his heart sank as he realised that she was burning with heat. She was muttering incoherently, but he caught the word *London* several times. Then she opened her eyes and said quite clearly, 'I must go to London! Now!'

'You can't go anywhere at the moment. You've hurt your head. You must rest.'

She resisted his efforts to put her back on the pillow and cried, 'But there isn't time, I tell you. You mustn't stop me. Let me go, let me go!' Eyes bright with fever and cheeks flushed with two spots of brilliant colour, she pushed his hand away with unexpected force and struggled to sit up. When he put an arm out to hold her back she grew even more agitated and shouted, 'You can't stop me! I won't *let* you keep me here!' Thrusting the covers back, she scrambled to get out of the bed, but before her foot even touched the ground she gave a cry and if James had not caught her she would have fallen to the floor. He could feel the heat of her body through the fine linen of the nightgown. She was burning up with fever.

James put her back in the bed as quickly and as gently as he could and covered her up. Then he went to the door and shouted for a servant to send for Mrs Culver, who came hurrying into the bedroom in a surprisingly short time. 'I hadn't gone to bed—I thought something like this would happen,' she said briskly. 'Now, Master James, I'd like you to hold the young woman while I give her a sip of the draught Dr Liston sent. That's the way.'

The girl stirred as he raised her, but made no protest as Mrs Culver administered the sedative and James laid her back against the pillows. She was quiet again. Mrs Culver straightened the covers, and said firmly, 'And now I want you to leave her with me till morning, my lord. This is a sick woman and she needs proper nursing.

She'll be well looked after, never fear. One of the maids will join me in a minute. If she wakes and asks for you, I'll send for you. Meanwhile, you'd do better to have some rest yourself.'

James went to his room reassured. Years before, whenever he and John had been sick, they had only ever wanted Cully to nurse them. She was the best possible person to look after his mysterious and unexpected protégée.

To his surprise James slept for a few hours, but woke soon after dawn. He had not been disturbed during the night, and hoped this was a good sign, but he nevertheless threw on his dressing robe and hurried along to the green bedroom. The maid was fast asleep in a chair on the other side of the room, but Mrs Culver was leaning over the bed, bathing her patient's face.

'How is she, Cully?' he asked as he came softly into the room.

'She hasn't stirred all night, and seems to be breathing quite naturally. The fever has gone down.'

'That's good news! You must be tired. Let me take over.'

'I never need much sleep, Master James. And I

think…' She paused as the maid stirred and woke up. Then, with a critical look at James's state of undress, she raised her voice and said, 'I think I can say the patient is doing well, my lord. It's kind of you to be concerned. I'm sure it would be quite in order for you to visit her later in the day—after breakfast, perhaps?' She turned to the maid. 'Rose, go to the kitchen and tell cook to have his lordship's breakfast ready in half an hour. And if Mrs Gage is in the kitchen, ask her to come up here.' The girl turned to go. 'And, Rose! Remember to hold your tongue about this young woman!' Rose nodded and left.

Ater she had gone Mrs Culver said severely, 'My lord, I have to say that coming along here at this hour before you are properly dressed was very unwise. The sudden arrival of this young woman has given the servants enough to talk about already. It won't do to give them any more.'

James brushed this aside and asked, 'Why do you wish to see Mrs Gage?'

'She's a good nurse and knows how to keep a still tongue in her head. If you agreed, she could sit with the young woman during the day.'

'Surely I could do that!'

Mrs Culver said in an exasperated tone, 'What

have I just been saying? You mustn't do it, Master James! But there! I might as well talk to a five-bar gate! You haven't changed, and I don't suppose you will. You're just the same as you always were, forever rescuing something or other.' She cast a look at the girl on the bed and said, 'But this isn't cat or a dog or a bird or one of those wild animals you took under your wing! It's a grown woman, and you have to be more circumspect. People will gossip if you seem to be taking her into your care! She will have to go elsewhere as soon as she can be moved. To the parish, if necessary.'

'No, Cully! I refuse to leave her to the mercy of the parish.'

Frowning, Mrs Culver looked at him sharply and said, 'Just what is this person to you, my lord?'

James looked at the sleeping figure. 'I had never seen her before last night, if that is what you mean. I don't know who or what she is, or where she comes from. But you're wrong if you think she is some kind of vagrant, Cully. She's a lady, I'll swear. And she's in some sort of trouble—or even danger. Until she can tell us more about herself she will have my—*our* protection.'

Mrs Culver was still not convinced, but said resignedly, 'I hope your grandmother never hears about this, Master James. But for the moment you'd better get dressed and ready for breakfast. Doctor Liston will be here soon. He said he'd call in early this morning. Perhaps the young woman will be able to talk to us after he has been.' She gave a nod and added firmly, 'And then, when we know where she belongs, she can be sent back there the moment she is well enough.'

James had thought he would visit the girl as soon as he had finished his breakfast, but when he went upstairs he found he would have to wait. Doctor Liston was with her. It seemed like hours before the door of the room opened and the surgeon came out.

'Good morning, Lord Aldhurst.'

'How is she, Liston?'

'I'm pleased to say that I think she is out of danger, though she's still weak. She should be kept warm, given plenty of liquids and left undisturbed. I doubt the fever will return, but if it does you should send for me. Good day to you, my lord. Unless I hear from you sooner, I'll call at the same time tomorrow again.'

James looked in on the girl several times during the day, but found her asleep with Mrs Gage or one of the maids in attendance. They told him that she occasionally roused herself enough to sip a little water, but fell asleep again almost immediately. 'It's the best thing, Master James,' said Mrs Culver, when he expressed concern about this prolonged rest. 'As the doctor said, it's what that girl needs most.'

When he came to see her the next morning Dr Liston was just coming out of the room.

'How is she this morning, Liston? Not worse?'

The surgeon looked at him somewhat strangely. 'No, no! Her constitution is a strong one. She seems to have survived her exposure to the elements remarkably well. The head wound is healing nicely...' He paused. 'Her vision does not seem to be affected, and she speaks sensibly enough. But...'

'But what?'

The doctor hesitated, then put his hand on the door. 'Perhaps you should talk to her. She might remember you.' He held the door open for James.

Mrs Gage was at the head of the bed, plumping

up the pillows behind the girl. She gave them a last pat and then curtsied and withdrew. Sitting propped up against them the girl looked weary, but the hectic flush had died down, leaving her pale again, as white as the bandage she now wore round her head. Her eyes were open and clear as she looked across the room at him, but their expression of bewildered anxiety gave James a strong urge to hold her, to comfort her as he would a child, until that dreadful, lost look was chased away. But with Cully's warnings in mind he mastered the impulse and kept his voice normal as he came towards her.

'Good morning,' he said, sitting down by the bed. 'How are you?'

She hadn't taken her eyes off him. 'I recognise you. You're James Aldhurst,' she said. 'And this is your grandmother's house.' She paused and looked at him anxiously. 'Is that right?'

He nodded. 'Absolutely right,' he said.

She gave a sigh of relief. 'At least I've remembered that much.' She looked at him gravely. 'Good morning, James Aldhurst.'

'Good morning. I'm glad you remembered my name. Now tell me yours.'

'Didn't I...didn't I tell you?'

'No, not quite.'

'What do you mean? What did I say?'

James wondered why the girl was so reluctant to tell him who she was. He said slowly, 'You can trust me with all of it, you know. You've only told me your first name. Anne.'

Her look of eagerness vanished. 'Anne...' she said, and for a moment she frowned in intense concentration. Then she shook her head and the lost look returned. 'I...I can't,' she said. 'I don't know. I can't remember. I've tried and tried, but I can't remember.' Her voice rose as she repeated, 'Anne... Anne... Anne what?' She looked at him, her eyes full of anxiety. 'I can remember who you are, but I don't remember who I am! I...I seem to have lost my memory!'

James took her hand in his and said gently, 'No, you haven't. You remembered me, and you remembered where you are, didn't you? You're just still confused after that bang on the head. You'll remember the rest soon enough. Worrying about it would be the worst thing you could do. Let it come naturally. It will come back all the sooner, you'll see.' He smiled at her encouragingly.

Her fingers grasped his, and she gave him a

twisted smile in return. 'Yes, yes. It will, I'm sure
it will. Forgive me. I'm not usually as poor-spirited as this. It must be that bang on the head.'

'You see? You've remembered something about
yourself already! You're certainly not poor-spirited. That's a quite a relief! I'm not fond of poor-
spirited girls.'

She made an attempt to smile, but it failed.
'What happened? I don't even know how I got
here.'

'We brought you in after we found you lying
unconscious on the drive to this house. I think
you must have been there for some time. There
was a storm and you were very wet.'

'A storm? I don't remember that at all,' she said
wearily, turning her head away.

Doctor Liston came over. 'Lord Aldhurst, I
think my patient needs to rest again.' He caught
Mrs Gage's eye. 'Can you find something for
the young lady, Mrs Gage—a little thin soup or
gruel, something like that?'

'I'll see to it right away, sir,' said Mrs Gage.
She went out.

The surgeon turned to the girl on the bed and
said kindly, 'I'll call again tomorrow to see how
you are, but there's not much more I can do.

Temporary loss of memory is not at all unusual in a case like yours. You must not distress yourself, ma'am. I think you can depend on Lord Aldhurst to find somewhere for you to stay until your memory returns.'

'She will stay here, Liston,' said James decisively.

Doctor Liston looked surprised. 'It's good of Lady Aldhurst—'

'My grandmother is not here. But I am sure she would agree with me that Miss…Miss Anne must stay at Hatherton for the time being.'

The surgeon looked doubtful, but said, 'Very well, my lord. I shall come again tomorrow. Er…when are you expecting Lady Aldhurst to arrive?'

'I am not expecting her,' said James as he ushered the surgeon out of the room. 'Lady Aldhurst is in London and as far as I know is planning to stay there.'

'But in that case, surely the young lady—'

'Set your mind at rest. The young lady will be perfectly safe here, with or without my grandmother's presence. I don't make a habit of seducing defenceless invalids.'

The surgeon was shocked out of his professional

manner. 'Really, sir!' he exclaimed. 'Nothing was further from my mind! But convention would suggest... The Rector would possibly know of somewhere more suitable...' He looked at James's expression. 'Or if you wish, I could ask Mrs Liston if she would offer the young lady a room.'

'No, Liston. The young lady is *my* responsibility. I found her, and I shall look after her. Mrs Liston would not thank you for bringing someone who might be in danger into the house.'

'Danger?'

'You saw the girl's wrists. She has been kept somewhere against her will. Whoever tied her up may well want her back, and I suspect they may not be too scrupulous about their methods.'

'I see... Well...in that case it may be best to leave her in your care after all, Lord Aldhurst.'

'Quite.'

Doctor Liston was obviously shaken. 'I shall... er...I shall call again tomorrow—unless you think I shouldn't?'

'Please do,' said James.

He went back into the bedroom. The girl had taken the bandages off her wrist and was examining the scars.

'You heard,' said James.

'Yes. The door wasn't quite shut. I seem to be causing you a great deal of trouble.' She looked at him. 'You should have listened to Dr Liston.'

'Nonsense.'

'I mean it. What would your grandmother say if she arrived to find an uninvited stranger in her house? A nameless stranger at that!'

'You have a name. It's Anne.'

'Anne,' she said. 'It's a pretty name. But it doesn't somehow sound quite right.'

'It will do for the moment,' James said firmly.

'There's something else, Lord Aldhurst...'

'What is it?'

'You said... You told that doctor that he might be in danger if he took me in. What did you mean?'

'I didn't want an argument about where you should stay, that's all.'

She shook her head. 'Please be honest with me! What *are* these marks on my wrist? It wasn't just a story to put Dr Liston off. I *have* been tied up, haven't I?'

'It looks like it.'

'So there *is* danger... I knew it. I have this feeling...of some kind of threat...and...and something

I have to do… But I don't know what it is!' She held her head in her hands. After a few moments she looked up again. 'Why can't I remember?'

James heard the beginning of panic in her voice and said, 'Stop! Stop this at once. It won't do you any good, Anne. And you can forget about danger. I told you last night—you're perfectly safe here. Or…do you not trust me?'

'Of course I trust you. I have to. There's no one else.'

'Exactly. So listen to me! You will remember who you are, and where you have come from quite soon. And if you don't we shall set about finding out. But the first step is to get your strength back. Agreed?'

She nodded.

'Then give me a smile.' She smiled tremulously. 'Brave girl! Not at all poor-spirited.' He regarded her white face. 'Now where is Mrs Gage? Liston said you were to have something to eat and then a rest, and that is what you shall do. Ah! I can hear her coming. But you'll have to sit up straighter than that.' He bent over and put his arms round her to lift her higher in the bed.

It wasn't Mrs Gage who came in, but Mrs Culver. She gave a loud cough.

'I believe the doctor ordered some food for the patient, my lord. The maid is just bringing up some soup for her.'

'Ah, there you are, Mrs Culver,' said James, completely unaffected by the look of shocked disapproval on her face. 'Good. I'm sure Miss Anne is ready for it.' He grinned at the housekeeper unrepentantly. 'The pillows had slipped, Cully, and I was straightening them. That was all.'

Mrs Culver remained unappeased. 'That wasn't at all necessary, my lord. That is my job. It's what I came in to do,' she said austerely. She paused. 'Am I to understand that the young lady has now remembered her name?'

'No, but until she does we shall call her "Anne".'

'Very good, my lord.' She took the tray from the maidservant who had followed her in and put it on the bed. 'Now, Miss Anne, you must finish this all up, and then have a good rest. His lordship is a busy man, but he might find time to pay you a short visit this evening. Is that not so, my lord?' She gave him a severe look. 'A *short* visit.'

'Of course! Whatever you say, Cully.' James turned to the girl. 'Try not to worry. Enjoy that soup if you can. I remember it from my childhood. I wasn't too fond of it then, and I don't suppose it tastes any better now.'

'It's good, wholesome food and it didn't do your lordship any harm,' said Mrs Culver. 'Nor your brother, either. Don't listen to him, miss.'

After James had gone out, Anne took a sip of the soup. 'What is his lordship thinking of? This is delicious!' She finished the plateful eagerly, but refused an offer of more. Mrs Culver removed the tray and told the maid to take it out. Then, after she had tidied up and seen to Anne's needs, she sat down on the chair by the bed. 'I'll just stay till you are ready to sleep, miss,' she said.

Resting thankfully against the pillows Anne said, 'Lord Aldhurst is very kind. Have you known him long, Mrs Culver?'

'Ever since he was a little boy. His lordship and Master John lived here with their grandmother when the boys' parents were off on their travels.'

'Master John?'

'His lordship's younger brother.' Mrs Culver sighed. 'But he died, and now there are just the two of them left—Lady Aldhurst and his lordship.'

'Lord Aldhurst is not married?'

'Not yet.' Mrs Culver gave Anne a look. 'But I understand that he is as good as engaged. Before she left for London Lady Aldhurst was sure it was all settled.'

'So he...he has someone in mind?'

Mrs Culver nodded and said cheerfully, 'His lordship could have married any one of a number of young ladies, of course, but he and Lady Barbara have known each other since they were young. It would be a very suitable match.' She paused. 'And we'll all be very pleased when he does marry. It's time we had a new generation of Aldhursts running about the place.' She got up from her chair. 'But I can see it's time you had a rest. I'll get one of the maids to call in on you occasionally, but she won't wake you. Sleep is the best cure for most maladies.'

But sleep would not come to the girl in the bed. She had found the news that James Aldhurst was about to be married dispiriting. He was her rock, her safe place in the uninhabited wilderness that was her world at the moment, and, however unjustified, the thought that he was about to marry someone else was most unwelcome.

She lay awake, thinking about her rescuer. He

had been gentle enough with her, but she suspected he was not usually a patient man. He was an aristocrat to his fingertips, self-assured, his manner occasionally verging on the autocratic. But the servants seemed to like him. And there had been laughter in those grey eyes. Tall, athletic, dark haired, grey-eyed, with a sense of humour—James Aldhurst was a very attractive man.... And, she told herself, he was a man who was about to marry. It was better to stop thinking how attractive he was!

She looked round the room for something to distract her and her eye was caught by a mirror on the dressing table opposite the bed. With a shock she realised that she had not the slightest idea of what she herself looked like. Was she beautiful? Or was she plain? What was the colour of her hair, her eyes? She pulled a strand of her hair forwards and saw that it was dark brown. But her eyes? Did she have a squint? Was her nose crooked? Were there gaps in her teeth? She stroked her nose. It felt reassuringly straight. And when she ran her tongue over her teeth they all seemed to be there. That left the question of her eyes, and that couldn't be settled without looking in a mirror.

But the mirror lay tantalisingly out of reach. She sank back. Perhaps it would be better not to see herself at the moment... She would not be looking her best. A bandage was not an aid to beauty, and it was perfectly possible she had a black eye, too. She lay fretting about this for a full minute before she decided that it was no use—she had to get to that mirror!

When she first put her feet to the ground she was not so sure, but after a minute or two she managed to stand without too much difficulty. Taking one step at a time, she held on to the chair, the foot of the bed. So far, so good... She stretched out for the table...and suddenly her legs gave way and she lost her balance.

Rose heard the crash and came running in. When she saw her charge lying on the floor in a heap she ran out in a panic, calling frantically for Mrs Culver.

James had been out with the agent and had just come in. He was in the hall when he heard the maid's cries, leapt up the stairs three at a time and was stunned when he got to the bedroom door to see Anne lying in a crumpled heap by the chest of drawers. But before he even reached her she was struggling to get up, uttering a cry of frustration as she collapsed again, her feet tangled in her nightgown. Without a word he swept her up and took her back to the bed. He stood for a moment holding her in his arms, looking into the face so close to his.

'What happened?' he asked grimly. 'Who did this?'

Chapter Three

James's touch was having a strange effect on Anne. She stammered, 'I d-d-did.'

'What do you mean, *you* did? Who left you lying on the floor?'

'I fell. All by myself. No one else was here.'

'You fell? Why wasn't someone with you?'

'They…they thought I was asleep in bed.'

'So you should have been! What on earth were you doing over there?'

She hesitated, then hung her head and said in a low voice, 'I… I wanted to see what I looked like.'

'See what you…' James looked at the chest of drawers. 'Oh! The mirror!' He regarded her with astonishment. 'You wanted to see yourself in the mirror? Do you realise that you've just given me the devil of a fright! I thought for a moment you'd been attacked!' He started to laugh. 'What does it matter what you look like at the moment? Or did you think your bump on the head had given you a black eye?'

'It isn't at all funny!' she said, looking up indignantly. 'It's very natural to want to know what one looks like, and I have no idea.' After a pause, she added, 'A black eye wouldn't really matter, it wouldn't last. But...have I...have I a squint?'

This produced another laugh, but he quickly became serious and said, 'I'm sorry—I hadn't realised... No, there's no sign of a squint.' He studied her for a moment, then said slowly, 'In fact, I think your eyes are the loveliest I have seen in a long time.'

She was startled. 'What?'

He went on, still studying her intently. 'They are large, the dark blue of lapis lazuli, and they are straight and deep and true. And there's not even a hint of a black eye. Will that do?'

A delicate rose coloured her cheeks. 'I'd say it was more than enough, sir! Thank you.' She gave him a small smile. But something about the way he was looking at her confused her. She looked away and said nervously, 'Perhaps you'd better put me down before Mrs Culver comes in. She won't approve of your being here.'

Laughing, he said, 'Don't you think I deserve something before I do?' Then, when she looked up again, puzzled, he kissed her. The kiss was deliberately light and fleeting, nothing more than a casual caress, but her eyes widened and she stared at him in surprise. For a moment his grip tightened, but he put her carefully down on the bed almost immediately and said abruptly, 'I…I'll get the mirror for you. Then I'll find Mrs Culver or Rose.'

He handed the mirror to her. 'I think you'll be satisfied,' he said with a brief smile as he went out.

When Mrs Culver came in a few minutes later she found her patient lying on top of the bed, looking dazed. 'I'm sorry I was so long—Rose took some time to find me,' she said. 'I see one of the others has put you back, but why didn't they put you properly under the covers? I sometimes ask myself what those girls are thinking about, I really do! Let me straighten you up.' She picked up the mirror.

'What's this?'

'I wanted to see myself in the mirror.'

'Now, Miss Anne, you mustn't be worrying

about that sort of thing. You're not looking your
best at the moment, it's true. Your hair is dirty
and it's in a dreadful tangle, but a good wash will
sort out the worst of it. And it's only natural you
should look a bit peaky...'

'It isn't that. It's my memory—I didn't know
what I look like at all!'

Mrs Culver stared, then her face softened.
'That's a terrible thing, Miss Anne. I hadn't
thought... But don't you worry. We'll soon have
you looking a lot prettier than what you see in
that mirror at the moment. Now what do you
want to do? Do you feel strong enough to sit in
a chair while the maids change the bed?'

Meanwhile, James had left the house puzzled
and feeling in need of fresh air. 'Set your mind
at rest,' he had told Liston. 'I do not make a habit
of seducing helpless invalids.' And when he had
half-jokingly claimed a kiss as his reward, nothing had been further from his mind. Her wide-
eyed shock had at first amused him, but when
he looked into those dark blue eyes it had taken
most of his considerable self-control to put her
down calmly and gently—and leave her.

James Aldhurst rarely allowed his emotions to

run away with him. Personable, rich and eligible, he had been the target of matchmaking mamas and bored sophisticates alike from the day he first entered society. As a result he had learned discretion at a very early age. The young ladies regularly presented to him by their hopeful mamas had left him unmoved, and, though he had conducted affairs with several more experienced beauties with varying degrees of passion, he had never been in any danger of losing his head or his heart. The polite world had learned that, charming though Lord Aldhurst was, he seldom failed to be in complete charge of himself and the situation.

But what had happened when he had held the girl in his arms was disturbingly new, and he was at a loss to explain it. Cully would say it was a case of pity for her situation, and indeed, when he had first come across her, that was exactly what he had felt. But the feeling aroused a short while ago had little to do with pity. It had been totally unexpected, coming quite suddenly out of nowhere, and he was not at all sure he liked the unsettling effect it had on him. It was not only new—it was dangerous. And until he had recovered his senses it would be better for everyone if he kept away from the girl!

* * *

So it was a relief to arrive at the stables and find a need for immediate action. The damage done by the storm two nights ago was already being cleared away by men from the estate, and any evidence about what had happened would soon be lost for ever. Accompanied by Sam Trott, he found without difficulty the spot where she had been lying, just where an ancient, rustic bridge crossed a small stream.

James pointed to the path, which ran beside the stream. 'That path leads to the Portsmouth Road. Perhaps that was where she came from?' They climbed down to look more closely.

'You're right, my lord! Look!' Sam pointed to a large boulder that formed part of the support for the bridge. It had been loosened by the rain, and was sticking out over the path. 'I'd say the young lady fell as she was climbing up the path and hit her head on this stone. And then she clambered—no, crawled—up to the drive before she collapsed.'

They looked at the marks made by a girl desperately scrabbling up the bank. 'She's a determined lass, that one, all right,' Sam said. 'How is she? Has she been able to tell you what happened to her?'

'She can't remember anything at all before we carried her into the house. But she was running away from someone. There are rope burns on her wrists where she has been tied up.'

Sam was shocked. 'Can't she tell you who kept her or how she escaped?'

'Not yet. She could still be in danger. Pass the word on—I want to know if any strangers appear in the neighbourhood asking questions.'

'I'll do that.' Sam looked at the marks on the ground. 'She's a brave lass, whoever she is.'

They were so deep in thought as they walked back up the drive that they said little to each other. But as they neared the house Sam suddenly said, 'That young lady can't have come more than a few miles without being noticed. It was a bad night, but I'd be surprised if someone or other didn't see her. I'll ask Mr Norris and one or two of the farmers, shall I?'

'That's a good idea, Sam. There's very little Norris doesn't hear about sooner or later. Though there won't have been many travellers on the road that evening. It was a terrible night!'

'Indeed it was,' said Sam with some feeling. 'I

heard Mr Norris telling *someone* only madmen would go out in that storm when they could stay safely indoors.'

James grinned at this, but then said seriously, 'If I hadn't decided to carry on to Hatherton that night, your brave young lady would probably have died, Sam.'

'Aye, and that would have been a pity. Right, I'll be off to Norris and the rest, my lord.'

On his way back to the house James decided that he had exaggerated the effect the girl had had on him. He had promised her she would be safe, and the sight of her lying on the floor of the bedroom after apparently being attacked had thrown him off balance, that was all. Was it likely that a sad waif, who couldn't even re-member her own name, would touch him when so many accredited beauties had failed? No, he hardly needed to avoid her. Indeed, it would be cruel and unnecessary. She trusted him. She would expect him. By the time James entered the house he had made up his mind to keep his promise and visit her that evening—in spite of Mrs Culver's certain disapproval.

* * *

When Anne next woke up it was late afternoon. A fire was burning brightly in the fireplace, and for a while she watched its light flickering over the room. Then Mrs Culver came in, followed by Rose, who was carrying a tray. 'There you are!' she said, lighting a lamp. 'I was thinking I would have to wake you. Eat this up and then we'll put you in a chair by the fire for a while.' She disappeared while Anne was eating, but came back shortly, carrying a blue dressing robe. 'Your own clothes will be ready for you tomorrow, but meanwhile I've taken the liberty of borrowing this old robe of Lady Aldhurst's for you.'

In a short while Anne was sitting in front of the fire, trying not to wince as Rose did her best to bring her hair into some order. But the maid was skilled, and after some painful moments Anne's hair was brushed and tied back tidily with a ribbon.

'There, miss,' said Rose. 'You look ever so much better. His lordship *will* be surprised to see you looking so much more the thing.'

'That will do, Rose,' Mrs Culver was severe. 'I doubt his lordship will see anything of the sort! He has spent most of the day trying to find out

where Miss Anne came from, so it's most unlikely he'll visit her again today. He has better
things to do with his time.'

Mrs Culver was wrong. When James came in
he saw her in the hall and immediately asked how
Anne was.

'She is doing very well, my lord. She is awake,
and has eaten a good nourishing meal.'

'I'll see her, then.'

'Rose is with her at the moment. It really isn't
convenient. Besides, I'm afraid I gave orders to
serve your dinner in an hour.' She looked expres-
sively at the mud on James's coat and breeches. 'I
expect you will wish to change.'

'Oh, very well, Cully. I'll see Miss Anne after
dinner.'

'I expect she will be asleep, my lord.' The
housekeeper's tone was discouraging.

James had been about to go to his room, but
now he stopped and looked at her. Then, taking
her by the arm, he led her into the small parlour
off the hall. 'Cully, I have no wish to challenge
your authority in this house, but I shall see Miss
Anne sometime tonight. That girl is feeling com-

pletely lost at the moment and I intend to keep my promise to see her.'

Mrs Culver shook her head. She said, 'You always did go your own way, Master James. But I wish you'd be more careful.' She paused, then added with a touch of temper, 'The sooner that girl is out of the house the better!'

'Why are you so eager to get rid of her, Cully? It isn't like you to be inhospitable.'

'You may be sure I'll see that she is comfortable while she is here. But, I don't like mysteries, and there are too many about this girl you've brought into your grandmother's house. She may have been wearing a beggar woman's dress and boots when you found her, but the rest of her clothes are best quality, and you can tell by the way she treats Rose and the others that she's used to dealing with servants. And, for someone who was at death's door a night or two ago, she has recovered remarkably quickly...' Mrs Culver took a breath. 'I don't suppose you've learned anything more about her this afternoon?'

'It looks as if she came from the Portsmouth Road, though it's quite a distance to walk. Sam Trott is going to ask Norris and others if they have heard of anything. But she will stay here until I am sure she is safe.' When he saw the housekeeper's expression he added sternly, 'You and I are old friends, Cully, but we shall fall out if the girl comes to any harm through anything you do or say. I'd be obliged if you would keep these suspicions of yours to yourself.'

Mrs Culver drew a deep breath and said stiffly, 'My lord, I am surprised at you. In any matter involving the Aldhurst family my discretion has never been called into question. Your lordship may rely on it. Completely.'

'Good!'

'I will see that your lordship's dinner is ready when you are,' said Mrs Culver majestically. She curtsied and went out.

James shook his head ruefully. In deciding to come to Hatherton he had looked for time and peace to consider his future. Instead, he had been plunged into a mystery that threatened to wreck his relationship with one of his oldest allies in the house, as well as offending one of his grand-mother's most trusted servants. Cully might be right, after all—the girl was an unsettling influence and ought to go as soon as possible. If she regained her memory in the next day or two, he would see her safely delivered to her own people. If it looked as if it was going to take much longer than that, he would have to see that she went somewhere where she would be looked after in comfort. He and everyone else at Hatherton could then forget her.

When he entered the green bedroom later that evening, James found Anne dozing in a chair by the fire. The blue robe she was wearing was his grandmother's—he remembered it from his childhood. Her hair had been tied back, revealing an ugly bruise, vulnerable hollows under her cheekbones and dark shadows under her eyes. He came forwards and sat down quietly in a chair near to her. The bandages had been removed from her wrists, and he could see that they were healing. But the sight of cruel red lines still encircling her delicate bones angered him. She must have been in considerable pain.

When he looked up again he saw that her eyes were open and she was staring at him blankly. 'I thought I was safe,' she said quite clearly. 'I thought he hadn't seen me...'

'Who, Anne?'

The deep blue eyes were still wide. With a small

frown she said, 'Why are you calling me Anne? That isn't my name.'

'At last! You've remembered. *What is it?*' But the urgency in his voice had disturbed her.

Now wide awake, she said, 'Of course I remember! It's An...' She paused, wrinkling her brow in desperate concentration. 'It's...' But after a moment she put her hand over her eyes, and said with a sob, 'I almost had it! It was there! But it's gone again.'

James cursed himself for an insensitive fool at the despair in her voice. He took her hand away from her eyes. 'I'm sorry. I shouldn't have pressed you. Were you dreaming?'

'I think I must have been. I was passing an open door. The room inside was full of smoke...' She shook her head in angry frustration. 'I can see just the corner of that room—what use is that?'

'It will come in its own good time. Don't try to force it.'

'But I must! You have no idea what it is like—' She stopped, and almost visibly pulled herself together. 'I know you want to help. Mrs Culver said you were out today looking for clues—about me.' Her eyes searched his face, and then she gave a sigh and looked away. 'You didn't find any,' she said despondently.

'It's true that we didn't find many,' he said, 'But we found a few and we're working on them. You mustn't be unhappy. You're making wonderful progress. Who got you up? Mrs Culver?' She nodded, and he went on, 'My grandmother used to wear that robe when I was a child. The blue suits you.'

'Would Lady Aldhurst mind my wearing it?'

'She would be delighted. Anne—' He stopped. 'May I call you Anne, until we know better? I hope so—I have something for you.' She nodded and he produced a book from his pocket. 'This too is my grandmother's. I gave it to her when it was first published, and I think it is now one of her favourites. You might enjoy it. It's about a girl called Anne. It might amuse you while you have to stay indoors.'

Anne took the book. '*Persuasion*, by Miss Jane Austen.' She turned the pages cautiously then looked up with a tremulous smile. 'What a relief! I can read! I was afraid for a moment that I might have forgotten that, too.'

The uncertain smile undermined him. Forgetting his sensible resolutions, he drew her up and put his arms round her. After a moment, she said in a muffled voice, 'You must think me such a coward.'

'I think nothing of the sort,' he said. He held her for a moment or two, his cheek against hers, then he put her carefully back into her chair, and moved away to look into the fire. He said, 'All the same, I shouldn't be here at this time of night, holding you like that... The rest of the world would never believe it was innocent. I'm supposed to be protecting you. Mrs Culver is right. I must find somewhere else where you can be kept safe until you remember who you are.'

Anne considered him gravely. 'Am I not safe with you?' she asked.

'Of course you are!' he said forcefully. 'That isn't what I meant.'

There was a short silence. Then she said hesitantly, 'Are you afraid your fiancée might not understand the situation? Do you want me to go because she might be hurt or angry if she heard I was staying here with you?'

He turned round again in surprise. 'My what?'

'Mrs Culver told me you are to marry soon. Someone in London.'

'The devil she did! I wonder who the lucky girl is. Did she tell you that?'

'She mentioned a Lady Barbara?' said Anne hesitantly.

'Lady Barbara? Did she indeed?' He took a breath and went on grimly, 'Mrs Culver is mistaken.'

Anne looked at the frown on his face and said quietly, 'I'm sorry. I shouldn't have said anything.'

'I'm glad you did. I am *not* engaged. I never have been engaged, and if it were left to me I never would be engaged. This is my grandmother's doing! She and Cully are desperate to see me married off and producing heirs for Roade House, but I have no intention of letting my grandmother or anyone else dictate when and whom I should marry. No, it is for your own sake that you should go, not for the benefit of an entirely mythical fiancée.'

Anne got out of her chair and put her hand on his arm. 'Then let me stay here,' she said. 'You're the only one I trust at present.' She hesitated and then went on, 'I shall have to leave sometime soon, I know, but the thought of going out into the world before I'm used to the idea terrifies me.'

'What do you mean—have to leave? Who would make you?'

'I can't stay here for ever. I'm sure Mrs Culver would like to see the back of me as soon as possible. And if my memory never returns I shall have to find some other place, where I can earn a living without it. But...I know I'm a coward, but please don't send me away yet.'

James saw how pale and weary she looked. 'If your memory doesn't return, Anne,' he said gently, 'I'll make sure you're not left alone to find your way. Do you believe me?'

She nodded and he went on, 'But now I think you've had enough for today—let me call Rose or someone to see you to bed.'

Before she sat down, she hesitated and said, 'Will I...will I see you tomorrow?'

James shook his head. 'Not tomorrow.' She looked disappointed and he explained, 'I must spend the day at Roade, but I'll see you the day after. We could go for a walk in the garden if you are strong enough. Meanwhile, promise me you'll stay in this room while I am away. Walk a little, read your book—and try not to worry.' He went to the door and turned to bid her goodnight, but when he saw the droop to her head he found himself saying, 'I'll see if I can call on you tomorrow before I go out. Goodnight, Anne. Sleep well.'

Chapter Four

Rose was slow in coming, and Anne sat gazing into the fire for some time after James had gone. Her fears were briefly forgotten as she allowed herself to dream. So Mrs Culver had been wrong—James was not about to marry anyone, not engaged, and, from what he had said, didn't have anyone in mind either…

And after Rose had come and gone she lay awake, inventing a fairy tale to keep her fears about the future at bay. She would recover her memory, and turn out to be an entirely suitable bride for an Aldhurst—the daughter of an earl perhaps, or even a duke. They would fall in love, marry and live happily ever after at Hatherton. What would it be like to sleep with the man you loved, to have his arms around you, holding you, caressing you…? Her last thought before she finally fell asleep was that, though Lord Aldhurst was most unlikely to fall in love with *her*, she was more than halfway to falling in love with *him* already.

But Anne paid dearly for indulging in these romantic fantasies, with a series of nightmares. She was faced with a dark red door that she knew was familiar, but she struggled in vain to reach its knocker… Then, in the way of dreams, the door changed into a spreading pool of dark red blood, and, terrified, she fought to save the man lying at its centre, her heart racing and gasping for breath, struggling against the cruel hands that were dragging her away… Suddenly the hands holding her were James Aldhurst's hands, and she sobbed with relief as she looked again from the protection of his arms and saw that both the pool of blood and the body at its centre had disappeared. She turned thankfully back to him, but when she looked up, his face was cold and distant and he pushed her away, and gradually disappeared into the distance, deaf to her cries.

She woke up at last unrefreshed and lay for a while with traces of tears on her face, her mind full of the images in her dreams. They frightened and confused her—was there a clue to her identity in them? She puzzled over them for some time, but the images meant nothing to her. Her life before she had been found on the drive was still shrouded in grey fog.

And in the cold light of morning her romantic fantasy of the night before seemed more like the delusions of a lunatic. The end of the dream had been telling her as much. Lord Aldhurst would keep her safe until she knew what she was to do, but he could never consider her suitable to be his wife. Although Mrs Culver might have tried to deceive her about his marital plans, her warning was clear enough. He was the last of an ancient and distinguished family and the world would expect him to find a bride of equal rank. Wealthy, handsome, well born, with a duty to his family—why on earth should an Aldhurst ever look at penniless Miss Nobody of Nowhere, who was not even very beautiful?

For a moment she felt very sorry for herself, but was soon ashamed of indulging in so much self-pity. It was time Miss Nobody stopped being so poor-spirited, pulled herself together and started to take charge of her life instead of leaving it to others! She also had things to do!

* * *

When Mrs Culver came in an hour later she was astonished to see Anne walking round the room with grim determination.

'Whatever are you doing?' she exclaimed. 'You shouldn't be up for another hour at least. You'll wear yourself out. Sit down and rest. Rose will fetch your breakfast.'

Anne sat down gratefully in a chair and said, 'I'm not really ill any longer. My legs are weak, that's all, and they won't get any stronger if I don't use them. It's time I had some exercise. I don't intend to be a burden to you all any longer than I have to.'

Mrs Culver gave a satisfied nod. 'I'm sure I'm glad to hear you say that. And if you wish you can put on your own clothes again. I have them here. We've washed and pressed them for you, so they are perfectly clean.'

'Thank you. But I'm afraid *I* am not. Before I dress I should like you to bring water and a towel, if you would.'

The request was reasonable enough, and if Mrs Culver experienced a touch of resentment at the hint of command in this nameless nobody's voice it did not show. 'There's a bath in the dressing room next door—I'll get the maids to fill it. And Rose will wash your hair.'

An hour later, when Anne was sitting in front of the fire while Rose dried her hair, Lord Aldhurst walked in. 'Good morning,' he said with a smile, 'I've come to see how you are.'

'Th-that's very kind of you,' stammered Anne. 'I...I hardly expected to see you at all today. Though you did say...' Her voice faded. This wouldn't do. She pulled herself together, stood up and gave him a slight curtsy. 'Good morning.'

His eyes were on her hair, which was hanging loose in dark chestnut waves down her back. 'You look different,' he said.

'I should hope so indeed! Rose here has just spent a great deal of energy cleaning me up. And I feel much the better for it.'

He came forwards and, frowning, took up a lock of her hair. 'It's...it's a different colour. I thought your hair was darker,' he said.

Anne suppressed a smile and removed the hair from his fingers. 'No, my lord,' she said gravely, 'it merely needed to be washed. And now it is clean. I'm sorry if you don't like its colour, but that is what it is, I'm afraid.' She laughed and added, 'I consider myself fortunate. When I was a child it was much redder and I had a temper to match.'

There was a sudden silence. Then she said in a strangled voice, 'How do I know that?'

James nodded. 'I'm not sure, but it's a good sign. Your memory seems to be returning, if only in fragments.'

'That was a singularly unimportant fragment,' said Anne bitterly. 'My name would be more welcome.' Then she attempted another smile, and added, 'But beggars can't be choosers—I suppose I should be grateful for anything at all.'

There was another short silence, and then she went on in a more formal tone, 'Thank you for your enquiry, my lord. I am much better. I hope you have a pleasant day.'

He paused, then said, 'Have you breakfasted? If not, do you feel strong enough to come downstairs to have it with me?'

She was so taken by surprise that she didn't know what to say. 'With you? I...I thought you wished me to stay in this room?'

'I would like you to stay in your room while I am out—but you would be safe downstairs with me. Of course, if you would prefer not to join me...'

'No, no! I should like to! But I can't be seen downstairs with my hair like this.'

'Shall we say in ten minutes? I'll talk to Mrs Culver. And Rose can do whatever is necessary to your hair.'

He bowed and left the room. Rose was already busy with brush and comb, twisting and winding Anne's hair into a graceful knot on top of her head. When she had finished she gave it a final pat and said, 'There, miss! You look lovely. His lordship will be pleased!' She paused. 'But I wouldn't be so sure about Mrs Culver.'

Anne privately agreed with the maid, but she said coolly, 'His lordship will be relieved to see that I shall soon be strong enough to take up my own life again. And so will Mrs Culver. Thank you, Rose. Show me where the breakfast room is, if you please.'

If the caretaker at Roade House had expected to see James early that day then he would have been disappointed. James spent more than an hour over breakfast and the morning was half over before he finally rose from the table. Anne sat opposite him, a touch of colour in her cheeks and a swathe of glossy hair falling from the simple knot on top of her head. She was an altogether different creature from the pale waif he had rescued, and she intrigued and delighted him. Her dress, as Cully had said, was of poor material and very simply cut, a servant's dress, but she wore it with an air. Though he knew she felt vulnerable, even frightened, at her inability to remember anything about herself, no one would have guessed it from her composed manner. Her conversation was of necessity not about herself, but it was lively, sometimes displaying a touch of irony that perfectly matched his own, and occasionally revealing a keen sense of the ridiculous that made him laugh out loud.

Anne in turn was equally happy in his company. He talked with affection of his grandmother, and it was clear to Anne the bond between them was very close. She was obviously a woman of strong character, but he seemed to be amused rather than annoyed by her attempts to rule his life. Anne herself was amused at Mrs Culver's determination not to leave her alone with James. She was in and out of the breakfast room far more frequently than strictly necessary, clearly disapproving of this joint breakfast. But James ignored her frowns, and quite often called on her to confirm or add to what he said when he was telling Anne stories of his childhood at Hatherton. Anne observed with interest how quickly the housekeeper responded to James's charm. Before breakfast was over Mrs Culver was actually smiling again.

At last James reluctantly rose from the table and said, 'It's no use. If I am to keep my promise to Agnew I shall have to be gone. What do you plan to do today, Anne?'

Anne looked at Mrs Culver. 'I think I would be strong enough to do some work, if Mrs Culver has anything for me to do?'

'It's good of you to offer, Miss Anne, but I'm sure his lordship would prefer you to be resting in your room. And so would I.' Mrs Culver's tone was cool. James might be back in her favour but this didn't extend to his guest.

James frowned, but said nothing. Instead, he turned to Anne and held out his arm with a smile. 'Mrs Culver is right as usual. I'll see you to your room. The stairs are steep, and you are still not quite up to strength. I don't suppose you've started the book I gave you, have you?'

'No,' said Anne, looking at Mrs Culver's retreating back. 'I'm looking forward to reading it today.' Then as they slowly mounted the stairs, she said softly, 'You are wrong to tease Mrs Culver, Lord Aldhurst. I'm sure she has your interests at heart.'

'What does that mean?'

'I'm glad of your arm up these stairs, but it would have been quite easy to ask one of the servants to help me, and very much more...tactful. It's nonsensical, of course, but Mrs Cully sees me as a threat. She doesn't trust me.'

They had reached the door of her room. He opened it, then said softly, 'I'm not sure it's as nonsensical as you think, Anne.'

She looked up at him, startled. 'You don't trust me?'

'Oh, I trust you, of course I do! But you're definitely proving a threat to my peace of mind.' He added abruptly, 'I must go! Agnew will be wondering what has happened to me. Enjoy your day! Read the book and stay in your room! Please?' He turned towards the stairs, stopped, turned again and said, 'I'll look in on you this evening to see if you like the book. May I?'

'Of course,' said Anne. She pulled a face. 'I

think I can safely promise to be at home, Lord Aldhurst.'

She watched him race down the stairs, then went in, closed the door and hurried to the window. Two horses, one a powerful bay, were standing outside the front doors, held by a groom. James came out, mounted the bay and they moved off. Anne followed him with her eyes until he disappeared round a bend in the drive. Then she turned with a sigh, fetched the book and sat in a chair to read it. When Rose came in with a tray an hour later she was absorbed in the story of gentle Anne Elliot.

Later that afternoon Anne abandoned her book in favour of some exercise. She was walking vigorously round the room when Mrs Culver came in, a collection of clothes over one arm. She congratulated Anne on the progress she was making, then went on, 'I've looked out a change of clothing for you, Miss Anne, though if you carry on as well as you seem to be doing at the moment you may have left us before you need them all. I hope you don't mind—they are old dresses and such of Lady Aldhurst's.'

Anne was touched. 'Thank you, Mrs Culver. I'm sorry to be such a nuisance.'

Mrs Culver hesitated, and then she said, 'The underclothes may be plainer than you are used to, I think…?'

Anne was puzzled. 'Are mine so elaborate? I hadn't thought…' She lifted her skirt and examined the lace round the bottom of her petticoat. 'I suppose they are. This is beautiful. I wonder where it came from.' She looked up to find Mrs Culver regarding her with a strange look. 'You think I know? I only wish I did. I take it that the garments *are* mine?'

'They are indeed, miss. And very fancy they are, too.'

The touch of disapproval, which almost amounted to hostility, in the woman's voice, was accompanied by a very sharp look. Anne took a breath and said carefully, 'You obviously regard me with suspicion, Mrs Culver. Why?'

'I'm sorry if I've upset you. But I know that Lady Aldhurst's dearest wish is to see Master James married and with a family.'

Somewhat mystified, Anne said, 'That's very natural. I hope she wishes him to be happy as well?'

'Of course. And he will be, as long as he finds a wife from his own world, a lady of rank, breeding, a good *name* of her own that everyone knows. People in London don't like mysteries.'

Mrs Culver's intention was now plain. Though annoyed, Anne said calmly enough, 'You are worried that Lord Aldhurst might be distracted from this goal by me, perhaps? You needn't be, I assure you. But what have my clothes to do with it?'

'They're all wrong. Not even one of the kitchen maids here would wear the dress and boots you had on when you arrived. They're more like a tavern wench's things. But your underclothes are quite different.'

Anne began to laugh. 'You're suspicious because my chemise and my petticoat don't match my dress and boots? But that is absurd!'

Mrs Culver flushed unbecomingly. 'Master James brought you here, Miss Anne, and we've looked after you as well as anyone could expect. But—I'll come straight out with it—we still don't know who you are or where you came from.'

Anne gave her a twisted smile. 'Any more than I do.' There was an awkward, significant silence.... The colour rose in Anne's cheeks. 'Oh, come, ma'am!' she said angrily. 'You surely cannot think I'm play-acting!'

'I suppose not. But how can we be sure?'

Anne went to the window and stood with her back to the housekeeper until she had mastered her anger. Then she turned and said, 'I do not remember who I am or how I came to be lying on your drive. But I promise you that as soon as I feel I can face the world again I shall leave Hatherton, whether my memory has returned or not. Will that do?'

Mrs Culver looked uncomfortable. 'I don't want to be cruel, Miss Anne. But I know Master James, and I can see he's taken a fancy to you. And it mustn't go any further. It would break his grandmother's heart if he married badly. He is all she has left.'

'Yes, well, if that is the case we must hope that he doesn't actually fall in love with someone who is as unsuitable as I am,' said Anne crisply. 'But he is in no danger from me.' She took up her book. 'Now I think I've had enough of this conversation. Thank you for the clothes. When Lord Aldhurst returns you may tell him that I have a headache, and would prefer not to see him this evening.'

Mrs Culver found herself curtsying in response to the authoritative tone in Anne's voice, and left the room rather apprehensively, wondering if she was making a mistake. Those last sentences had sounded as if they came from someone of quality, not at all the owner of a shabby dress.

But she delivered Anne's message as requested that evening. And Master James's air of disappointment reassured her once again that she was doing the right thing.

After Mrs Culver had gone, Anne sat at the window for some time with the book on her knee, but it lay unread. She was deep in thought. The housekeeper's suspicions were ridiculous, but Anne could not disagree with her basic message. The sooner she left Hatherton the better. She sighed and set about some serious thinking....

She reflected again on the previous night's dreams. The red door—where was it? She could almost believe she had actually tried and failed to knock on that door, and not just in her dream... She had been excited, full of happy anticipation, she remembered... But though she tried to hold on to it the picture dissolved and turned into a pool of blood. She heard her own voice shouting hoarsely, 'No! No! It can't be!' and she suddenly felt sick. She thrust the image violently away out of her mind, and the pool vanished. But she was still shivering with horror... James's book slid to the floor as she jumped up and walked agitatedly round the room, resolutely keeping her mind blank. She *would not* remember, it was better *not* to remember...

After a moment or two she had calmed down enough to sit down again and turn her mind to other matters. Was there a clue in the petticoat and the rest of her clothes? Had the boots and dress belonged to someone else? But who could that be...?

When Rose came in Anne was wearing nothing but the blue robe, anxiously examining her underwear.

'Help me to look at these things, Rose,' she said. 'There must be *something* about them that will tell us where they came from.'

'I'd say that they were especially made for you, Miss Anne. You can tell that by looking at this shaping. But there's nothing else. And this dress is just like one the girls in the village wear.'

Anne pushed the clothes away dispiritedly. 'I'm quite tired. I think I shall go to bed, Rose. Mrs Culver knows I don't wish to see...anyone tonight.'

Rose nodded sympathetically. 'You've done too

much today, miss. But his lordship will be sorry not to see you.' She said no more as she busied herself helping Anne to prepare for bed, but just before leaving the room she asked if Anne would like a glass of milk later on. 'It's a long time till morning, Miss Anne. A glass of milk might be welcome. I won't wake you if you're asleep.'

Too weary to argue, Anne nodded her head. She was already half-asleep by the time Rose had made up the fire, drawn the curtains and slipped quietly away.

She slept soundly and dreamlessly for several hours, but woke up when she heard her door open. The fire had died down somewhat, but there was enough light for her to see someone entering the room and approaching the bed.

'Rose?'

'I'm afraid it isn't Rose.' James Aldhurst put the glass of milk he was carrying down on the table by the bed, picked up her candlestick and took it over to the fire. In a few minutes the soft glow of candles was creating a pool of light round the bed.

Chapter Five

'You shouldn't be here!' whispered Anne.

'It isn't late. No later than when I came last night. How is your head?'

'My head? Oh, yes, my head! It's much better, thank you. Why did you come?'

'I was afraid you might be ill again. So when I saw Rose with the glass of milk I said I would deliver it.'

'You shouldn't have done that. Mrs Culver—'

'Mrs Culver is in bed with a headache. Let me help you to sit up.'

He leaned over, and supported her with one arm while he rearranged her pillows. 'There! Now drink the milk.'

He handed her the glass and sat down on the edge of the bed. She sipped it, looking at him warily over the rim of the glass. He took the glass from her and said, 'I have some news for you.'

Anne leaned forwards eagerly. 'You've found out who I am!'

'No, no! Nothing as helpful as that.' When she sank back disappointed against the pillows he went on, 'But it might be a beginning. There was a coach accident the night we found you. It's thought that the driver took a wrong turning a mile or two back along the Portsmouth Road and ended up stranded by a stretch of flood water. He tried to get back over Firland Cross Bridge, which any local knows is barely wide enough for a cart, let alone a full-sized coach. The coach lost a wheel and crashed into the stream.'

'Who was he? Where is he now?'

'Ah, that's the problem. He can't have been very seriously injured. The coach was a complete wreck, so he took the horses and abandoned it. He has disappeared.'

Anne didn't respond. She was staring into the darkness, her eyes full of horror. James went on, 'It's probable there were two of them, but if so the other one has disappeared, too. There were two horses. Two horses and two men.'

'Two men. One on the box, one inside,' whispered Anne, her eyes wide and unfocused. 'That's all. Only two. One on the box and one inside.

Don't give up hope! There are only two of them. One on the box and the other—' She suddenly gave a scream and thrust out her hands in a frantic gesture to save herself. 'Aaah! Oh, please God, *help me!*'

'Anne? Anne!' James took her by the shoulders and shook her. For a moment she was rigid, staring at him without seeing him. Then she relaxed, gave a shuddering sigh, and threw herself into his arms. He held her close as she said hoarsely, 'The coach overturned and water was rising inside it. I thought I was going to die. But I fought…and suddenly I was free… The stream was cold, but it wasn't far to the bank… And afterwards I ran and ran. I had such a pain in my side, I didn't know where I was going, but I dared not stop. I could hear them behind me… Then I slipped and I was so sure they would catch me again…'

She was shivering, and he held her fast, stroking her hair. 'Hush, hush. You didn't die, they didn't catch you, and you're quite safe here with me.'

She lay in the circle of his arms and gradually the shivering stopped and she was quiet. Still holding her, he sat, thinking over what she had just said. This was without doubt the coach that had carried her into the district. He must have a look at it tomorrow.

That was for tomorrow, but tonight he was beginning to realise exactly what Anne had been through. She had at last remembered something, but he could almost wish it had remained buried for her sake—the horror of the accident, her helplessness as the water rose inside the coach, her certainty that she was about to drown… And then her panic-stricken flight, which had ended in her collapse on the drive at Hatherton. Throughout it all was her refusal to give in, her determination to survive. Sam had called her a brave lass, but he didn't know the half of it. James was visited by a fierce desire to defend her, to find the villains who had put her into such mortal danger, and make them suffer for it.

He sat holding her for a little longer, surprised again at the depth of his feelings. They were a far cry from the light-hearted flirtations, the short-lived affairs, which had earned him his grandmother's disapproval. But he wasn't sure that that lady would approve of his growing interest in Anne, either. In fact, he was damn certain she wouldn't! He could hear her now, not shouting—his grandmother never shouted—but with a voice icy with anger. 'What are you trying to do, James? Ruin us? Make us the laughing stock of the scandal sheets? Have you considered what the world will make of this? Barbara Furness, Mary Abernauld, Clara Paston—all of them the cream of London society! And now you insult them and me by spending your time with a...a nameless nobody. Aldhurst of Roade House and Miss Who Knows What of Nobody Knows Where! I won't have it, I tell you! I won't have it!' Yes, he was quite sure his grandmother would not approve. Shaking his head ruefully, he put Anne gently back against the pillows. For the moment it was more important to establish her identity. He looked at her. There were traces of tears on her face, but she looked very beautiful. He bent over and kissed her cheek. She murmured a small protest, but didn't wake. James picked up one of the candles, blew the rest out and left.

The next day he had an early breakfast, collected Sam Trott and was soon on his way to the site of the accident. It promised to be a fine spring day, and as he rode along he decided he would take Anne for a walk outdoors when he got back.

Fresh air and new surroundings would be good for her. She would be safe in Hatherton's walled garden, sheltered from prying eyes as well as any cold winds, and he was sure she would enjoy it.

How would he feel if today was the day her memory came back? Glad, of course, there was no question of that. The present state of affairs couldn't last for ever. And if she remembered her proper place in the world he must help her find her way back to it. The thought was surprisingly unwelcome and he thrust it aside and concentrated instead on what they would find at Firland Cross.

They had no difficulty in finding the coach. The flood waters had by this time completely subsided, and someone had hauled it out of the stream and left it on the bank.

'There's nothing much here,' said Sam, clambering over the wreck. 'You wouldn't get more than a guinea or two for the whole lot. And I tell you, Master James, it can't have been a comfortable ride for anyone, let alone someone with their hands tied together.' He was now rummaging inside. 'It's completely empty. There's nothing here at all.'

James was walking along, examining the bank.

He bent down and called, 'Look, here's where the horses got out. The ground is soft after the rain and you can still see their hoof marks. And this must be where our girl escaped. See?'

Sam didn't reply, and when James looked up he saw that the groom was out of the coach and standing on the bank, his eye fixed on a figure walking purposefully down the hill with a gun in his hands. James abandoned his search and joined him on the bank, but he laughed as the bluff, homespun figure approached, 'It's all right, Sam. It's one of my grandmother's tenants, Holford from Firland Farm—though he's put on some weight since I last saw him. Good day to you, Mr Holford.'

'Well, bless my soul, if it isn't Master James! How are you, my lord?' The farmer put the gun under his arm and shook hands. Then he gave a great laugh and said, 'I thought for a minute you were one of them ruffians come back to have another look at that coach.'

'Ruffians? What ruffians?' asked James with interest.

'Nat and I saw a couple of suspicious characters round that coach few days ago. I don't suppose you remember Nat, my lord? He's my youngest boy.'

'Of course I do. He must be fourteen or fifteen by now.'

'Aye, and he's a strapping lad, though he's just fourteen.'

'These "suspicious characters", Mr Holford. You've seen them before? Spoken to them?'

'No, we haven't. And we didn't have a chance to speak to them the other day, either. They ran off as soon as they saw us coming down the hill. They were likely looking for something, but there wasn't anything to find. Nat and one or two of the men had pulled the wreck out of the stream the day before, but there wasn't much left in it—just an empty purse and a bit of rope.'

'Let me know if the men come back again, Holford. And if you still have that purse I'd like a look at it.'

'Here's the purse, my lord. You can have that with pleasure, but we threw the rope away.'

James was turning the purse over in his hands. As Holford had said, it was empty, but when he pulled it flat he could see that it had a monogram of sorts embroidered on one side. An *A* and a *C*... AC... Anne C...?

Holford's voice broke into his thoughts. 'If we happen to find anything else I'll send Nat over with it, shall I?'

'I'd be obliged if you would.' James spent a minute or two longer with Holford, but left as soon as he could. The purse was not much of a clue, but it might provide the trigger for Anne's memory. He would show it to her when he got back.

Meanwhile, Anne had woken up, and when she found that she could remember everything from the night before she was full of eager anticipation. Perhaps this morning...? But the excitement died away again when she discovered that her name was still a blank, along with the rest of her past. For a while she was despondent at the thought of spending yet another day without a name, but then Rose came in, and by the time she was dressed she was more cheerful. Lord Aldhurst had invited her to breakfast the day before. She might be invited to join him for breakfast again today. At the very least he was sure to pay her a visit to see how she was. Rose went away and Anne sat waiting for him.

But it was Mrs Culver who came, and when

Anne reluctantly asked after Lord Aldhurst she told her he had already left the house.

Her disappointment was so intense that, before she could stop herself, she asked, 'Did he...did he leave a message for me?'

The housekeeper shook her head. 'He probably forgot,' she said with a touch of satisfaction. 'His lordship can't inform anyone and everyone about his plans for the day. He's a busy man.' She put her tray down and busied herself setting the table by the fire. 'He has a number of friends in the district, of course. Or he might be up at Roade House with the caretaker there. After all, that's why he came to Hatherton in the first place, though he hasn't so far done much about it. One visit to Mr Agnew, that's all—and that didn't last long.' She put the last touches to the table. 'Your breakfast is ready, miss.' As she left he room she added, 'One thing I do know is that he won't want to waste any *more* time. Lady Aldhurst will expect him back in London before long.'

Lower than ever in spirits, Anne ate her breakfast alone, and then, determined to put her disappointment behind her, walked vigorously round

her room until she was quite out of breath. Lord
Aldhurst had his own life to lead, she told herself
as she marched round. He had already been extraordinarily kind to her, and she must not expect
more. Perhaps he had been embarrassed by her
breakdown last night, and was keeping his distance. Or perhaps he was visiting friends in the
neighbourhood. The neighbours might have a
beautiful, eligible, suitable daughter... She realised she had come to a standstill, and with an
impatient shake of her head she started off round
the room again. This would not do! The sooner
she accepted that James Aldhurst was out of her
reach, and worked out how to leave Hatherton,
the better! From now on she would concentrate
on getting stronger and forget how interesting he
could be, how charming, how very handsome...
She realised with a start that she had stopped and
was gazing into space yet again! She must stop
being such a lovesick idiot! Anne pulled herself
together and circled the room several more times
until she had calmed down. Then she picked up
her book with determination and began to read.

But when James eventually came in the book
was on her lap and she was sitting, gazing out of

the window. She jumped when he spoke, and her book fell to the floor.

'I'm sorry if *Persuasion* was not to your taste,' he said, picking it up and replacing it. 'I was so sure it would be. How are you?'

'I am well, thank you,' she replied, doing her best to disguise her pleasure at seeing him. 'And I loved *Persuasion* and would like to read some more of Miss Austen's books.'

'You've finished it? Good! I have another in mind for you, but we'll leave that for later.' He came round to examine her more closely. 'You looked surprised when I came in.'

'That was because I wasn't expecting to see you.'

'Why not? You must have known I'd be back if only to see how you were after last night. Do you still remember what you told me? It was quite harrowing.'

'Yes. I can remember everything I said—every word. But no more than that.' She paused, and added bitterly, 'Certainly not my name.'

He put a sympathetic hand on her shoulder. 'Don't lose heart, Anne. I have something here that just might help. Look.' He produced the purse the farmer had found in the coach. 'Does this mean anything to you? The initials could be yours.'

Anne held the purse in her hands for several moments, staring at it. Then she turned it over, smoothed it with her finger, held it up. 'A... C... *A* for Anne? *A* for Annabel? Alice? Amy? And C... *C* for what?' She shook her head and thrust the purse back into his hand. 'They could be my initials,' she said abruptly, 'but as far as I know I've never seen the thing before.' She jumped up, walked away and stood with her back to him. 'I just don't remember it!' she said in a stifled voice.

He gazed at her in silence for a moment, then said, 'It's too sunny a day to waste indoors. How would you like to see the garden? Hatherton is proud of its gardens.' She hesitated, uncertain what to do. 'It would be good for you,' he said persuasively. 'You won't be cold. The garden is sheltered from the wind—a shawl would be enough. I've brought one for you and I've even borrowed a hat from Rose.' When she still remained silent he put the shawl round her shoulders and a simple flat straw hat on her head and led her over to the mirror. 'There—see how pretty you look! Not a squint or a black eye in sight! Shall we go?'

He led her downstairs, along a corridor to the back of the house and out into the warm spring sunshine. Anne stopped to breathe in the fresh, herb-scented air, and then, with a sudden lift of spirits, she smiled at him and said, 'Thank you.'

James smiled back at her and said, 'Wait till you see what comes next!' He took her along a stone-flagged path, which ended in a gate set in a high wall. 'This particular garden is my grandmother's creation,' he said as he unlocked the gate. 'It's her special place, though now she leaves the work to her gardener while she sits and watches what he's doing. Whenever she is at Hatherton this is the place you are most likely to find her, no matter what the season.'

He opened the gate, and she went through and stopped to feast her eyes on the garden inside. It was set against a tranquil background of grey stone walls and soft greenery, a garden full of spring, with clumps of rich golden daffodils, creamy jonquils, an array of scarlet tulips... She forgot her troubles as she wandered on, bending down now and again to admire pale yellow primroses or to take in the scent of dark purple violets. Pots of lavender and rosemary, beds of roses, lilacs and honeysuckles climbing up the walls, hinted at pleasures to come, waiting to give the garden colour and scent when the spring flowers had gone.

James sat on a bench, content to watch Anne as she walked along the paths, stopping to sniff a flower, gently finger a leaf or examine a bud. This was the first time he had been able to observe her at a distance, to see her as someone he might meet socially at a garden party, or at one of his friends' houses. Her dress was simple, her boots serviceable rather than elegant, but she moved among his grandmother's flowers with grace and inborn pride, an aristocrat to the tips of her fingers.

She came back to the bench and sank down gratefully beside him. 'Thank you. Your grandmother is a genius. And you are very kind.' She hesitated, and then, not looking at him, she said, 'I have an apology to make. This morning when you went out without…without saying anything, I wondered if you were tired of me and the problems I had brought you. Mrs Culver kept telling me what a busy man you were, and after… after last night I thought you wouldn't want to waste any more of your time on me. I know your opinion of poor-spirited females, you see, and last night I was disgracefully poor-spirited! I'm sorry for burdening you so.'

'*Burdening* me?' he said, amazed that she had so little idea of what he thought of her. 'What a ridiculous notion! The more I see of you the more I wonder at your courage.'

'I'm n-not at all b-brave,' she stammered.

'Oh, yes, you are. But what on earth made you think I had deserted you?'

'I was...I was disappointed. And stupid. Mrs Culver told me you had gone out without leaving word and I thought...'

'Ah! I see. You thought we would have breakfast together again, was that it? I wanted a look at that coach and was up and out too early to call on you before I left. But...' he gave her a smile and took her hand '...before I went I had planned to bring you out here when I got back. Does that make you happier?'

His hand round hers felt warm and comforting. She nodded, and said, 'I should have guessed that you would look for the coach. Did you find it?'

'Very easily—one of the farmers had already hauled it out of the stream. He found the purse—together with a piece of rope.' Stroking her wrists with his thumbs, he said, 'I can guess what the rope was used for. And I had great hopes of the purse. But it didn't help, did it?'

She shook her head and her feeling of happiness vanished, 'That's just it. *Nothing* seems to help!' She got up and walked away, suddenly struggling for calm. 'Why is it?' she burst out. 'Why on earth is it that I remember the names of most of the plants in this garden, but *can't remember my own*? You cannot imagine what it feels like to live with only half a mind. I'm in limbo!'

James followed her and drew her back against him. 'Nonsense! You're not in limbo, you're in the garden at Hatherton, and you're living with me, not half a mind. I'm better than that.'

This made her laugh in spite of herself. 'Indeed you are!'

'Tell me what you've been doing today. I suppose Cully told you where I was?'

'She wasn't sure. She said you might be visiting your friends, or calling at Roade House.'

'I'm surprised at Cully! She knew precisely where I was going and what I was doing, because I told her. I was sure she would pass it on to you.'

'Mrs Culver thinks I'm a bad influence on you. She's afraid I'll distract you from what you're here for. I don't know what that is, of course. Why *are* you here at Hatherton?'

'I'm here to see what ought to be done to Roade House.'

'Roade House?'

'The big house up the valley from here. Sit down on this bench and I'll tell you about it. My great-grandfather built it. He was already more than rich enough when he married an heiress, Christina Roade. They decided Hatherton was too small and too old-fashioned for them, so they built a mansion on the side of the hill half a mile up the valley and called it Roade House.' He stopped and she wondered why he frowned. 'The house…the house has been…has been practically unused since my grandmother moved out of it after my grandfather died. It needs a lot of attention.' Almost reluctantly he said, 'Would you like to see it? If the weather is as good tomorrow I'll show it to you. Could you could manage that?'

'I'm sure I could.'

'Or—better still—do you ride?'

She cocked her head and gave him a mock-reproachful look. 'Now how would I know that, Lord Aldhurst?' Then she laughed and said cheerfully, 'But I expect I do. I could certainly try.'

James looked at her animated face, and secretly congratulated himself on distracting her from her problems. 'We shall see tomorrow. I have an idea my mother's riding things are in the attics here. I'll get Cully to look them out.'

'Mrs Culver will no doubt be delighted,' said Anne drily.

'Cully is all right. She'll come round in time.'

'Not if she sees me as a threat to her darlings! How long has she been in service with the Aldhursts?'

'All her life. She came as a girl when my grandmother was first married and has been with her ever since. Don't worry about the riding things—she'll look them out tomorrow morning. So, would you like to ride up to the House with me?'

'Weather, ability and Mrs Culver permitting, I think I would. Thank you!'

'Now I have another suggestion to make!'

'Which is?'

'I shan't ask you if you play chess—you'll tell

me you don't know. But we shall see what you can do.'

'When? Now?'

'Tonight. I must go soon to have a word with one of the farmers, and will probably eat with them... Shall we try a game when I come back? It won't be late.'

'I'm perfectly willing to try, though I give you no guarantees. Where shall we play? Much as I like my bedroom, I don't think Mrs Culver would approve.'

'We won't risk it. I'll order a fire to be lit in the library and we shall play there. Would you like that?'

'Very much!' James saw her pull the shawl up round her shoulders, looked at the slanting shadows in the garden and said firmly, 'I think it's time we went in, don't you? And, after I've seen you to your room, I shall find Mrs Culver and tell her our plans.'

Anne went upstairs in a more cheerful frame of mind. James had made her feel a real person again with something to contribute, something to look forward to. The feeling was probably temporary, but it was pleasant while it lasted. At the door to her room he held her hand, and said, 'Till tonight, Anne.' His eyes lingered on her mouth, and she thought for one heart-stopping moment he was about to kiss her. But he shook his head ruefully and walked to the stairs. He turned and looked back. 'Till tonight,' he said again.

She went in and shut the door.

Chapter Six

Now that she was alone Anne found she was tired after her walk in the garden. She went over to her chair by the window and sat down. Her thoughts were full of James Aldhurst, his warmth, his concern for her, his refusal to let her despair. She somehow doubted that many of his London friends had seen this side of him. Certainly not the beautiful, well-connected Lady Barbara. He had described London to her over their shared breakfast, the busy streets, the houses, the balls, the soirées. She closed her eyes and saw herself in a white silk dress, gliding down the room on his arm, the centre of admiration…

'Miss Anne! Wake up, Miss Anne!' Someone was shaking her shoulder. It was Rose with her evening meal. As she arranged Anne's tray she

said, 'You must have done too much this afternoon, miss. You've tired yourself out.'

'I was glad of a rest afterwards,' Anne admitted. 'But I'm sure the fresh air did me good.'

'What did you think of her ladyship's garden?'
Rose talked to Anne as she busied herself about
the room, tidying up. When she had finished she
paused, and then said, 'The fire in the library is
already lit. The room will be nice and warm for
you. You could wait there for his lordship if you
wished.'

Anne looked with amusement at the maid.
'Thank you. Yes, I think I will,' she said calmly.
'I suppose the whole household knows that we
are to play a game of chess there tonight?'

'Well, Miss Anne, there isn't much that escapes
us. Most of us are related one way or another,
and the ones that aren't have been here for years.
But we don't talk to outsiders. Would you like me
to brush your dress and do your hair before you
go down?' Anne nodded and Rose went on, 'It's
a real shame you haven't anything else to wear—
especially when there are so many clothes in the
presses upstairs. You're a bit taller than her ladyship, but there are some that belonged to his lordship's mother which would fit you very well.'

'I'm quite happy with this dress, Rose, especially if you would give it a brush. Mrs Culver did bring some others for me, but you're right. Both dresses are rather short.'

'Hmm! Those were only fit for the rag bag, if you ask me. There are much prettier ones upstairs.' She gave Anne a look. 'But perhaps Mrs Culver doesn't want you to look pretty.'

'I am very happy with whatever she brings, Rose. Beggars can't be choosers. But I would like you to do my hair. You have such a good touch.'

'You're no beggar, Miss Anne! Supposing I took some of the lace off your petticoat and made a collar for that dark dress of yours. It wouldn't take more than half an hour and the dress would look much better. Shall I?'

Anne smiled. Rose's enthusiasm was very appealing. 'Why not?' she said.

And when Anne put the dress on again an hour later she was amazed at its transformation. The cheap servant's dress with its high fastening and long, ill-cut sleeves had changed into something quite different. Its high-necked bodice now had a white collar and cuffs edged with lace, turning its wearer into a demure Quaker girl of a bygone era. Rose had finished by brushing Anne's hair into neat bands and winding it all on top of her head in a coronet of polished chestnut. 'I knew it would look right on you, Miss Anne! I just knew it! I wonder what his lordship will think.'

'I wonder what Mrs Culver will think, Rose! You must finish off now. You'll be in trouble if you spend much more of your time up here. But I do thank you for your work.'

'Mrs Culver has gone out and won't be back for another hour or more. I've always wanted to be a lady's maid, Miss Anne, and doing things for you these past days has been a real pleasure.'

'Well,' Anne said, laughing, 'if I turn out to be a lady, and if I need a maid, I shall send for you.'

Rose grinned. 'Better be careful, Miss Anne. You might turn out to be a Duchess, and what would a Duchess do with a maid like me? Would you like me to help you downstairs?'

Anne entered the library, and stopped short at the sight of the shelves of books, the smell of leather, the faint scent of pine logs on the fire, the rich colours of Oriental rugs, decanters with golden contents, glasses scintillating in the light... She had never been in this room before, but the mixture was potently familiar. Sometime, somewhere, she had spent a good deal of her leisure in a room very like this one. Quite when and where that had been stayed lost in the dark recesses of her mind, but this time she refused to be depressed. Tonight was a night to put aside her problems, a night to be enjoyed.

It was still early, and she knew James would not be there for some time. So she wandered round the room looking with interest at objects on display—a sword used in 1645 by a Royalist Aldhurst on the wall above the fireplace, a tiny linen cap worn by an Aldhurst baby in 1510, and a letter from Queen Anne to James's great-great-grandfather in a small glass-topped display table. Then she looked along the shelves for a book, and was soon sitting by the fire, in the excellent light of a branching candlestick, happily dipping into a copy of *Pride and Prejudice.*

So when James came in he was faced with the enchanting sight of Anne lost to the world in a book held in slender white-cuffed hands. The light of the candles in front of her had turned her chestnut hair to copper flame, her face was in profile, a pure line through cheek and delicate throat down to the white of her collar, her dress a dark background to the whole. For a moment it could have been a picture by some Dutch artist, and he wished he could find someone to paint it—a study of contrasts, light and shade, warm chestnut flame and cool white, the stillness of the figure and the leaping firelight... But she looked up and the moment had gone.

'This is a surprise!' she exclaimed. She put the book down and came towards him, smiling and holding out her hands. 'You're here much sooner than I expected.'

He took her hands and held her away from him. 'I managed to get away early. I'm glad to see that you don't look at all tired after your outing. Where *did* you find your new dress?'

Anne laughed. 'Thank you! It's a very old one created by Rose with help from a frill from my petticoat. I'm pleased you like it.'

'I like it very much, though I'm not sure why— Puritan girls are not usually my style!' He led her back to her chair. 'When I came in you looked so contented reading your book that I hardly dared disturb you! Do you still want to try a game of chess, or would you prefer to read?'

'I can read when I'm alone. I'd like a game of chess with you.'

James moved the book and the candlestick from her table and Anne watched in fascination as he unfolded the top and revealed a board inlaid with squares of black and white. As he laid the chessmen out on the board he named each one to her—king and queen, bishop and rook, knight and pawn—and demonstrated the moves each one could make.

'Good,' he said. 'I think you know enough. We shall begin. We'll have a practice run first.'

Anne looked at him. He was very confident. She wondered whether to tell him that she knew she could play. She had, in fact, known as soon as she had seen the chessmen. But she decided it would be more fun not to tell, and this evening was a time for fun.

James pushed one of his pawns forwards and waited. Anne hesitated, looked at him doubtfully and then responded. She made some deliberate mistakes, but not too many of them, and listened attentively as James explained where she had gone wrong. After a while he announced that they could play in earnest.

* * *

The game went slowly at first as Anne paused before each move, apparently trying to remember what he had told her. James, who was renowned throughout London for his opinion of people who hesitated too long at cards or chess, was not at all bored. He made his moves when it was his turn, and otherwise sat back and took pleasure in watching the girl opposite him. The fresh air of the afternoon seemed to have done her good. Her cheeks had more colour in them, and her eyes were clear and full of animation. She looked very lovely, though one of her braids had come unfastened and a lock of hair was resting over her shoulder. It fascinated him—it seemed to have a life of its own in the flickering light of the fire, and he could very easily imagine the red-headed child she said she had been...

Time passed. Anne was now wearing a frown of concentration as she studied the board in front of her, and James was intrigued to see the tip of her tongue appear as she deliberated. He had seldom seen anything so innocently seductive, he thought, moving his bishop.

'Er...I'm not sure what I should do now,' Anne said.

James looked at the board. 'Isn't your queen in danger?'

'Not if I take that bishop with my knight. Like that. Is this where I say "Check"?'

James looked at the board again, this time more closely. 'You've managed to get my king in check! How did that happen?' he asked blankly.

'Perhaps you weren't concentrating? In fact, James, I don't think you can move your king at all, can you? Isn't that—what was the word? It means "The King is dead".'

'Checkmate!' Slightly annoyed with himself, James apologised and suggested they should try again.

'I would love to! I must remember that word— *checkmate*,' Anne said thoughtfully with a hint of mischief in her eyes. And when James laid out the pieces again he told himself he must treat this game a little more seriously. It wasn't fair to Anne to make such careless errors.

But by the time James had discovered that his previous defeat was not solely due to his own carelessness, it was already too late. Anne was once again in a commanding position.

He looked her in the eye. 'I concede defeat,

ma'am. And I deserved it. I made a cardinal mistake, one which I haven't made since I was a boy at school.'

'What is that, sir?' asked Anne innocently, her eyes sparkling with amusement.

'I underestimated my opponent. Where did you learn to play like that—at your father's knee? Whoever taught you must have been a master!'

'I have no idea who taught me, of course. But I do know I've played a great deal. I confess I knew I could play as soon as we started,' she said, starting to laugh.

'You mean to tell me that you were leading me by the nose right from the beginning?' demanded James. Anne found the expression of outrage on his face so comical that she couldn't suppress the laughter bubbling up inside her. Eyes brimming with mirth, she tried to say something, but could only manage to nod her head helplessly.

James came round the table and pulled her up from her chair. He looked at the laughing face so close to his own, and said severely, 'You ungrateful little imp! I ought to punish you,' and gave her a shake. A giggle escaped her and then he too started to laugh.

When she could speak again Anne said, 'I apologise! But it was just too irresistible.'

He was still holding her, a smile lingering in his eyes. 'I forgive you. It was worth it just to see you laughing like that!' After a pause he went on, 'However, now that I know how good you are, you won't beat me again!'

With a militant light in her eye she said, 'Oh, won't I? We shall have to see! Another game, sir?'

They sat down to another game, but this time they proved to be so well matched that it grew later and later and still neither had won. James had to send for more candles and a little refreshment to sustain them, and eventually it was midnight before he finally said, 'You're a very worthy opponent, but you must be tiring. I think that, my dear, is checkmate.'

Anne sighed and nodded. 'That was a brilliant trap of yours. I didn't see it coming. Thank you! It was a good game, and I enjoyed it. But *next* time…'

James smiled. 'Next time we shall at least begin on an even footing, my deceiver! And I shall look forward to it.' He stood up and held out his hand. 'But now, if you are to be fit to accompany me to Roade House tomorrow, you should go to bed! I'll see you upstairs.'

At the door of her room he stopped and bowed. 'Thank you for a most...instructive evening. I shall see you tomorrow. We don't know how well you ride, but after tonight's experience I shall think twice before challenging you to any kind of race—at least before I put any money on the outcome. Sleep well.' He bent his head and for one heart-stopping moment she wondered if he was about to kiss her. But he hesitated, then nodded without saying anything, and departed along the corridor. Anne was left wondering at his behaviour, until she heard another door close somewhere in the distance. Mrs Culver was keeping guard....

Rose was waiting for her in her room. As she helped Anne to undress she said, 'The riding clothes and boots for tomorrow are in the dressing room, Miss Anne. Mrs Culver brought them in about half an hour after you had gone downstairs. She wanted you to try them on. She's been in since once or twice, and wasn't very pleased when she came the last time and found that you and his lordship were still in the library.'

'That's a pity,' said Anne. 'But I don't think I shall bother trying them on tonight. Lord Aldhurst and I have had a royal battle of wits and mine are quite worn out.' She yawned. 'I'm sorry to have kept you up—you needn't have stayed, Rose.'

'Mrs Culver said I had to. Besides, it's what ladies' maids do, isn't it? Goodnight, Miss Anne.'

Anne smiled as she fell asleep. Rose could not yet be described as a perfect ladies' maid. But her friendly chatter was a welcome contrast to Mrs Culver's dourly dutiful approach.

The sun was shining in through the window when Anne woke the next morning. It was another fine day, and she had slept soundly with no dreams to disturb her. She sat up, revitalised and excited about the forthcoming excursion to Roade house. First, she had to see if the late Lady Aldhurst's riding clothes fitted her—the boots were the most important, for if she couldn't wear them she couldn't ride, and would have to walk. She leapt out of bed and went into the dressing room. James's mother had dressed expensively and well. The riding habit of dark green Circassian cloth that hung against the clothes press had been tailored by a master, its severe cut softened with braiding down the front and a small white ruff at the neck. A beaver riding hat was on the chair beside it, together with soft leather gloves, and below on the floor were boots of supple, rich brown leather, all of them the work of first-class craftsmen. After days spent in ill-fitting boots and a dress that was, despite Rose's efforts, basically shabby, Anne's feminine heart was bursting to wear such an altogether desirable outfit. She was struggling with the boots when Mrs Culver came in.

'Oh, you're in here!' she said. 'I wondered where you might be.'

Anne stiffened, but decided to ignore any implication in the housekeeper's words. 'As you see, Mrs Culver,' she said coolly, 'I was looking for the clothes you were asked to put out for me, and have found them. Thank you. I shall need help in putting them on, particularly the boots. Have you come to help me, perhaps?'

'Rose will be here in a moment. His lordship will see you in the breakfast room when you are ready.'

'Please thank him and tell him I shall be with him in half an hour.'

Mrs Culver left and Anne sighed at the house-keeper's continued resentment. But she cheered up a few minutes later when Rose came in with her ready smile and willing hands, and before the half-hour was up she was dressed and ready to go downstairs. Rose was more than satisfied with the overall result. 'It's almost twenty years since those things were worn, Miss Anne, but you'd never guess it. From what I've heard the late Lady Aldhurst was always up to the minute in fashion, and her clothes fit you very well. That colour might have been meant for you, and I like the little ruff.'

'Let's hope I can live up to my finery when I'm on a horse, Rose. I expect I can ride, but I don't know how well!'

'I am sure you'll find you ride very well, miss. I just know you will. But don't wear yourself out again today. You're still not all that strong, and there's a lot to see in Roade House. It's much bigger than Hatherton, but it's a beautiful place. It's a shame it's been empty for so long. We're all waiting for his lordship to marry, and then he might settle down and live up at the house—for some of the year, at least.'

Anne put aside the thought raised by mention of James's future marriage and went downstairs.

She was nervous. Today for the first time she was wearing the sort of clothes worn by a lady of the house, not a servant. She felt at home in them, but what would James think of her? Would he regret his offer to take her riding when he saw the beautiful clothes his mother had worn on the back of a waif, a stray, someone without name or status?

He was already at the table, but as soon as he saw her standing shyly in the door he got up and came over to her. For a moment he stood looking at her, and then he lifted one of her hands to his lips. 'Good morning,' he said, smiling. 'I think you slept well last night—you're looking better than ever today. Did you?'

'Very well, thank you. With no dreams.'

'Chess is obviously good for you. Now, come to the table—you must fortify yourself. Honey? Toast? Meat?'

Their conversation over breakfast was as lively as it had been the first time, but James reluctantly cut it short. 'There's a lot to see at Roade House. If we are to ride there and back and still have time to inspect the place properly we must set off quite soon. Are you ready?'

Ten minutes later they were outside the front of the house where Sam Trott was waiting for them. He had with him James's bay and two other horses, both mares.

'I see you've found what I asked for, Sam,' said James, carefully inspecting the mares, one a little chestnut and the other a bay like his own. 'But we'll see what Miss Anne thinks of them.' He turned to Anne and patted the chestnut mare standing patiently by the groom. 'Would you care to try this one? She's pretty, don't you think? And a highly suitable mount for a lady.'

'And the other one?'

'This is Fuela. She's a good horse, but I should warn you that this one has a mind of her own. She needs to have it made clear to her who is in charge.'

'Then I'd like to try her, if I may.'

James exchanged a smile with Sam. 'What did I say?' he murmured. Sam nodded and offered to help Anne mount. The two men watched on the alert, ready to come to Anne's rescue as Fuela sidled and curvetted and tried a few dance steps, but their help wasn't needed. Anne let the horse have her way for a minute or two, then took her firmly in hand and made her walk sedately round the drive. 'She's a beauty!' she cried as she brought Fuela to a halt in front of them. 'I'd love to ride this one.'

James mounted his bay. 'I was almost sure you would. Right! It's this way. One thing to remember—if we see any strangers we'll keep well away and let Sam deal with them.'

They set off down a branch of the drive that soon turned into a bridle-path lane leading up the valley through woods and meadows. It was a fresh spring morning, and the countryside was alive with small creatures going about their business after their winter rest. The path took them through woods, and Anne exclaimed in delight at the buds on the horse-chestnut trees, which were already showing a hint of green, at the catkins on the silver birches dancing in the slight breeze, at the blue haze of bluebells pushing their way through the dead leaves of the previous season. James grinned at her frequent cries of, 'Just look! Look at that! And that over there!' and as the woods gave way to open fields he was hard put to it to answer her eager questions about the blackthorn bushes bordering them, and the flowers sheltering on the banks on either side of the path. As the path wound its way steadily upwards through woods and fields he watched her lift her face to revel in the sunshine, to savour the scents blown by the breeze.

When they emerged at last into the open and joined the carriage road connecting the house to the main highway, Fuela scented the possibility of a run and grew restive.

'Do you feel like letting her have her head?' asked James. 'The ground between here and the house is perfect for a gallop.'

Anne didn't wait to answer. She and Fuela took off down the drive before James had finished speaking. But he soon caught up with her, and together they raced towards the big house which was appearing in the distance.

'That was…glorious!' Anne gasped when they finally drew up. 'I'd forgotten just how exhilarating a ride like that can be. Thank you, my lord, a thousand times! But I hope you won't think me too feeble—I must rest for a minute or two just to get my breath back.'

For a moment James found it impossible to say anything at all. On their way up Anne's spontaneous response to everything she had seen and felt had amused and touched him. And now she was laughing up at him, so openly, so full of vitality, that he could not take his eyes off her. She was so unlike any woman he had ever known. The pale invalid had changed into a bewitching, laughing girl with a capacity for enjoyment, a spirit of strength and independence that amazed and delighted him. In a situation that would have destroyed many another she could still laugh, still be in turn mischievous, courageous, passionate, vulnerable, proud, and now at this moment so full of vivid life. A man would never be bored in her company, never have to wonder what to say next....

And then he remembered that without him she was still effectively helpless until her memory returned, and he wondered what he was to do about her. For someone who throughout his adult life had sedulously avoided any serious commitment, the thought that Anne depended on him so completely was astonishingly attractive....

'Lord Aldhurst?' Anne was giving him a puzzled look, and he realised he had been staring at her for too long.

'I'm sorry,' he said. 'Shall we go on now to the house? Agnew is expecting us.'

As they approached the house Anne looked around her and saw that the third Lord Aldhurst had been a man of taste as well as riches. Roade was built in the Palladian style, of pale, creamy grey Portland stone brought all the way from Dorset—no doubt at great expense. It stood proudly on rising ground, its stately facade in perfect classical proportions, with pedimented pillars, symmetrical rows of windows and a graceful balustrade.

James's great-grandfather had given his new house the setting it deserved, too. It was surrounded by a beautifully landscaped park, with scattered specimen trees and banks of shrubs and bushes. It even had a lake fed by the stream that flowed on down the valley to Hatherton, and as they came nearer Anne could see a gracefully arched bridge that carried the road over the stream close to where it left the lake.

The surprising thing was that it was all in excellent order. Anne could hardly believe that the house was unoccupied. 'It's not only lovely, it's so well cared for! But no one lives here?'

James frowned. 'Not at the moment. I suppose I shall have to live here sometime, but not yet. This place may be beautiful, but it holds no happy memories for me.' He looked unusually stern for a moment, then he started again, 'Agnew takes pride in looking after the grounds and does an excellent job. He has responsibility for the house too, but is less interested in that. I think you'll find a difference inside.'

Slowly, it seemed to Anne almost reluctantly, James led the way through a pair of handsome gates out of the park and into the gardens surrounding the house. They circled round and stopped in front of the steps and porch of the main entrance, where Agnew was waiting for them. After a brief conversation with him, James escorted Anne inside. Here she came to a sudden stop and looked around in silence. 'It takes my breath away,' she said in a whisper, gazing up at the lavishly decorated white-and-gold ceiling, at the lofty Corinthian columns, which flanked the elaborately carved double door case opposite, at the paintings above each door.

'My great-grandfather would be delighted to hear you say that,' said James with a short laugh. 'The entrance hall to Roade was meant to impress. I believe he spent more on this room than on the rest of the house put together. Do you like it?'

Anne hesitated. 'I think *like* would be the wrong

word. *Admire* would be better. I am certainly impressed.'

'AsachildIfounditoverwhelming.Frighteningly so.'

'It needs something to soften it. But then, if a family lived here, they would have flowers in urns, tables with possessions left on them,' Anne said, turning round and viewing it as she spoke.

'It never had anything like that when I lived here with my parents, I assure you. Come, I'll show you the other rooms.'

Their progress through the house was slow as Anne ignored the dust and cobwebs and admired everything she saw. She exclaimed at the view from the master bedroom window, was enchanted by the intimacy of the small parlour used by the ladies of the house, and lovingly traced with one finger the figure of a little mouse carved into the rich decoration of the library. Gradually, as James looked at the house through her eyes, it came alive for him too, and he began to see it as it could be, instead of the bleak place it had been in his early childhood.

When they entered the music room she turned to him and said, 'This looks just right. Listen!' Her voice echoed round the room as she sang a short cascade of notes. 'I knew it! It's perfect for sound! I wonder what that piano is like...' Without waiting for permission she walked over to the piano, which occupied most of one corner, sat down and played a chord. 'It's hardly out of tune at all,' she said delightedly, and started to play an enchanting little piece, a waltz, which James had heard recently in one of London's most fashionable drawing rooms. His hostess had claimed that it had arrived for the first time from Vienna just two days before.

'Who taught you that?' he asked.

Still playing, she shook her head at him. 'Really, my lord! I'm surprised at you. You should know better than that by now. I've no idea, of course!'

She finished the waltz and got up. 'Someone who loved music designed this room,' she said, gazing round wistfully. 'I'd like to live—' She stopped, took a breath and said brightly, 'What else is there to see?'

James ushered her out into the entrance hall again. 'I saved the best till last. I think you'll like this next room even more.'

Chapter Seven

James opened one half of a pair of double doors and ushered Anne into the room beyond. It was dark inside, and she stood by the door while he unfolded the shutters on three tall windows in the opposite wall. Then, as light flooded in, her first impression was one of airy grace. Delicately carved girandole mirrors filled the spaces between the windows and ornamented the walls to left and right, and the plasterwork ceiling was exquisitely decorated with classical figures and garlands, which were repeated round a finely carved white marble fireplace. When she walked over to the window she could see the lake, with its picturesque bridge in the foreground and a prospect far beyond over the valley to distant woods and fields.

But as she turned and looked more closely she could see that the room showed the same evidence of neglect she had noticed in the rest of the house. The gilded mirrors were lacklustre, the fireplace was covered in dust, and the large chandelier, which hung in the centre of the room, was enveloped in a cotton shroud. The shutters had been closed because the curtains that should have been hanging at the windows were missing, and the few pieces of furniture were all protected by soiled Holland covers. Her footsteps echoed emptily as she walked about the room, and it seemed to her that, like the rest of the house, it was lying asleep, waiting for someone to come and bring it to life again.

'It's such a pity,' she said impulsively. 'This room is much too beautiful to lie empty like this. It should be full of people enjoying themselves, dancing, laughing…'

'I believe it was when my grandfather was alive. He and my grandmother were fond of entertaining. But once my father inherited Roade it all came to an end. The house was hardly ever occupied. He and my mother were never in England for long enough.'

'They travelled?'

'Everywhere. All the time.'

'Did they take you with them?'

James gave a short laugh. 'What an idea! We would have been far too much in the way. No, my brother and I were looked after by servants here at Roade until my grandmother took us in hand. That's why I like Hatherton so much better. John and I were very happy there. My chief memory of this place is one of loneliness, of a house that was cold, unwelcoming...'

Anne's heart ached for the small boy who had been treated with such indifference. She must try to help blot out those memories. So she shook her head and said with conviction, 'Oh, no! That wasn't the fault of the house. Just look at this room! It positively begs you to feel at ease in it, to dance. Come! Quickly, while I still have that music in my mind!'

She smiled at him bewitchingly and held out her hand. James hesitated, then laughed and took it. He bent over it in a bow and said, with a solemnity belied by the twinkle in his eyes, 'May I have the honour of this waltz, ma'am? Er...riding boots and all?'

Anne fluttered her eyelashes at him over an imaginary fan and said, 'Why, of course, my lord! And we always dance in riding boots at Roade. It's a family tradition.'

Still laughing, James put his other hand on her waist, gave her a nod and they started off down the room. They discovered that they were in such perfect step that no music was needed. In spite of the riding boots she was not at all stiff or awkward, but was as light as a feather in his arms, immediately responsive to the slightest pressure of his guiding hand. And soon they were lost in a strange enchantment, and forgot that they were dancing in an empty room, without music, and dressed for riding rather than a ballroom.

When at last Anne held up her hand and said, 'I'm breathless again!' he stopped, but did not immediately release her. His hands still firmly at her waist, they looked into each other's eyes in silence for a long moment, until he slowly bent his head and kissed her.… This, their first kiss, was like nothing she could have imagined. It was neither light-hearted nor careless, no impulsive gesture made in laughter or mock anger, but deliberate and very, very sweet. Anne felt her whole being melting in response to its slow delight. When it came to an end he looked deep into her eyes, then, tracing her features one by one with his finger, said softly, 'What the devil am I to do about you? A short while ago I didn't even know you existed, and now I can't think what life would be like without you. You make me laugh, you intrigue me, you enchant me with your smile, and you can turn my heart over with one look from those lovely eyes of yours. You can even take a small boy's unhappy memories and magic them away with your warmth and gaiety. And you waltz like a dream. I think you would haunt this room for ever if I were to let you go.'

The spell was broken. For a brief hour or two she had put aside harsh reality and been part of a world of fun and laughter, of love and a vision of what life with James could be. But now reality was back. 'But you must,' she said sadly. 'Before very long I'll *have* to go.'

'Why? Why, Anne?' he demanded.

'You should know that yourself. I…I'm not a suitable person for you. You have a family, a distinguished name. I haven't even the *memory* of one!'

She removed herself from his arms and stood at the window with her back to him. 'You've been so kind to me, so patient. When I'm with you I can sometimes forget what is wrong with me. Yesterday and today I foolishly put the real state of affairs out of my mind and indulged in dreams. Dreams of what it could be like if we discovered that I was...that I would be a suitable partner for you. But the truth is that I'm a girl without a past, without a home. I suppose I belong somewhere, with someone, but no one seems interested in looking for me—not even the men who took me in the first place.' She turned round and faced him. 'It's perfectly possible that I will *never* remember who I am.'

'I refuse to believe that. You've already remembered something of your past. The rest will follow, I'm sure of it.'

'Oh, yes!' she said with a sob. 'I remember the nightmares. I remember how to play chess. I remember how to ride, how to play the piano and dance the waltz. But none of it means very much when I don't have any idea where I *belong*—' She broke off, and tried to calm herself. But then she cried out, 'Oh, it's all so impossible! I don't want to be dependent on anyone, but where can I go in my present state? What can I possibly *do*?'

'This must stop!' James came over to her and took her quite roughly into his arms again. At first she fought to escape, but suddenly she gave a cry of despair and melted against him. Soon they were holding each other in a fiercely pas-

sionate embrace, the world around them forgotten once more in an explosion of feeling.
Eventually he murmured, somewhat unsteadily,
'Anne! Darling Anne! You'll stay with me, of
course! You must.'

She shut her eyes and stayed quietly in his arms
for a moment. Then with a sigh she moved away,
shaking her head. 'I'd give anything to accept.
But I can't.'

'Why not?' he demanded.

'Hatherton has been a retreat for both of us, but
what about your life in the world outside? Your
position in society? Any sort of scandalous liai-
son would break your grandmother's heart, you
know it would. And you love her too much to do
that to her.'

'There must be a way...' he said, frowning.

'I don't see one. I won't be your mistress. And
that is what I would be if I stayed with you now.'
He made an involuntary gesture of protest, but
she continued in passionate despair, 'I couldn't be
anything else. Who knows? I might be engaged,
married, a widow...or even a criminal, like the
men who drove that coach—I just don't know—'
She broke off and turned away. After a moment
she said wearily, 'There's no point in saying any

more. I don't want to argue, but I won't let you ruin your life. I must leave you, find somewhere else to stay.'

'No!' he exclaimed. Taking her hands in his, he said, 'Anne, listen to me. Give me a little more time to find out who you are. Just give us a little more time.'

It was much harder to behave rationally than Anne had imagined. But, she promised herself, she would not let him persuade her to stay for very long. Soon she must leave Hatherton, with or without his help.

'A few more days, then,' she said. 'And now, James, I think I've seen enough of your beautiful house. I'd like to go back to Hatherton.'

The sun had moved round, and the path down through the valley was in shade. The atmosphere on the ride back was very different from that of the morning. They were both quiet, both deep in thought. James was busy with plans for the future. It was vitally important to find out who she really was. Anne was also busy, but her plans were less happy. The afternoon's events had made it clear to her that she must leave Hatherton within a few days. Even if she were ready to live with him, counting the world well lost for love, at some point in the future he would be forced to make a respectable marriage for the sake of his family. Better by far not to embark on a course which would, *could*, only lead to unhappiness, certainly for herself, probably for James, and quite possibly his future wife as well. No, no, it would be better for everyone if she enjoyed the short time left to her and then disappeared. She saw that they were very nearly back at Hatherton. With determination she put these gloomy thoughts out of her mind and turned to James.

'James, let's forget all this for tonight! I enjoyed our game of chess. May I have the pleasure of beating you again?'

He turned to her in relief. 'You may try. I shall enjoy the battle, of course. But don't build your hopes too high on the outcome.'

After that they talked of chess and Roade and the gardens—anything but the real battle that was just beginning. At the house she let him help her dismount, and together they went inside. At the door of her room he said, 'I hope you'll dine with me tonight before our game.'

'But—'

'Don't argue, Anne,' he said, opening her door,

and coming in with her. 'It's a harmless enough request. There'll be no arguments, no passionate scenes, no strong emotions. I'd enjoy your company, and can't believe you wouldn't enjoy mine. We shall dine in style, and conduct ourselves in a rational, civilised manner, with talk of London scenes and London society. Perhaps something will even stir your memory.'

Anne said drily, 'Since I don't remember ever studying London scenes or meeting London society, the conversation will be somewhat one-sided, but I'll do my best to respond.'

He laughed and put his hands on her shoulders. 'That's my brave girl,' he said, bending his head to kiss her.

Good resolutions are all very well, thought Anne dizzily, but when breaking them leads to such delight it...is...so...much...harder...to keep...them...

Mrs Culver's voice broke in on them a few minutes later. 'Excuse me, my lord.'

Flushed and confused, Anne broke away and moved to the window. James had to work hard to control his annoyance, but he managed to speak calmly enough. 'What is it, Mrs Culver?'

'I'm sorry to disturb you—'

'So you should be, Cully, so you should be. Why don't you knock before coming into a room?'

'You must excuse me, my lord. I was only going to ask Miss Anne if she knew where you were. I hadn't expected to find you here in her bedroom. Until now it has never been necessary to knock before coming into the room of a guest in your grandmother's house.' She threw a glance full of disapproval towards the girl in the window.

'Well, what is it?'

'You have a visitor, sir. One of Mr Holford's boys is here.'

James nodded. 'I'll be down in a moment.' He turned and went over to the window. 'Anne? You will have dinner with me tonight?'

Conscious of Mrs Culver's hostile presence at the door, Anne murmured reluctantly that she would. James gave her an encouraging smile and said softly, 'Don't worry. I'll explain to Cully. She'll come round.' He took Anne's hand and held it to his lips. 'Till tonight then.' On his way out he said, 'Cully, I'd like you to look out one of my mother's dresses for Miss Anne to wear tonight when she dines with me. A pretty one.

For a special occasion. Now, where is Master Holford?'

'He's in the dining room, my lord.' Mrs Culver followed him downstairs, but Anne knew that before long she would be back. The housekeeper had undoubtedly been shocked at the scene she had just witnessed, and James's reference to a 'special occasion' would not have reassured her. She must now be convinced that her Master James was in imminent danger of falling into the toils of an unscrupulous wanton.

She leaned her head against the window. Now more than ever she needed to think coolly and rationally. It was so *tempting* to take what happiness she could and so ruin both their lives. She would not do it. No, if James would not see reason she must find a way of escaping from Hatherton without his help. She thought wryly that Mrs Culver would be more than willing to assist her—the housekeeper would do everything she could to get rid of this threat to her beloved Master James!

Meanwhile, downstairs James was examining what young Nat Holford had brought to show him. 'I found them after you'd gone, my lord,' he said.

'Where were they? Inside the coach?'

'No! They were in the stream farther up. There are letters on the ring.'

'So there are,' said James thoughtfully, fingering the fine gold chain Nat had brought. One of the links had been broken, as if it had somehow been torn from the wearer's neck, but it was attached with a firm knot to a heavy gold ring set with a black stone. The chain had unmistakably belonged to a woman. The ring was equally unmistakably a man's.

James examined the ring in silence. It had an engraved monogram—*HJC*. And when he held it up he could see an inscription running round inside. It read, *With all my love from your own devoted AC*. The message was damnably clear...

'They must have belonged to someone in the coach,' he said to the boy eventually. 'I'd like to keep them.'

'Pa said you was to have 'em,' Nat said, eyeing the chain enviously.

James gave the boy a twisted smile. 'Which would you prefer, Nat? These, or a golden guinea?'

After the boy had left, a happy smile on his

face and a gold coin in his fist, James studied the ring, with the look of a man who had just been dealt a mortal blow. It was certainly a very handsome ring—the sort parents would give to a son on achieving his majority. Or a godfather might give to a favourite godson... But the message inside it made it seem more than likely that 'AC' had given it to 'HJC' on the occasion of their betrothal or...marriage. With a muffled curse he thrust both ring and chain onto the table at the side and went upstairs to his room.

Anne was still standing by the window when, just as she had expected, Mrs Culver appeared. She had a dress draped over one arm.

'I've brought you this,' she said. 'It's been folded up in a clothes press for years. Rose will smooth it out later. It's short, but it has a matching petticoat, which will give it more length.' She held the dress up for Anne's inspection. Made of striped silk brocade, the dress was in the style of the previous century, forty years exquisitely out of date, with a narrow waist, low-cut bodice and a full skirt.

'I couldn't wear that! It's far too beautiful!' exclaimed Anne.

'It's what his lordship wants, though it isn't his mother's,' Mrs Culver said, laying the dress out on the bed. She gazed at it for a moment then turned to Anne again. 'Lady Aldhurst—*my* Lady Aldhurst—used to wear this when his lordship's grandfather was alive. I was just a housemaid in those days, but I can still remember it.' She paused. 'He and Lady Aldhurst entertained a lot up at the big house. They both loved Roade. My lady and her husband were very close. So close that when his lordship died Lady Aldhurst moved into Hatherton and refused to see anyone for months.'

The housekeeper stopped, and Anne asked, 'Was that when the walled garden was created?'

Mrs Culver nodded. 'But then, when she heard how her two small grandchildren had been more or less abandoned up at Roade, she brought the boys here to live.' She hesitated, then said, 'Their father was…a disappointment to Lady Aldhurst, though she never said anything, of course. But we all knew. As long as he and his wife had the means to travel, all the Aldhurst lands could have gone to rack and ruin for all he cared. He didn't even bother with his own sons. It was left to their grandmother to bring them up…'

Mrs Culver was silent for so long that Anne wondered if she had finished. But she shook her head and went on, 'Then they were killed, both of them, Lord Aldhurst and his wife. Master John died soon after. It was left to his present lordship to rescue the Aldhurst estates. And Lady Aldhurst has worked for and worried about them ever since.'

She looked down at the dress again and stroked its folds into shape. 'My lady is not well,' she said. 'She's in London for treatment now. But she won't rest until she can be sure that the Aldhursts will survive. Master James is her only hope. She's waiting for him to marry and take his place at Roade. You saw the house today. It needs attention. It needs Lord Aldhurst and his wife to come and live there. And so do the rest of us.'

She straightened the folds in the dress where she had disturbed it and came over to Anne. She was pale, and her hands were clasped so tightly that the knuckles showed white. Anne waited for what she knew was coming. Mrs Culver said, 'I'm still not sure what to make of you, Miss Anne. You could be what you claim to be—you could be a girl who had an accident and lost her memory. But you promised me you would leave

Hatherton as soon as you were strong enough. I think that time has come, don't you? Or was I wrong? Do you have altogether different plans?'

'I don't have any kind of plans,' Anne said evenly. 'What do you mean?'

'You look and act like a lady, but, when all is said and done, you're a girl without a home. From what I witnessed just a few minutes ago in this room, you could be planning to find one here. His lordship is so taken with you that it wouldn't be difficult to entice him into an affair, one which would do him no good at all, and might well kill his grandmother.'

Anne was so stung at the injustice of this that she was on the point of saying something she would later regret, but she stopped herself. In other circumstances she would have been touched by the woman's blind devotion to her mistress's interests. After a moment she had recovered enough to say calmly, 'I may have lost my memory, Mrs Culver, but I still have principles. I *do* intend to leave Hatherton, and have told his lordship as much.'

Mrs Culver said grudgingly, 'If I'm wrong about your motives, I apologise. But it's obvious that you and his lordship are getting…closer with every day that passes. The longer you stay the harder it will get.'

'But even you must see that I cannot simply disappear without having an idea of how or where I am to go!'

After a moment, Mrs Culver said, 'Perhaps you would like to go to London? The first night you were here you appeared quite desperate to go there.'

Anne shook her head. 'I don't remember that,' she said wearily.

'That's a pity. But if that is what you want I might be able to help. My brother calls here twice a week on his way to London to see if we wish to send any fresh produce or messages to her ladyship. In fact, he'll be here tomorrow. I could arrange for him to take you with him.'

'Tomorrow!'

'If that is too soon, he will call again in three days' time.'

'I...I couldn't go tomorrow. At the moment I have no idea what I would do when I got there.' Anne suddenly realised just how vulnerable she was. In fact, without James's support she was destitute! She looked at Mrs Culver, hesitated, and then said stiffly, 'To begin with, I haven't any money. I'm sure you're aware that I have nothing but the clothes I arrived in!'

Mrs Culver was not to be put off. 'I am sure my brother could find respectable work for you in London. The Season is just about to begin, and it's getting quite busy. I could let you have a little money to tide you over for a day or two.'

'No!' Anne cried. 'I'm ready to work, but I won't accept any favours from you, Mrs Culver.'

'I wouldn't regard it as a favour to you, Miss Anne. It would be for the benefit of Hatherton.'

Anne turned back to the window and gazed out blindly. It hurt to see such hostility in someone else's eyes, especially when she knew how little she deserved it. But hostile or not, Mrs Culver had suggested a relatively safe way she could escape from Hatherton.

She said at last, 'You couldn't wish more desperately than I do that my memory would return so that I could leave Hatherton safely, but it seems I'll have to face the world without it. But I won't go before I think I'm ready.'

'I hope that won't take too long. Otherwise I shall be forced to warn her ladyship what is going on here.'

'I understand,' said Anne wearily. 'Thank you, Mrs Culver. Send Rose up, would you, please?'

Rose came up, exclaimed over the dress before pressing it very carefully, helped Anne with her *toilette*, arranged her hair and last of all helped her to put the dress on.

'You look lovely, miss!' she exclaimed. 'Just like the picture of Lady Aldhurst in the dining room. It's a real pity you haven't any pearls to go with it. Lady Aldhurst is wearing some lovely pearls in that picture.'

Rose's uncomplicated admiration was very comforting. Anne smiled at her and said, 'Perhaps I could wear a length of ribbon round my neck instead of jewellery? I've seen a portrait of my grandmother wearing one.' She stopped short. 'A portrait of my grandmother...' she said slowly. 'I remember a portrait of my grandmother...' Rose was looking at her with eyes like saucers.

'It's coming back,' she said. 'Your memory— it's back!'

Anne frowned, but after a moment she sighed and shook her head. 'No,' she said, 'it was just another sudden flash. Of a painting I've seen. It's gone again.'

Rose looked sympathetic. 'That's a real shame, Miss Anne. But you do look a real picture and no mistake. I'll get a piece of ribbon.'

Anne had a last look in the mirror before she went downstairs. The black velvet ribbon served to emphasise the slenderness of her neck and the proud carriage of her head. Her face was delicately flushed, and her dark blue eyes looked almost black in the soft light of the candles. She felt she had never looked more beautiful, and wondered wistfully if this was how James would remember her after they had parted.

'I'm ready,' she said.

Chapter Eight

James was waiting in the hall. He came to the foot of the stairs and held out his hand. 'You look…magnificent,' he said, giving her a little bow before putting her arm on his to lead her into the dining room. But Anne was disconcerted. There was a subtle change in James's manner that worried her, and for a moment she wanted to run back upstairs and change out of her finery into her familiar, simple black dress. He seemed distant, like a stranger, in his evening clothes and immaculate linen, and in the formal way he had spoken. It was so unlike him not to see how nervous she was. But underneath those formidable manners he was still James, still her rescuer, her comforter…and her love. And since she would soon have to leave him she would make the most of this evening. So she lifted her chin, smiled and said gaily, 'Fine feathers, my lord, even if they are borrowed and a little out of date.'

He gave her a slight smile. 'Beauty, my dear, is never out of date.'

Anne was once again chilled by the lack of warmth in his manner. There was surely something more to it than just an excess of formality. What had happened between this afternoon and this evening to cause such a change in him?

In the dining room, gleaming silver and glasses reflected the light of branched candlesticks on a table set for two. A bowl of flowers scented the air, and a pink camellia lay by her plate. It was a setting for lovers, she thought, for romance. But where were *they* this evening?

James saw her to her chair and took the seat opposite. While two of the maids served them, he smiled courteously at her and said, 'I'm afraid we lack the necessary footmen here at Hatherton. When my grandmother is in residence she keeps a full complement of staff here, but most of them accompany her to London. However, I believe Mrs Culver does very well. She has been in service here for a long time. My grandmother trusts her absolutely.'

Was this the man who, such a short time ago,

had held her so tightly that she could hardly breathe, while his lips had covered her cheeks, her eyes, her mouth, with passionate kisses? Servants or no servants, she had expected to see a feeling warmer than *courtesy* in his eyes, to hear more than polite small talk when he spoke!

She lifted her chin again and replied with a passable imitation of his tone, 'From what I have seen, the house seems to me to be extraordinarily well run, Lord Aldhurst. And the garden you showed me yesterday is particularly delightful, too.… Tell me, what plans do you have for Roade? The house has such potential.'

There was a short pause, then he said curtly, 'None at the moment, I'm afraid. They will have to wait.'

Anne winced. Roade and its associations were not, it seemed, to be discussed. There was another awkward silence while she absorbed and dealt with this. Then she said brightly, 'But I believe you promised to tell me about life in London. I understand the Season is almost upon you? When does it actually start?'

James described some of the events of the Season to her, and Anne responded as best she could with questions and comments. But the banter and laughter that had been such a feature of their breakfast together were altogether lacking. When the servants finally withdrew the silence lasted even longer than the previous one.

Finally, Anne decided she would take no more. She said, 'I don't think I can belong to the polite world after all, Lord...Lord Aldhurst. If this conversation is a sample of what I am to expect, I should prefer to find that I do *not* belong! The activities of London society appear to me to be singularly boring!'

James's manner was more natural, though still cool, as he replied, 'I've often thought the same myself! However, it's clear from your supply of small talk that at some point or other you've been taught the social graces. It's odd that you don't seem to recall any of it. Very odd.'

'Perhaps my previous life is buried deeper than we think. What has there been so far, apart from a few nightmares? That I had red hair when I was a child...I can play chess, and the piano, and ride. And this evening I remembered a portrait of my grandmother. It isn't much, is it?'

'Your grandmother? Can you describe her?'

'It's just a portrait. She was wearing a dress in the same style as this, and she is wearing a ribbon like this, too. I remember thinking how beautiful she was...'

'So are you, Anne.' The words seemed to come of their own volition, and were said with all the warmth she could wish for. He met her eyes, then looked away and said, 'I'm sorry.'

'James! What is wrong?'

He hesitated, then seemed to come to some conclusion. 'I want you to look at something.' He went over to the side table and, after staring down at it for some time, came back with a chain in his hand. Letting it dangle from his fingers, he asked, 'Is this familiar?'

Anne took the chain from him and examined it. 'I think it's made of gold,' she said. 'And it has a broken link... No, it doesn't mean anything to me. Where did you find it?'

'Holford's boy brought it this afternoon. It was in the stream not far from the coach.'

Anne shook her head again. 'It's like the purse,' she said. 'I suppose it must be mine, but I don't remember a thing about it.' She looked up to see that he had gone back to the side table.

'James, what is it? There *is* something wrong. What is it?' Anne got up and went over to see what was holding his attention. But as soon as she reached him he turned round and pulled her to him, wrapping his arms right round her, holding her head tight against his chest, resting his cheek on her hair. 'What is it?' she asked, putting her hand up to his face. His own hand briefly covered hers, then he released her and led back to her seat. 'Sit down and I'll show you. It may be nothing.'

He waited till she was ready, and then put a ring down on the table in front of her. 'The chain I've just shown you was knotted round this.'

Anne looked at the ring and was overcome by a powerful sense of urgency. She picked it up and studied it. 'I…I… This is different…' She leaned forwards and turned it this way and that in the light of the candles, giving particular attention to the monogram. James leaned forwards as her eyes met his. He looked very tense, as if expecting a blow.

'So this *does* mean something?' he said.

'I don't know what!' she said slowly, 'But I know it's important…very important. It's not my ring, of course. It belongs to a man…'

She stroked the black stone gently with her finger…and jumped as James banged his fist on the table and said angrily, 'Anne, I can see that! Read what it says inside!'

She held it up again. 'With...all...my love... from...your own...devoted A...C...' She looked up. 'From your own devoted AC... And the initials on the stone are HJC...' She looked at him in shock. 'James? You think *I'm* AC?'

'Of course I damned well do! Who else could it be? The initials *AC* were on that cursed purse. The purse was in the coach, and this ring was found within yards of it, very near the spot where you escaped. Of course you're AC—' He broke off and walked several paces away from her. Then he turned and said angrily, 'You say it's important to you. From the way you were fingering it a moment ago, I'd say it means a great deal more than that. You were stroking it with affection, as if it belonged to someone you loved. I want to know why! I want to know why you were wearing it on a chain round your neck. I want to know the meaning of that accursed inscription! As you say, it's a man's ring, Anne. *Whose is it?*' He leaned over her again, and she was afraid for a moment he was going to shake her. 'Don't you remember *anything*, dammit?' he asked fiercely. 'For God's sake, woman, *try!*'

This behaviour was so unlike him that she stared at him in shock. Then shock turned to apprehension as the reason for his behaviour throughout the evening, his anger, now became clear to her. 'You think *I* gave this ring to someone...to someone dear to me. As a betrothal ring?'

'Or was it a marriage ring?'

'No!' She jumped up and walked away, shaking her head. 'No! That can't be!' She turned and came back to him. 'I can't be married, James. I can't!'

He took her hands in his, grasping them so tightly that it hurt. 'How do you know?'

'Because...because of the way I feel about you. I couldn't possibly be married to someone else.'

He shook his head as if he wanted to clear it of some demon, but he failed. His next words shocked her once again, this time beyond measure. He dropped her hands and moved away from her. Studying her coolly, almost objectively, he said with a hint of cynicism, 'Really, ma'am! Are you really so incredibly naive? So innocent of the world and its ways? Do you really not know that London is full of married women, devoted to their husbands, but who find it very easy to accommodate a lover as well? I've had what you might call a personal acquaintance with one or two such ladies myself.'

'James!' Shocked, hurt and angry, she pulled away from him and fled to the other side of the room. Her distress seemed to bring him to his senses, and for a moment he stood like a man waking from a nightmare. Cursing his stupidity, he shook his head in disgust and, in a voice full of remorse, said, 'I'm sorry, I'm sorry. I should never have said such a thing. Not to you. I don't know what came over me. The truth is that I haven't been myself since I saw that ring. I have never felt like this before. Never felt so...so jealous. And a moment ago, when you said it was important to you, I was *insanely* jealous of this HJC. It's a damnable feeling!'

'James, listen to me,' she said quietly. 'This ring has a significance that I can't explain, because the reason is buried in this wretched memory of mine. But I am absolutely certain that I don't love HJC in the way you are thinking. I can't at the moment even remember who he is, and I couldn't imagine ever forgetting *you*.' She gave a bitter little laugh, which ended in a sob. 'But as you say, I might be married to him.'

James stifled a curse. 'Yes, dammit. Unhappily

married, and only too willing to forget him!' He walked away again, pacing the room impatiently. At last he said, 'It won't do. We have to find out the truth. We've waited long enough for your memory to come back. I have a business appointment with the family lawyers in Guildford tomorrow. I'll ask them for names of reputable investigators. The men I sent to make enquiries along the Portsmouth Road haven't brought back anything useful. They found the coach, but the villains who were in it have vanished, and that trail is cold. We can't wait any longer to find out who you are. I'll set it all in motion tomorrow.'

'And if you find that I *am* a married woman?' asked Anne quietly.

There was an appreciable pause. Then James said heavily, 'I don't know. I just don't know. You may remember you love him after all. How can I be sure that what you feel for me isn't just gratitude, not love? You've had to trust me, had to depend on me... I suppose you might have come to think you love me.'

'James, it's not like that at all. I know, I am quite *sure*, I love you!'

'Do you, Anne? I'm no longer sure about anything at all.'

This time the silence was long and heavy.

'Then there's nothing more to say, is there?' she said sadly, turning towards the door.

'Anne! Wait! Don't go. We may be quite wrong!'

'You mean the ring may not be mine? That some farmer's wife, who just happens to have AC as her initials, dropped it in that stream on her way to market? I don't think so, James.'

'Wait until I've spoken to our lawyers in Guildford. They may have some suggestions. I'll see you tomorrow after I get back. Meanwhile we'll hope it isn't as bad as we think.'

'Yes, James. We'll do that,' said Anne wearily.

They went up the stairs together, but he stopped at the door of her room. Holding her face between his hands, he looked into her eyes. His expression changed when he saw what was in them. 'I want to believe you, Anne,' he said. 'You have no idea how much I want to believe you!' He kissed her, and said softly, 'I'll see you tomorrow evening. It will all turn out well, I know it will.' He kissed her once more with such gentleness that she almost broke down. Then he opened her door and waited for her to go through.

Anne leant with her back against the door and listened to his footsteps receding. The pain of letting him go was so acute that she could hardly breathe. But she knew she must leave Hatherton without delay. The ring was even more important to her than she had let James see, and if she was indeed married he might well become involved in a scandal that could ruin for ever his chances of leading a normal life at Roade with a wife and family of his own. His early start for Guildford the next day would give her an ideal opportunity to escape.

She looked down at the ring, which was still clutched in her hand. It looked so harmless, lying there in her palm. Once again assailed by a feeling of urgency, she was certain that she had made the right decision. Something vital concerning the ring lay buried in her memory. But what?

When Mrs Culver came Anne had already taken the dress off and had gathered her few possessions together. 'I've changed my mind,' she said. 'If your offer to help me escape tomorrow still stands I shall accept it...' She paused, swallowed her pride and added, 'And I would accept a little money, too, which I will repay as soon as I am able.'

To her relief, Mrs Culver made no comment,

but nodded and picked up the dress. 'I'll bring what you will need when I come back after putting this away.'

She returned a few minutes later with a thick shawl, a bonnet and a small carpet bag. 'I've put a few things in it,' she said, 'things we don't need anymore. They'll do you for a while. The bonnet and shawl are to keep you warm on the journey to London. And I can give you three guineas. It's not much, but my brother is a good man—he'll see that you get paid employment before too long. His lordship will set off for Guildford at eight or thereabouts. Be ready to leave soon after.' She hesitated. 'I...'

'Please don't say anything,' said Anne. 'I know how glad you are to see me go. No doubt Lady Aldhurst will be grateful, too. His lordship...his lordship might...might not understand at first. But I know I am right to...to save him from making a mistake. I shall leave a note for him to make it clear that this...this was my decision, not...not anyone else's. Thank you, Mrs Culver.'

The housekeeper gave a little curtsy. 'I shall see you tomorrow,' she said.

* * *

The next morning Anne was at the window when James rode off. She watched him till he disappeared out of sight round a bend in the drive. Then she turned away and put the last few things in her bag. Lady Aldhurst's copy of *Persuasion* she left on the bed, on top of the nightdress she had been given to wear when she had first arrived. Rose came in and was astonished to see that she was already dressed.

'I'd come to help you, Miss Anne,' she exclaimed.

Anne smiled. 'It looks as if I shall have to learn to do everything for myself from now on. I think I've done pretty well, don't you?'

'It's not right! You're a lady if ever I saw one! Mrs Culver—'

'Don't, Rose! Mrs Culver has only done what I asked. But you could find me a longer piece of ribbon if you would.'

Rose disappeared and came back with a length of silk ribbon. 'Will this do?'

'Perfectly!' She threaded the ribbon through the ring and hung it round her neck, concealing it under the neckline of her dress. 'That's safe now.' She gave Rose an apologetic smile. 'I'm afraid I have nothing else. I can't give you anything to remember me by. But I do thank you for your kindness and help. I…I hope to see you again one day. Goodbye.'

'I wouldn't take anything, Miss Anne. And I'm coming with you to the door. I want to make sure Mr Cobden will take good care of you. You're not yet all that strong.'

Anne laughed shakily. 'Please don't tell him that! He expects me to work! I shall be perfectly all right. You really mustn't worry.' She put a note addressed to James on the chest of drawers, cast a glance round the room, and went downstairs to the kitchen door where Mrs Culver's brother was waiting. Mrs Culver was there, too. 'I've had a word with Hal,' she said. 'He's sure he can find you something, and you can help his daughter in the house until you do. And I do thank you, Miss Anne, for what you are doing today.'

'Like you, Mrs Culver, I have my loyalties and obligations.'

'I believe you do.' With this Mrs Culver took Anne to meet her brother. He wasted no time on courtesies, but said, 'It's time we went. Now stop your fussing, Sarah—I'll give your messages to

Eliza and the children. If Miss Anne is ready, we shall be off.'

In no time Anne was on her way, following the route James had taken not an hour before. But when they reached the Portsmouth Road her driver turned the gig north towards London, instead of south to Guildford. Each milestone reminded her that she was leaving Hatherton and her life with James farther and farther behind. Mr Cobden was not a talkative man, and the chill of the morning gave her an excuse to huddle inside her shawl, seeking comfort. But the only grain of comfort she could find, and it was small enough, was when she felt the ring through the thickness of her dress. Somewhere in London, she was sure, lay the answer to the mystery surrounding it. And if she solved *that*, she might solve the other, bigger mystery—the question of who she was.

Mr Cobden travelled at a good pace, and by mid-afternoon they were in London itself and turning north up Park Lane towards Oxford Street.

Halfway up Park Lane they came to a stop. It was a chaotic scene. A high-perch phaeton had collided with a curricle, and their wheels were immovably locked together. Their two owners were so busy trading accusations and insults that they were quite oblivious to the traffic rapidly building up around them. The road was completely blocked.

'It'll be some time before those two have sorted themselves,' Mr Cobden grumbled. 'We might just as well sit back and have a rest! There's not much else we can do.' Anne looked around her. The gig had stopped just level with a street leading off to the right, and at the end of it she could see a hint of trees. The scene was hauntingly familiar… Her heart started to beat rapidly, and she found she was suddenly trembling. She had to see what was in that street. She couldn't wait a moment longer. With a muttered apology to Mr Cobden she leapt down from the gig.

'Miss Anne! What's wrong?'

'It's all right, Mr Cobden,' she said hurriedly. 'Henrietta Street. That's where you're going. I shan't forget.' She grabbed her bag from the back and darted across the road, narrowly escaping being run down by a delivery cart.

'Miss Anne! Come back! You'll get lost…'

Mr Cobden's shouts fell on deaf ears. Once on the other side she gave a brief look back at the gig.

The traffic was moving again and Mr Cobden was quite unable to do anything but follow it. She felt a moment's regret, but the force that was driving her was too strong for her to go back. She walked slowly, looking from one side to the other. It wasn't long before she was transfixed by the sight of a house with a dark red door... She recognised it instantly. It was the door in her dream.

Everything else was forgotten as she stared at it. After a while she had gathered enough courage to walk up to the door and knock.

It was opened by an elderly man in the dress of a superior manservant, who regarded her dowdy bonnet and shawl, her clumsy boots and her carpet bag with a look of withering scorn. She realised in a panic that she had no idea what to say or whom to ask for, and thought for a moment that he was about to shut the door on her, or fetch another servant to chase her away. But as she looked up his face was suddenly transformed. Scorn changed to recognition, rapidly followed by rejection, then he looked again.

'Miss Calverley?' he asked doubtfully. He turned round as someone came up behind him and an anxious voice asked, 'What is it, Blandish? Is there some news?'

'My lady, I...I don't know...I don't know what to think. It's a young person at the door. It...it could be Miss Calverley herself.'

'*What*? And you've left her standing there? Let me see!' The owner of the voice appeared. It was a woman, tall, and with a cool air of elegance. But, on seeing the girl at the door, her face lit up with joy, she gave a cry of astonished delight and flung her arms round Anne. Drawing her inside she hugged and kissed her over and over again. 'Antonia!' she exclaimed. 'Oh, Antonia, thank God you're safe! Where have you been? Oh, I can't believe it! Come in, come in! Blandish, don't stand there gawping like a fish, take my niece's bag and shut the door. Oh, this is wonderful news!'

Bewildered and dazed, Anne let herself be ushered into the inner hall. It seemed dimly familiar. She took a step forwards, and suddenly dazzled by a shaft of sunlight coming through the window above the stairs, she could hardly see anything at all for a moment. Then she peered into the semi-darkness as someone at the other end of the hall came running towards her. It was the man she'd seen in her dream lying in a pool of blood... She screamed, and then memory flooded back, wave after wave of it, drowning her, choking her... She felt herself falling...falling, and everything went black.

Chapter Nine

Antonia

Antonia opened her eyes. The room was in darkness except for a small lamp in its opposite corner, and she wondered where she was. Then she saw a familiar figure sitting at her bedside, and realised with a huge sense of relief that she was in her aunt's house in London. She was safe!

She tried to speak, but her throat was dry. Alerted by the slight sound, Lady Pendell got up and leaned over the bed. 'Antonia! You're awake at last! Would you like some water, my dear?'

Antonia nodded. 'Thank you,' she croaked, struggling to sit up. She drank deeply and then sank back.

Her aunt eyed her and said, 'How do you feel?'

'My head is aching a little, but I'm so happy

to see you, Aunt Pendell. How...how did I get here?'

'We don't know! You arrived out of the blue last night, came into the hall and then you...you screamed and fell down in a faint. You dropped like a stone. I've never seen anything like it.' She put a cool hand on Antonia's forehead. 'You might have given your head a slight bang, but the surgeon didn't think you were otherwise hurt. We put you to bed and you've slept like a baby ever since.' She added with a shudder, 'But your scream...it was enough to make one's hair stand on end.'

Antonia sat up again and clutched her aunt's hand. 'Who was the man I saw in the hall?'

'My dear Antonia, you must know who that is—you've known him all your life! He's your father's right-hand man.' Then, as Antonia continued to stare at her blankly, she said, 'It was Lawson, of course.'

Antonia was absolutely still. After a moment she said, 'That isn't possible. Lawson is dead—' She stopped and swallowed hard.

'My poor child, I assure you Lawson is very much alive and nearly out of his mind with concern over you. He is so relieved to see you here at last. Where *have* you been? We were beginning to think we would soon have to tell your father—'

'Tell Papa what?'

'That you were missing, of course! But he was so weak after the journey up from Portsmouth that we've kept it from him till now. He thinks you've been confined to your room with a bad cold since he arrived.'

'Papa is here in London?'

'He arrived two days ago.'

Antonia said thoughtfully, 'It's taken me two days to get here…'

'Antonia, it's been much longer than that! Lawson has been looking for you for over a week! We've been getting desperate. I would love to know what happened to you, but we've no time to talk about it at the moment. Your father is asking for you. Now that he's getting stronger it's been more difficult to put him off. He won't be satisfied until he has seen you for himself.'

'I'll go straight away.'

'One of our maids will help you dress. There's been no sign of yours, though the carrier arrived with your trunks some time ago—they are all unpacked.'

'Martha is with her sister in Marylebone.'

Lady Pendell frowned. 'Whatever is she doing there? No, there's no time—you can tell me later.' As she left the room she said, 'Remember to be careful when you talk to your papa, Antonia.'

Antonia scrambled out of bed and ran to the door. '*How* long did you say Lawson was looking for me?' But she was too late. Her aunt had disappeared.

She sat down on the bed again. She must have misheard. Lawson couldn't have been looking for her for *over a week*! Wrinkling her brow, she tried to picture what had happened before she had got to her aunt's door, but her mind was a complete blank. Then the maid came in and she decided to leave it till later. Her father mustn't be kept waiting any longer.

When Antonia tapped on her father's bedroom door and went in, Sir Henry was sitting in a chair by his bed. Someone had obviously told him to expect her, for he had his eyes fixed on the door and smiled when she appeared. She hurried over and knelt down beside him. 'Papa!' she said softly, taking his hand in her own and kissing it.

'I'm so glad to see you at last,' Sir Henry said,

adding testily, 'Your wretched aunt and Lawson here have been conspiring to keep you away from me for too long.'

The man standing on the other side of the chair said, 'That was for your own good, and well you know it. You had enough to cope with. You didn't need to catch a cold in the head from Miss Antonia as well.' Antonia could hardly take her eyes off him. In his late fifties, wiry, with grizzled hair and bushy eyebrows, Lawson was her father's groom, guide, bodyguard and general factotum. He had been part of her life as long as she could remember. She shivered as she remembered the last time she had seen him, lying on the dusty street in a pool of blood. She had been quite certain he was dead....

'You're not still ill, are you?' her father asked. 'These colds are the devil to get rid of.'

Gratefully, she turned back again and replied, 'No, I'm quite well now.'

'Good! What about the papers? Did you manage to deliver them to the right man? I'll have my ring back, please.'

Antonia fingered the ring, which was hanging round her neck. 'I can't let you have it yet, Papa.

I still have the papers. But I'll take them to the Foreign Office very soon.'

Sir Henry looked at her in silence for a moment. Then he said, 'They should have been with the Foreign Office by now. Croxton is a slippery customer, and he'll use every moment we give him to make his position with the Prince Regent more secure. Why else would I have taken the risk of sending you to London without me? What held you up?'

Lawson made an involuntary gesture, but before he could say anything Antonia replied swiftly, 'Some of the...some of the...the depositions had been badly translated and I had to rewrite them. Then I was...I was ill, as they told you. But they'll be ready and delivered tomorrow.' She smiled coaxingly. 'Come, Papa, the Croxton affair is nearly over. You've done the major part, and can safely leave the rest to me. Delivering the papers is easily accomplished. Lawson and I will take them the minute they are ready.'

'You have my ring? You will need it for identification.'

'Of course...' She held it out for him to see, and saw with surprise that a piece of ribbon had replaced its chain. She hurried on, 'It's time you forgot Lord Croxton and concentrated on my début. I hope you're fit enough for Lady Carteret's reception next week—isn't that when you are planning to present me to the London *ton*? I hear they're a formidable lot, highly critical of newcomers, so we must both be in top form. You've promised me a husband out of it, remember!'

Her father smiled. 'As if you couldn't already have had your pick of Europe's finest!'

'Ah, but I want one of those rich English "milord's" with an eyeglass and a drawl, and acres of English countryside. And a house, no, a mansion, in the centre of it...' Antonia faltered as a picture of the house was suddenly clear and complete in her mind—a house of creamy grey stone, high on a hill and with an arched bridge over a lake... It had a white-and-gold entrance hall... and a carving of a little mouse.... Her heart gave a jump and for a moment she was inexpressibly sad.

She pulled herself together when she saw her father's stare. 'Can you think of anyone, Papa? He needn't be clever,' she said brightly.

'Don't talk such nonsense, child! You wouldn't survive for two minutes with a man whose wits and interests didn't match your own, however rich he was. I hope to do better for you than that. There are one or two young men at the Foreign Office...'

She had achieved her object. Her nonsense had distracted him. After a while she saw he was ready to rest again, and, promising to see him the next day, she left. Lawson followed her.

As soon as the door shut behind them she took Lawson's arm and marched him down the stairs and into the small room where Lady Pendell was waiting for them.

Here Antonia hugged Lawson, wiped a tear from her eye and said, 'Oh, heavens, Lawson, never do that to me again. What happened to you?'

With a look and a little nod in Lady Pendell's direction, Lawson said gruffly, 'Never mind me, Miss Antonia. I lost a deal of blood, but a bit of a rest soon put that right. As soon as I was on my feet again I asked about in Portsmouth, and found you'd been carried off by a man called Briggs. I caught up with him in Putney. He told me there'd been an accident and that you'd escaped. What happened to you? I searched the length of the

Portsmouth Road, but couldn't find you or the coach.'

'Lawson tried to tell me he was sure you'd make your own way here somehow or other,' said Lady Pendell. 'But I can't say I was reassured.'

'Begging your pardon, ma'am, you don't know Miss Antonia as well as I do. She doesn't lose her head. You weren't there to see how she dealt with a couple of brigands in Spain.'

'No,' Lady Pendell said faintly, 'I'm happy to say I wasn't.'

'She has always been a capable lass in tight situations,' Lawson said proudly. He turned back to Antonia. 'I didn't stop looking. I searched that road three times. But a week went by and I couldn't find any trace at all. That was when I started to get worried.'

'So my aunt *did* say you were looking for me for over a week?'

'You were missing for nearer two. I didn't start straight away.'

Antonia protested, white-faced, 'But that's impossible! I came straight here! I suppose I got confused—I seem to remember banging my head after I'd escaped...and I can't quite remember what happened after that. But I haven't been anywhere else.'

Lady Pendell looked more concerned. She took her niece's hand and led her to a chair. 'My dear, you've been missing ever since you left Portsmouth, and that was nearly two weeks ago. You *must* have been somewhere else. Where?'

Antonia stared at her aunt. 'I don't know...' She looked at them both in bewilderment, then said slowly, 'I suppose I have to believe you. But all I can remember is that I escaped from the men Lawson told you about and came straight here. In a cart... I remember a cart!'

Lawson shifted uneasily. 'Er...Miss Antonia...'

'Yes?'

'It's those papers... Sir Henry wants them delivered as soon as possible. We could talk later about the rest. Do you really have them? Or was that just a story to keep him quiet?'

'Martha has them. I gave them to her to look after while we were still in Portsmouth. Then, when I saw the men catching up with us, I bundled her into the London coach before they came round the corner, and told her to wait for me at her sister's. So she escaped with Papa's papers and the men followed me instead. We can go and collect them straight away.'

'Not before you've been seen again by the surgeon,' Lady Pendell said very firmly.

'I haven't come to any real harm, Aunt Pendell. A headache is nothing!'

'From what I've been hearing you've been in serious danger from the moment you left Portsmouth. Your father should never have allowed you to travel without him.'

'He had to! The papers—'

'The papers, the papers! What *are* these papers?'

Antonia hesitated. 'They're very confidential.'

'Your uncle was a diplomat, too, Antonia. I know how to keep secrets. So while Lawson sees about the carriage you can tell me about them. You are not leaving this house until I know what's going on.'

Lawson nodded and went and Antonia said. 'Papa has been working on a special assignment for the past year which involved one of the Prince Regent's closest friends. The Foreign Office had heard some worrying rumours about the source of his fortune. If they were true, there was a risk that the Prince could be involved in a huge scandal, so Papa was asked to investigate. The rumours proved perfectly true. The Prince's friend is part of a ring of extortion and corruption all round the Mediterranean, and the proof is in those papers.'

'But why this urgency?'

'Because the Prince is planning to confer one of the highest honours in his power on Lord...on this man! It's very important he knows the truth before he does!'

'Lord Croxton—he's the one, isn't he?—is a very unscrupulous man. Henry should never have let you take such risks, and I shall tell him so.'

'You mustn't! Papa isn't yet well enough to be told I was missing!'

'Why not? You can't keep it a secret for ever!'

'Please, Aunt, please leave it to me to tell him!'

After some persuasion, Lady Pendell agreed to leave it to Antonia to break the news to her father, but the delay caused by the discussion meant that it was early evening before Antonia got away.

James had also arrived in London. After their disastrous dinner party two nights before, he had spent a sleepless night wishing he could forget his behaviour, and haunted by Anne's distress. He, who had always prided himself on his detachment, had been totally unprepared for the feelings aroused by the discovery of the ring, his furious jealousy at the idea that Anne might already belong to someone else, be betrothed or even married. He had had to exercise considerable self-discipline to speak at all rationally during the meal, and then, when his worst fears had been confirmed, when Anne had admitted that that accursed ring was important to her, he had forgotten how vulnerable she was and had given way to his own anger, had spoken to her in a manner he had never before used towards any woman. He was ashamed at how deeply he had upset her.

His only excuse, and it was an inadequate one, was that he had found himself in a situation which was entirely foreign to him. His relationships with other women had been lightly begun and as lightly ended. His relationship with Anne had been growing and changing so rapidly that until that day he had had no idea just how very different it was, how important she had in fact become to him.

The following morning he had almost gone to

see her before he left, to try to put things right, but then had decided to leave it till the evening. What could he have said to her? The situation at Hatherton could not continue as it was. Something had to be done about it, but he was damned if he knew what. Anne ought to leave Hatherton before long, but how could he bear to let her go? And where *could* she go? One or two people he knew in Guildford might suggest a few of the answers, and after he had spoken to them he would make sure he got back to Hatherton in good time to talk to Anne.

As soon as he had arrived in the town he had sought out an old army friend, a medical man who had treated men whose memories had been lost through some sort of shock in battle. He had listened with interest to James's carefully edited account of 'a friend's' memory loss and said finally, 'It sounds to me as if you're giving your friend exactly what she needs for the moment. She has been through an extremely threatening experience and has quite *literally* put it out of her mind. All the evidence would suggest that the memory loss is temporary, and it will very probably return as soon as she feels fit enough to deal with whatever it was that happened. Whatever

you do, do *not* tell her who she is. Let her remember it for herself.'

'I couldn't tell her if I wanted to, Edgar. I have
no idea who she is.'

'Really? So this is an act of charity?'

'You could say so,' James had said, avoiding
his friend's eye.

'An intriguing situation. I admire you for it.
You are obviously concerned for her, James. It
will hasten her cure if you show her your concern. Make her feel protected. Give her a sense
of greater security. And...let me know what
happens.'

James had then dealt with the rest of his business, including a short consultation with his lawyers, and had set off for Hatherton in good time.
On the way back he had considered his friend's
advice, and found himself faced with a dilemma.
According to his friend the worst thing he could
do would be to send Anne away to fend for herself.
On the other hand, they could not stay together at
Hatherton for much longer. Their feelings for one
another had reached a point where some sort of
crisis was inevitable. But Anne might be another

man's wife, and it would be dishonourable to ask her to betray him by staying on at Hatherton.

Moreover, it had occurred to him in the night that, the longer Anne stayed, the more likely it was to reach the ears of the gossips that James Aldhurst was entertaining a young lady at his grandmother's country retreat. Then the fat would really be in the fire! Whatever her status, single, betrothed or married, nothing then could save Anne from scandal. *His* reputation might suffer, but hers could be destroyed for ever.

In the end he had decided that there was only one sensible thing to do. The next morning he would go to London to talk to his grandmother. She must be persuaded to offer Anne a home until her memory returned, or her identity was established. Meanwhile, there was still time to see Anne that evening... and when he arrived he had gone straight upstairs to look for her. But Anne was not in her room, and when Rose told him that she had left Hatherton he could hardly take it in.

'She can't have! Where would she go?'

'Mrs Culver's brother took her to London, my lord.'

'*What*? When?'

Rose had taken one look at his face and faltered. 'This morning. Miss Anne left a note for you... It's here.'

James had read the note in silence, then dismissed Rose and sent for Mrs Culver. 'I believe I told you once,' he had said, keeping command of himself with difficulty, 'that Miss Anne was to stay here until I was sure she was safe. And now you have sent her away!'

'Master James, I can explain—'

'No,' James had said curtly, 'you will listen. I warned you at the time that you and I would fall out if Anne came to any harm through anything you said or did.'

Mrs Culver protested, 'But she wanted to go. And she's safe enough, I swear! She's with—'

'With your niece in London. I know. Tell me, if you please, how Miss Anne is to support herself there? She has no money, no clothes...'

'I...I gave her some money. I had a little put by. And she can work in my niece's house until she finds something better...' Her voice had faded as she had seen James's expression.

'I hope you kept something for yourself, Mrs Culver. If any harm has come to her, you might find you have need of it, I promise you.'

'Your grandmother is my mistress,' Mrs Culver had said somewhat truculently. 'I did it for her. And there's no harm—'

James had lost his temper. 'No harm?' he had said, his voice trembling with rage. 'No harm? You have sent a vulnerable, gently bred girl— for she is a lady, make no mistake about that—to earn a living as a servant! If her memory never returned, you would have her condemned to work as a skivvy, with no protection, no hope of escape from a life of drudgery. And you claim it was for my grandmother! Lady Aldhurst would not thank you for it, believe me! You have never done a worse day's work in your life! But at least I know where to find her. And tomorrow I shall take her to stay with my grandmother in Brook Street, where she will be treated as a guest.'

'Master James—'

'Please leave me your niece's address, and see to it that my groom and the stables are informed of my wish to leave for London as soon as it is light tomorrow.' He had gone to the door and held it open. 'Now go! Leave your niece's direction in the hall. I don't wish to see you again before I know that Miss Anne is safe.'

* * *

Left alone in Anne's bedroom, James had looked round. The room was full of her—pale and motionless in the bed, in a chair by the fire in his grandmother's blue robe, clinging to him in the grip of a nightmare, laughing at him over the game of chess... She had left the copy of *Persuasion* on the bed. What sort of a life would he have if he never found her again? But that was nonsense. Cully had at least ensured that she was safe for the night. And in the morning he would collect her and take her to live with his grandmother until... Until what? Until she remembered that she had a husband? A family, even? No! He refused to believe it! Anne was his.

And so he had come to London in search of her. By noon he was on Henrietta Street, where he was devastated to learn that Anne had abandoned Mr Cobden's gig in the middle of Park Lane, and had not been seen since. His plans had fallen apart.

Mr Cobden's good turn had gone disastrously wrong, and he was full of self-condemnation. 'I should have pulled in, I know I should. But everyone was shouting and yelling, and I couldn't see where to stop. I didn't expect her to do such a thing, my lord. She was that quick I couldn't prevent her.'

'Exactly where were you when Miss Anne left the gig?'

'About halfway up Park Lane.'

'Near Grosvenor Square?'

'That's it! We halted about there. Miss Anne ran across the road towards the Square. If you ask me, my lord, she knew where she was going. As soon as I could I went back there and was out till it was dark looking for her, but there was no sign of her anywhere. She must be with someone she knows.'

Cobden was still apologising when James left him and rode on to his house in Brook Street. He was at a loss. Find Anne he must! But how could he do that when he didn't even know her real name? Grosvenor Square and the streets leading off it were the only clues he had.

So when he arrived in Brook Street he left the horses with his groom and walked towards the Square. It was early evening and the large houses here were beginning to bustle with life. Carriages came and went, grooms and maidservants hurried in and out. Where *was* she? Not sure what he was hoping for, but reluctant to give up, he walked round the square, stopping to look down Upper Grosvenor Street towards Hyde Park. This was the way Anne had come after jumping so unexpectedly off the gig. Perplexed and worried, he walked slowly on towards Brook Street. A carriage going at a good pace overtook him just by the corner. As it passed he caught a glimpse of its passengers—a man and a girl. His heart leapt at the sight of the particular angle of the head, the familiar profile... The girl was Anne. It couldn't be anyone else!

The carriage was disappearing rapidly in the direction of Oxford Street, and he ran after it like a madman. But he lost sight of it when it turned and vanished among the milling crowds of horses, carts and coaches which filled one of the main arteries of the town. For some minutes he stood staring at the traffic, unable to believe that he had lost her after being so close to finding her again. But, wherever Anne had gone, she was at least safe, not roaming lost in the streets of London. She had been smiling when he saw her, and was clearly not in the carriage against her will. It was no hired vehicle, either, but privately owned, with some sort of a crest on its door panel.

He walked back to Brook Street, his mind full of what he had seen. Apparently Anne had found a refuge somewhere in the region of Grosvenor Square. With time he was sure he could find her again. But what if she didn't want to be found? What if her memory had suddenly come back and she had joined the gentleman whose ring she had worn round her neck? She had told him she couldn't remember anything about HJC, but she had taken his ring with her when she fled, though its chain had been left on the table. Had she suddenly remembered how important HJC really was to her? Was he more important to her than James Aldhurst?

During the sleepless night that followed this was the question that kept him restlessly pacing his room. Everything he knew about Anne, the magic of her touch, her kisses, her words, would seem to make such an idea impossible. At long last he had found 'the right woman', and he had been sure that she had loved him in return. But… and the thought was unwelcome…wasn't it also possible that she *had* remembered who she was, and had not been willing either to face a shameful scandal herself, or to see him involved in one? This was the doubt that haunted him.

By morning he had come to a decision. He could not abandon his search for Anne. He had to know for certain that she was safe, was being looked after. And if she was free he would do everything he could to persuade her to come back to him, to convince her that their love for one another was worth fighting for.

But where was he to start?

Chapter Ten

Antonia collected her maid and the all-important papers, and with a sigh of relief delivered them the next day to the Foreign Office. She still had no idea where she had been for those ten days of her life, but she seemed to have suffered no harm, and, by some miracle, it hadn't yet come to the ears of society. She was sure there must be a simple explanation and that, given time, she would remember it. For that reason she continued to put off telling her father about it.

Sir Henry's health slowly improved, and he was able to accept Lady Carteret's invitation to be the guest of honour at a ball to be held at Marchant House the following week. Lady Pendell swiftly commissioned London's foremost modiste to make her niece an appropriate gown for this, her first appearance in London society. Antonia had accompanied her father on his travels as unofficial ambassador to the great and the powerful all over Europe, and as a result had a self-possession that many an older woman would envy. So she made it plain that she had no wish to wear what Lady Pendell thought suitable for her London début. 'At twenty-three I can hardly be described as your average débutante,' she said. 'I would find it very difficult to act as demurely as you seem to think I should. And I would just look silly in white frills, with a wreath of roses on my head.'

'My dear Antonia, as far as London is concerned, you *are* a débutante,' said Lady Pendell firmly. 'And if, as I hear, you can deal with a gang of Spanish brigands, surely you can manage to act a little out of character here in London! I will let you off the roses—your mother's pearl-and-crystal aigrette will do very well instead. But you will wear white.'

Antonia protested, but her aunt was adamant. However, when they visited Madame Rosa's establishment in Bruton Street, Lady Pendell agreed that Antonia's choice of a dress of white, self-striped silk, its neckline and hem richly decorated with tiny gold-and-crystal beads, was ideally suited to her niece's gracefully confident manner. Antonia herself was delighted with it, and soon she was looking forward to her first view of the phenomenon known as London society at Lady Carteret's ball.

James Aldhurst, however, was *not* looking forward to Lady Carteret's ball. Not in the slightest. He had failed to find any trace of Anne, though he had spent hours haunting the streets round Grosvenor Square until some of the servants in the big houses had started to look at him with suspicion. And as time went on without a sign of her he began to fear he would never see her again. He could not bear the thought. He had had such hopes. Anne would have taken away the hurt of his bleak early childhood at Roade, and made the place habitable for him. Together they would have built a life there, the sort of life his grandparents had enjoyed and his parents had never wanted.

In short, James Aldhurst had fallen in love for the first time in his life, and he had lost the woman he loved. London had seemed dull enough before he went to Hatherton, but now it was a desert. The thought of having to talk civilly to all the colourless, uninteresting girls he was bound to meet, to face the predatory looks of their mamas, or indeed to dance with anyone who was not Anne in his arms, appalled him. Normally charmingly courteous to everyone, he became morose and taciturn, even with his grandmother.

He was aware that she had been puzzled by his reluctance to talk about Hatherton since his return, and had no wish to increase her curiosity. But he was so preoccupied over dinner one night that she grew annoyed.

'What on earth is the matter with you, James? Where have your manners gone? You're not listening to a thing I say!'

'I'm sorry. Forgive me, ma'am.'

'That's not enough. I don't want an apology. It's time you explained your behaviour.'

'I'm not sure what you mean,' he said warily. 'I was not aware my behaviour was any different—'

'Of course it is, and you know it! First, you arrive out of the blue and baldly announce that you have left Hatherton for the foreseeable future. Second, when I ask you why you have cut your visit short, all you say is that Roade is well enough for the moment. Then...' she paused '...*then* I am told that on the day you arrived in London you were seen running up Duke

Street like a madman, and that you have taken innumerable walks in the neighbourhood since. I can't imagine it's for your health. In fact, to me it looks remarkably as if you are looking for someone. As for this evening—you have been sitting mumchance over the dining table, quite obviously not hearing half of what I've been telling you, not even when it is about the Croxton affair.'

'Croxton? What did the Prince finally give him? A marquisate or a dukedom?'

'There you are! If you had been paying better attention you would know that Lord Croxton seems to have lost the Prince's favour. Far from being granted a dukedom, he has been banished from the royal presence. All sorts of rumours are flying about, including the suggestion that he has been told to leave the country, but the Prince is keeping his own counsel, so no one knows for sure why. And society seems to be taking its cue from the Prince. Croxton is not getting the attention or respect he used to enjoy. I'm not at all sorry for him—he is a most unpleasant man.'

She waited, then went on, 'Still no comment? Do you know, James, if I didn't know you better I'd say you were in love.' She waited again. 'Did you know that Barbara Furness and her family have returned from Scotland without an announcement of any kind—not even an engagement?'

James smiled for the first time in days. 'What did I tell you?' he said.

'As you can imagine, speculation is rife among the gossips. Did Rothmuir not come up to scratch? Or did she decide not to marry him after all? If so, how *could* she have raised poor Rothmuir's hopes like that only to disappoint him? London can't decide whether to express sympathy or disapproval!'

'She never intended to accept Rothmuir. She won't care what people say about her.'

Lady Aldhurst looked fixedly at her grandson. After a pause she said slowly, 'If she can bear to face the tabbies, Lady Barbara might well be at tomorrow night's ball. But she will need friends.' She paused, then said, 'It will give you an opportunity to talk to her…?'

He said with a touch of impatience, 'You are wasting your time, ma'am. I've told you, there is not the slightest possibility that I will ever offer her anything more than friendship, and perhaps support in facing the tabbies. But no more. Not the slightest possibility!'

He said this so emphatically that his grandmother gave an exclamation of annoyance and rose abruptly from her chair. James came round the table to her and offered her his arm. She walked to the door, through the hall and into her room in offended silence and sat down in her favourite chair while James poured out two glasses of brandy. As he handed her one of them she tapped her stick angrily. 'I am disappointed in you, James. I sent you down to Hatherton to give you time to consider the future. You seemed at the time to be willing to think about your duty to the family. But you appear to have come back with your mind more than ever set against marriage.'

James said nothing, but stood twirling the empty glass in his hand. She watched him for a moment or two and her anger faded. Her eyes softened and she said more gently, 'I think I was right. You *are* in love. Who is she? And what has happened to make you so unhappy?'

James went to pour out another brandy. He offered it first to his grandmother, but when she refused it he drank it down and said abruptly, 'Her name, I think, is Anne. I wanted to bring her here to you. But I can't find her. I've thrown Hatherton into confusion, I've reduced Cully to tears, but all that counts for nothing beside the fact that I've lost Anne. Have you heard from Cully at all?'

'No, I haven't. James, what is this all about? Who is this girl? You obviously met her at Hatherton.'

'Sam and I found her the night we rode down...'

James slowly told his grandmother the story of Anne, ending with an account of his return to Hatherton from Guildford. He told her what Anne had said in the note she had left for him, and told her of his attempts to find her since. He ended by saying, 'I'm sure that if you were ever to meet her you would understand why I feel as I do.'

For a moment there was silence in the room. His grandmother had listened attentively and now sat, obviously considering how to reply. After a moment she said slowly, 'I don't propose to lecture you, James. This isn't the moment, though you are aware of my hopes and plans for the Aldhurst family. It seems to me, however, that this girl has faced the situation more realistically than you, and has made up her mind to end your association. She said as much in her letter.' James shook his head and was about to speak, but Lady Aldhurst tapped her stick on the floor and went on impatiently, 'No, let me finish. She may well love you, but she must know that you would risk becoming a social outcast if you either lived with her or married her after a divorce. She left Hatherton of her own free will, and at a time when she knew you were not there to stop her. What is more, she appears to have found a refuge of some sort since. She might even have recovered her memory and gone back to her husband! No, no! My advice to you must be to forget her.'

'You are assuming she is married,' said James, tight-lipped.

'It seems likely. There's the ring.' She frowned. 'You seem very sure she was honest. But *was* she? After all, you knew her for hardly more than a week. She told you she was a prisoner in that coach—but perhaps the coach belonged to her husband? She might have been running away from an unhappy marriage and this was an attempt to stop her. Drastically, perhaps, but within his rights. Or...perhaps the situation was even worse? Who was the man in the pool of blood? Her friend? Her lover? An accomplice? No, no,

James. Give her up—you are better without her. Especially as she apparently doesn't wish to be found.'

James turned away. After a moment he said, 'I don't believe that Anne is dishonest, and I find it very hard to believe that she is married. She is as true, as straight as any man could want. I won't give her up. I can't. At the very least I have to know the truth. I have to!'

Lady Aldhurst sighed and shook her head. 'Then I can only hope that the truth isn't too hurtful when you do find it.' She shrugged her shoulders and added less sympathetically, 'Meanwhile, I expect you to show some spirit, James. Take me to the Carterets' ball tomorrow night. Honoria Carteret has managed to snare Sir Henry Calverley as her guest of honour, which is a real feather in her cap. You could make your acquaintance with his daughter—he will probably have her with him. And who knows? The girl might help you to forget this unfortunate affair at Hatherton.' Ignoring the impatient shake of his head, she went on calmly, 'If Barbara Furness is there too you can support each other in your misery. But for heaven's sake don't give the tabbies more food for gossip!'

* * *

On the night of Lady Carteret's ball, Antonia sat at her dressing table, gazing at herself in the mirror. Someone had left a bowl of violets on the table, and their delicate scent hung in the air. Martha had brushed her hair till it shone, and, in defiance of current fashion decrees, it had been drawn back from her face and coiled high at the back of her head in the Spanish fashion. The pearl-and-crystal aigrette she had inherited from her mother was held in its folds. Her eyes were large and dark in the candlelight, her cheeks delicately flushed. Madame Rosa's white dress suited her perfectly, but her neck and shoulders looked rather bare. 'I could wear a length of ribbon round my neck instead of jewellery,' she thought, and was visited by a strange feeling that she had sat in front of a mirror and said exactly the same thing not long before. She was still trying to remember where it had been when Lady Pendell came in carrying a leather case and opened it to show her a magnificent string of pearls. 'Your father wants you to wear the Calverley pearls tonight, Antonia. They belonged to your grandmother.'

'I know,' said Antonia, absently. 'She's wearing them in one of the portraits in the dining room.'

Lady Pendell frowned. 'There isn't a portrait of your grandmother in the dining room, my dear.'

'Isn't there? I could have sworn... Are you sure? She's wearing an old-fashioned striped brocade dress, with these pearls. I can see it quite clearly.'

'Your grandmother's portrait is in the salon, and she is wearing a ribbon round her neck, not pearls. It was quite a fashion in her day. Her dress is of flowered silk. I don't know which portrait you have in mind, but it isn't that one. I don't remember a striped dress in any of the others, either.'

Antonia saw that her aunt was looking worried, and made herself laugh. 'Don't look like that! I must have been thinking of someone else's portrait, that's all. Would you help me to put the pearls on?'

But after her aunt had left Antonia went back and stared into the mirror. The scent of violets was tantalisingly familiar... She saw herself wearing an old-fashioned striped dress with a black velvet ribbon round her neck. Her eyes were dark in the candlelight, her cheeks were flushed and one long curl rested on her shoulder. She looked like a girl about to meet someone she loved. The scent of the violets was getting stronger... For a moment Antonia was full of excitement and intense anticipation... Then the image faded, and she saw herself once again in her new white dress, with her mother's aigrette in her hair and her grandmother's pearls round her neck. The feeling of anticipation faded, leaving behind it an inexplicably sharp sense of loss—a feeling that was becoming increasingly frequent....

She got up and walked restlessly round the room. Was she suffering from hallucinations? The reflection had been very clear, but when had she ever worn a striped, tight-waisted, low-cut dress, like the one in the portrait? The dress was at least forty years out of date. She felt a shiver run down her spine. This was not the first time she had had a curious flash of...of what? Memory? Whatever it was, she was always left with the same pain in her heart, the same haunting sense of loss. Anxious not to worry her father, she had not talked of them. But tonight the image in the mirror had been more vivid, and the feeling of loss more intense than ever before. That girl had looked so happy...

She shook her head impatiently. She was being absurd! It was nothing—merely nerves at the prospect of the ball. What she saw in the mirror was Antonia Calverley in her grandmother's pearls, about to have her introduction to London society.

No one observing Lord Aldhurst escorting his grandmother to Marchant House the next evening would have thought there was anything amiss. They were a handsome pair. Lady Aldhurst, straight-backed and dignified, hardly using her silver-topped cane, wore black as usual, but her dress was of heavy corded silk, the lace round her shoulders was Honiton, and her diamonds flashed and glittered in the light of the flambeaux surrounding the entrance. Lord Aldhurst, looking completely at ease in superbly cut evening clothes, ushered his grandmother up the steps, bowed over his hostess's hand with a smile, waited for Lady Aldhurst to finish her conversation with the Carterets, and then accompanied her into the crowded rooms. Many a female heart fluttered at the sight of his tall figure as he made his way slowly past them, and some even hopefully fluttered their eyelashes. But he ignored them all, merely nodding at one or two friends without stopping, until he found somewhere

where his grandmother could sit in comfort to observe the scene and exchange gossip.

'Thank you, James,' said Lady Aldhurst after she had greeted two of her cronies. 'If you can manage to steer one of those flunkeys in my direction, I shall be perfectly happy to let you go!'

'I shall fetch whatever you want myself, ma'am. And I have no wish to desert you at the moment. Brandy? Ratafia? A glass of fruit punch, perhaps?'

'I'll have the fruit punch. It won't do me any harm—the Carterets are too cheese-paring to make it strong enough. But it's probably better for me than wine.' James nodded and set off in search of the refreshment tables. When he returned his grandmother was deep in conversation with her companion. She accepted the punch and beckoned to him to sit in the empty chair next to her. 'Lady Carson here has been telling me about tonight's "lion".'

'Lion?'

'Come, James, I told you! Honoria Carteret always manages to have someone of distinction at her evening occasions, and, as I thought, tonight she has snared Sir Henry Calverley. She must be delighted with her success—he has lived very quietly since his arrival in London. In fact, this is the first time he has been seen in public since his return from overseas.' She glanced at James with a gleam in her eyes. 'You might even meet Sir Henry's daughter tonight, James. He will probably have her with him. This will be her first appearance too.'

'She is certainly here,' said Lady Carson. 'Sir Henry would apparently like to find a husband for her. But, dear Lady Aldhurst, look over there. Is that not Barbara Furness over by the arch? Have you heard how she treated poor Rothmuir? I wonder she has the impudence to appear to-night. And why on earth is she standing there alone? The girl has no sense of at all of what is proper!'

The ballroom at Marchant House had a long row of arches that formed a narrow arcade running down one side. Large urns stood at intervals in niches in the wall and tonight they had been filled with trailing greenery, which had been lifted up to decorate the arches above. Perhaps conscious of the charming picture she made, Lady Barbara Furness stood under one of these, a slender figure in green, with honey-gold curls framing a perfect face. She was gazing wistfully at the scene before her.

Lady Carson went on, 'They say her mother threatened to cast her off, but as usual Furness supported his daughter. And I must admit the prospect of living permanently in the Highlands of Scotland married to a man twice her age must have seemed daunting. One might wonder why she was foolish enough to consider it.' She paused. 'On the other hand, the poor girl's reasons for wishing to leave London were perfectly understandable. Perfectly!' she added, giving James a basilisk stare of disapproval.

James returned her look with one of his most charming smiles, excused himself to his grandmother and went over to greet Lady Barbara. She looked at him gratefully and said, 'Oh, James, I am so glad to see you. I was beginning to think my friends had deserted me tonight. People can be so very unkind.' Her slight lisp was enchanting, but her green eyes looked at him sadly, as if he was her sole source of comfort in a cruel world. However, James had known Barbara Furness for many years, and was not at all deceived. Some unfortunate swain, probably Harry Barcombe, was even now fetching her shawl or her fan or a glass of lemonade, and another would be eagerly waiting for his chance to serve. The tabbies could condemn her as severely as they wished—Barbara did not give a fig.

Years ago she had been sincerely in love with his brother, John, but Lady Furness had refused to let her daughter 'throw herself away' on a younger son. James privately thought that if John had survived just a year or two longer Barbara would have married him with or without her mother's consent. But John had died, and since then she had developed into an accomplished flirt. James was frequently amused by the cavalier manner in which she treated her suitors, but he was not above criticising her for it, especially when it involved one of his friends.

'Where is Harry?' he asked.

'Harry? Oh, yes. He went to fetch me something to drink. I was so thirsty. He wanted me to go with him, but I was hoping to see you, so I stayed here. I've put your name down on my card for the next dance.' She held it out. 'See?'

He gave her a stern look. 'Barbara, I'm happy to see you back in London. But I hope you are not going to start your tricks again. Harry is a friend of mine. You hurt him once before. You mustn't do it again. If you don't intend to marry him, then you must leave him alone.'

'He's a younger son. Mama wouldn't let me marry John, and she would never let me accept Harry, either.' She looked at him over her fan, a characteristic touch of mischief in her eyes. 'Now if *you* were to make an offer...'

'You know very well we shouldn't suit. Tell me why you told the world that you were leaving for Scotland because I had broken your heart. I'm not even sure you have one to break. Was it to punish me?'

'I was *very nearly* broken-hearted, James! I had fallen out with Harry completely. And then you were so rude about the way I had treated him... So I gave in to Mama's decision to take me to Scotland, just to show I didn't care. I never had the slightest intention of marrying Rothmuir, of course. Do you know, James, Rothmuir was old, but he was very sweet! When I explained the situation he was so understanding!'

James began to laugh. 'What on earth did you say to him?'

Barbara gave him a mischievous look. 'That was easy! I didn't actually have to say much at all, once he had met Mama. A few tears from me, a few acid comments made by Mama when she didn't know he was listening, and he decided to remain a bachelor. He kissed me fondly, hoped we had enjoyed our stay with him, and bade us all a relieved farewell.'

When James had finished laughing, he said, 'You still haven't told me why you pretended that *I* was the cause of your misery.'

'I did it on impulse—to punish you for telling me it was my fault that Harry and I had fallen out. I thought you were very unfair! But I only said it to Lady Carson.'

'You must have known that was as good as telling the whole of London!'

'Er...was there a *great* deal of gossip about us, James?' she asked innocently, looking at him over her fan.

'I didn't care about the gossip, but there was enough to upset my grandmother. Harry wasn't too pleased either, and, if he hadn't believed me when I said it was rubbish, I might have lost a friend. Don't ever do it to me again! And I'd advise you not to risk tormenting Harry any more, either. He's fonder of you than you deserve, but his patience won't last for ever. Here he comes now.'

Harry Barcombe, looking rather warm in his Guards uniform, beamed as he came towards them, carefully carrying a glass of lemonade. 'There you are, my dear,' he said cheerfully, handing it to the lady with a little bow. Then he turned to his friend. 'What are y'doin' here, James? I thought you were still at Hatherton. Lady Aldhurst isn't ill again, is she?'

'No, no! Her health is a lot better than it was. She's over there with Lady Carson...'

The music started at that moment, and Lady Barbara tapped her foot and looked wistful again. 'Harry, I would really like to dance with James, but now you have brought me this drink, I can't. I have nowhere to put it. Please get rid of it for me.'

'No, no!' said James. '*I'll* look after the drink and *you* can dance with Harry. Remember what I said!' He took the glass and turned to put it down by the urn inside the niche. And as he did so he caught a glimpse of a girl at the other end of the arcade. The carriage, the tilt of the chin, the burnished chestnut hair... She turned, and when she saw him she smiled. The glass in his hand tipped over, spilling what was left in it on to the floor, but he didn't notice. Deaf to Barbara's little scream of dismay, deaf to Harry's 'Good Lord, James!' he pushed his way as quickly as he could through the crowds to the other end of the room. That girl was Anne!

Chapter Eleven

It took James some time to make his way through the crowd, and he lost sight of Anne for a moment. But then he saw her. She had turned away and was talking and laughing with a group of people, most of whom he knew. He came to a halt, shaken by a sudden spurt of anger. He would have expected her to look for him, wait for him, even come to meet him. What the devil did she think she was doing? And why hadn't she let him know she was safe before now? She must know how worried he had been. He started pushing his way through the crowd again. But as he drew close enough to see her more clearly he began to wonder if he was making a mistake. Superbly dressed in white and gold, with a gleam of pearls and a glitter of crystal, this was a perfectly self-possessed young woman, fully at ease with some of the most distinguished people in London. She was totally different from the vulnerable girl he had known at Hatherton. Could his Anne *possibly* have changed so much? Or had his longing to find her again deceived him into seeing her in a stranger? He stopped to watch.

'She's lovely, isn't she?' He had been joined by Charles Stainforth, a friend of his grandmother's and a notorious gossip.

Still not certain, James nodded, and said as casually as he could, 'Who is she? I'd like to meet her.'

'My dear fellow, half of London would like to meet Miss Calverley!'

'Miss *Calverley!* Sir Henry Calverley's daughter?' James concealed his astonishment with an effort. He *had* indeed deceived himself. Anne could not possibly be Antonia Calverley. She had spent over a week with him at Hatherton, and the absence of Sir Henry Calverley's daughter would certainly have raised speculation and comment. He had heard nothing and, more to the point, neither had his grandmother.

'I don't think I've seen Miss Calverley before,' he said cautiously. 'How long has she been in London?'

'I believe the Calverleys came up from

Portsmouth quite recently. But I'm not surprised you haven't seen them. Sir Henry hasn't been well, so they haven't mixed in society as yet.'

He stopped and regarded James with a twinkle in his eye. 'I can see our lovely newcomer has made an impression on you, James. I'll willingly introduce you if you wish. You're just the sort of fellow she ought to meet. In fact, I'll do it now— her father is a colleague of mine.' He took a step, then stopped. 'Ah! It looks as if you'll have to wait a while. Prince Friedrich is about to take her off for this waltz.' He turned to James and said regretfully. 'That's a real pity. The girl would have done better to wait for you, James. Prince Fred may have been born in Vienna, but his waltz is definitely Berlin!'

They watched as Miss Calverley was led out on to the floor. Sir Charles went on, 'You know, of course, that the girl's father is the man who put an end to Croxton's hopes of a dukedom?'

'Calverley? How on earth did he manage that?'

'I'll tell you, but you must keep it to yourself. Calverley uncovered some unpleasant facts about the sources of Croxton's wealth.' He sighed. 'The Prince has never shown much discrimination, but he couldn't ignore what was in Sir Henry's report. So Croxton lost the royal favour, together with any hopes of a dukedom—or anything else. In fact, he's been told to leave England before the end of the month.'

'That's pretty harsh, surely? Where will he go?'

'He's lucky to escape worse! I should think he'll go to the West Indies. He has several estates there. Don't feel too sorry for him, James. The details in Sir Henry's report are pretty nasty. The country is better off without a man like Croxton, and so is the Prince. I believe he's here tonight, but the word is already starting to spread. He's finished in London.'

'So that was all Calverley's doing?'

'Yes. And if I were Calverley I'd watch my back. Croxton isn't a man to forgive or forget easily.'

James was listening with only half his attention. His eyes were on the pair waltzing past them. Miss Calverley was smiling at her partner with a delightful air of interest, but James was as certain as he could be that she was bored. He couldn't have explained *how* he knew, but he knew. The feeling of familiarity grew stronger as he continued to watch her. This was no stranger. He was sure in his bones that this was Anne, whatever Sir Charles or anyone else said!

'Shall we join our hostess?' he said. Sir Charles readily agreed and they went over to the group that included Lady Carteret and her guest of honour.

It was difficult, but James managed to maintain a calmly courteous manner while he waited for the dancers to return. He wanted to see Anne's reaction when they met again, to hear what she had to say, how she would explain herself. Sir Henry had just been borne off by his hostess to meet someone else, so he was unable to talk to Anne's father. But her aunt had stayed behind, and James, who already knew her slightly, exchanged a few words with her. He was surprised at the lack of warmth in her manner until he realised that she must have heard the story of Lady Barbara's so-called broken heart, and shared society's disapproval of him. It was perhaps wiser not to touch upon the subject of her niece. He moved on to greet other friends in the group, flirted lightly with Sally Jersey, who was an old friend, and waited. But he never lost track of the slender figure in white and gold circling the floor with her elephantine partner.

'You shall dance the next waltz with her, James,' said Lady Jersey with a look of sympathetic amusement. 'The poor girl deserves a treat after our estimable Prince Friedrich's efforts. He has trundled her round the ballroom like a gun carriage! And *you* dance like a dream!'

'Thank you. I...I would like that,' he said, his eyes still on the dancers.

'I prophesy the girl will be one of the Season's successes, don't you? You'll have your work cut out to make an impression on this one.' She added with a sly look, 'Or will she too end up going off to Scotland with a broken heart?'

James turned towards her with one eyebrow raised and said, 'I'm surprised at you, Lady Jersey! You, above all, ought to know that Barbara Furness was simply enjoying herself at my expense.'

'Of course, I know that, James! You've occasionally had a quite devastating effect on a number of young ladies, but the silly creatures must take a share of the blame. As for Lady Barbara—I didn't believe that story for one moment. Her love of mischief probably got the better of her. I have to say that this last business with Rothmuir was the outside of enough. Her tricks can be quite amusing, but this went too far.'

'Her love of tricks is not so amusing when it upsets people I'm fond of!'

'You mean your grandmother? Then I'm sorry to have teased you. Look, the waltz has finished, and Miss Calverley and the prince are returning. Do I detect a look of stoical suffering on her face? No, her manners are much too good for that. She really is delightful.' Lady Jersey held out her hand. 'Miss Calverley! I have someone here who wants to meet you. Let me introduce Lord Aldhurst.'

Anne had looked beautiful dressed in borrowed finery on her last night at Hatherton, but tonight she almost took James's breath away. He bowed and smiling into her eyes, said, 'Miss Calverley?' He added very softly, 'So that's your name!'

The dark blue eyes widened in surprise, but the expected recognition was not there. If anything she looked puzzled, and a little wary. 'Of course it is, Lord Aldhurst! What else would it be?'

James almost laughed. So this was to be her game! Pretending she didn't know him. It was understandable. He could hardly expect her to reveal to the assembled company that Sir

Henry Calverley's daughter already knew James Aldhurst very well indeed. Sally Jersey was looking interested, and it wouldn't do at all to rouse her curiosity—she was second only to Sir Charles in her love of gossip. For the moment he would have to play the game with her. He shook his head, laughed and changed the subject. 'Lady Jersey was telling me that you have spent some time abroad. Where was that, Miss Calverley? Spain?'

'Everywhere, I think. My father's work has taken us to most of the countries in Europe.' She eyed a young man coming towards them, and said with a cool smile, 'I'm so glad to have met you, Lord Aldhurst, but I'm afraid you'll have to excuse me. I believe Lord William is about to claim his dance.'

Before James could say anything more she was gone again, and when he next caught sight of her she was moving up the room in a lively set of country dances. Lady Jersey was now talking to someone else and James was left to himself, a prey to conflicting emotions. He was convinced that Miss Calverley and Anne were one and the same, but how on earth had her absence at Hatherton remained unnoticed? And why was she behaving so indifferently towards him? Apart from that one spontaneous smile when their eyes had first met—surely a smile of recognition?—she had not given the slightest indication, not even a flicker of an eyelash, that she had ever seen him before. She was certainly a better actress than he would have expected.

Miss Calverley returned eventually, looking flushed and animated. Her partner offered eagerly to take her in search of refreshment, but James protested, and Lady Jersey, who seemed to have taken up his cause, supported him.

'Lord William, alas! I have promised Lord Aldhurst that he may dance the next waltz with Miss Calverley, and I think he must be the one to look after her till then.' William Chatteris's face fell, but Sally Jersey was too influential a woman to argue with. He bowed and went away.

Miss Calverley's eyes sparkled and she said with a slight touch of rebellion in her voice, 'How kind of you, Lady Jersey! But I *am* just a little thirsty…'

'Of course you are, my dear! And I have found you the perfect partner. Lord Aldhurst has the best reputation in London for dancing the waltz, and he is second to none in his ability to take care of his partners! He'll find somewhere pleasant for you to enjoy a cooling drink before the next dance.' Miss Calverley looked for a moment as if she was about to object, but then made a charming little gesture of acquiescence. His heart missed a beat as she took his arm, and without thinking he put his hand on top of hers and smiled at her. She drew a sharp breath, took her hand away and walked off without him. With a shrug at Lady Jersey, who was shaking her head at him, James followed her.

Miss Calverley carefully avoided any contact as they made their way through to the anteroom where refreshments were being served, and James began to feel angry again. She was making a mistake if she thought she could play games with him for much longer. He found a seat in a corner, fetched a glass of fruit punch for her and wine for himself, and sat down facing her, a touch grimly. Much as he wanted to know why she was behaving like this, why she had run away, wanted to demand why she had not been in touch with him, to remind her of what they had meant to each other, he knew he must keep his feelings in check. The room was crowded and, aware that he was always the subject of conjecture and gossip, he sipped the wine, then said calmly, 'I am doing my best to understand you, Anne. Why are you behaving like this?'

Her manner became even cooler. 'Anne was my mother's name, Lord Aldhurst. Mine is Antonia. But I'm afraid it is not generally used by anyone but my family and close friends.'

'Friends! Dammit, we—' James controlled himself with an effort. 'I would say we were a great deal more than that!'

'I cannot imagine why you should think so, sir,' she said, and this time her voice was icy. She stood up. This was no acting. James would swear that the young woman standing before him was genuinely offended.

Conscious of curious eyes all around, James got up too and said, 'I...I seem to have made a mistake for which I apologise. Would you...would you prefer to go back to the ballroom?'

The music was just striking up, and James waited in silence until his partner nodded frostily and they went to join the dancers on the floor. His thoughts were in turmoil. Against all the evidence, he had been quite sure that this was his Anne, but now he was questioning his judgement again. If this was acting, then he had been totally mistaken in her character. No woman who had professed to love him as Anne had could possibly behave like this, however afraid of discovery she might be. He had seen no warmth in those dark blue eyes, no awareness of him as a person she loved, or even as someone she knew! Indeed, she had so far shown only polite indifference, changing to anger when she thought he was being over-familiar. Was he making a serious mistake after all?

The waltz gave him no reason to change his mind. He failed to engage her in conversation, and for the most part they went round in silence. And although James danced with all his usual expertise, neither he nor, apparently, his partner, enjoyed it. Miss Calverley was stiff and unyielding in his arms, and kept an even greater distance between them than the most rigorous chaperon would have demanded. In fact, he thought bitterly, she had been more at ease, danced more gracefully, with Prince Friedrich!

His heart ached when he remembered his last waltz with Anne at Roade. They had danced in a neglected house, in an empty room, with neither orchestra nor company, and yet it had been magical. She had melted into his arms as if they were one person.

Damn it, what sort of idiot was he? He loved Anne with everything in him. How was it *possible* not to be sure whether this woman was the love of his life—or someone he had just met?

The memory of the waltz at Roade persuaded him to try one last time. As they went up the room to rejoin the others he said carefully, 'I have offended you again, Miss Calverley, by using your name too freely. For that I apologise. But do you... do you really not feel that we have met before?'

They were nearly there. As she turned and curtsied she said with a scornful smile, 'Really, Lord Aldhurst, I am obliged to say that I am disappointed! I had expected a less...*tired* approach from a gentleman who is said to be the most skilled charmer in London. Ever since I was old enough to wear long skirts, gentlemen all over Europe have been assuring me that we have met before—usually because they wanted something from my father. I'm not sure what you want, but my answer is still the same. I'm quite *certain* we have *not*...met...before!'

Her words stung. James was angry, but he was damned if he would let her see it! He smiled lazily at her and said softly, 'Then I have to apologise again. I have been underestimating you, Miss

Calverley. I see I shall have to invent another approach, especially for you!'

He bowed and turned away. This…shrew could not possibly be his gentle, vulnerable Anne! She was a complete stranger, the opinionated daughter of a senior diplomat, and he had been tricked by an astounding likeness into making a fool of himself. And now he would have to start the search for the real Anne all over again!

He walked swiftly across the floor to where his grandmother was sitting. Sir Charles had joined her, and James listened for a while, still able to smile at their strictures on the couples on the dance floor in spite of his heartache.

Then Miss Calverley glided past on the arm of yet another partner. He watched grimly. She still reminded him of Anne with almost every one of her movements: Anne in his grandmother's walled garden, an aristocrat to the fingertips; Anne with laughter in her eyes, holding out her hand to him in the saloon at Roade inviting him to dance; Anne coming down the stairs in his grandmother's dress on the last fateful evening they had spent together… Oh, God, what if he never found her again?

His grandmother's voice recalled him to Lady Carteret's ballroom. 'James! James, Sir Charles has told me that the girl dancing with Arthur Porteous is our famous Miss Calverley.'

'She is, ma'am.'

'James has already danced with her,' Sir Charles said.

'Indeed? Why didn't I see you?' she demanded. 'And why didn't you bring her to me afterwards to be introduced?'

'Miss Calverley is in great demand,' James said curtly.

Lady Aldhurst's eyes widened and she gave him a penetrating look. To his relief, however, she didn't comment. She turned instead to Sir Charles. 'Have you too met Miss Calverley, Charles?'

Sir Charles was eager to talk and full of praise for Miss Calverley. Unwilling though he was to listen to any more about her, James had soon heard enough to put the seal on his conviction that he had indeed been mistaken. It was well nigh impossible for Miss Calverley to be the girl at Hatherton. Her resemblance to Anne was simply one of fate's crueller tricks.

'She's a most enterprising young lady, a true heroine,' said Sir Charles. 'I don't know what her father would have done without her. He was taken ill, you know, halfway to England. He has a very good manservant, but it was his daughter who nursed him for the rest of the voyage, and after they had landed, she was the one who saw to all the arrangements for travel to London. An intrepid young person! Once they were here she brought his papers personally to the Foreign Office.'

'She seems to be devoted to her father?'

'They are well nigh inseparable. In fact, I'm not sure what he will do when she marries.'

'Does she have someone in mind, Sir Charles?' asked Lady Aldhurst casually.

'Not that I've heard. Sir Henry's attack of fever was pretty bad. He was tired out by the journey up from Portsmouth and had to rest, so we haven't heard or seen much of him or his daughter since they arrived. But as far as I know there hasn't been the slightest hint of any engagement. I very much doubt there is one—I know for a fact that Sir Henry still wants his daughter to meet more people of her own age in London. But if you ask me she won't have any difficulty in finding a husband. She's a real charmer.'

Well, that's a matter of opinion, thought James grimly.

'I must see if I can do anything,' Lady Aldhurst said. 'What is Sir Henry's direction?'

'He has a house in Upper Grosvenor Street. His sister, Lady Pendell, has been looking after it while he has been abroad. You probably know her, Lady Aldhurst.'

'Yes, I do. We've met on numerous occasions. She is a widow, but mixes quite freely in society.'

James could stand no more. The motive behind his grandmother's intention of getting to know the Calverleys was only too clear, and he wanted none of it. He excused himself and went in search of more congenial company.

He found Harry alone and in a melancholy mood. Lady Barbara had ignored his name on her card and had gone to dance with someone else. James found him a drink and took him to a spot from which they had a good view of the floor. Couples came and went, and at one point Lady Barbara passed by and cast up her eyes at them as she was jogged along by her over-enthusiastic partner.

'She'll never agree to marry me,' Harry said morosely.

James decided at least to do someone else some good. 'Barbara loves you as much as she can love anyone,' he said firmly. 'But she enjoys teasing. You could easily persuade her to marry you if you put your mind to it.'

'Her mother wouldn't agree. I'm a younger son.'

'Harry, you were one of the bravest men I ever had in my command in Spain,' said James briskly. 'Where the devil has your fighting spirit gone? It's my belief that after this last escapade in Scotland Lady Furness would be only too pleased to marry her daughter off to a present-able young man such as you, with a pedigree as long as yours, younger son or not. You may never inherit your father's title, but you're not poor. You've more than enough to support Barbara in the style her mother would like. Don't let Barbara tell you differently.'

Harry's face brightened considerably. 'D'y'know James, I hadn't thought of that! I think you might be right. I'm obliged to you, old chap! Thank you! I'll just be off to catch her at the end of this set of dances.'

James watched him go, then turned to look

round the room. Lord Croxton was nearby, his eyes fixed on a group making their way across the now empty floor, their progress constantly impeded by people stopping to talk to them.

'Look at them,' he sneered. 'Look at the way they're all fawning on him—Sir Henry Calverley, the white knight of Westminster, damn him! And his lovely daughter...' He drank his wine and then laughed unpleasantly. 'I could tell you a thing or two if I wanted to—' He stopped, threw a quick glance at James and frowned, his face closing up. Then he was gone.

James felt a cold shiver down his spine. He had never liked Croxton, but this man now was like a dangerously injured animal. Someone should warn Calverley to be careful.

James's grandmother was still talking to Sir Charles, though he was obviously on the point of leaving her. As he moved away Lady Aldhurst looked around, caught James's eye and beckoned him with an imperious wave of her hand. As soon as he reached her she said, 'I should like to meet these Calverleys, James. Frances Pendell would be happy to introduce us. Would you be kind enough to ask her to bring them over?'

James was reluctant to have any more to do with the girl who was so like, and yet so unlike, his Anne, but he couldn't think of an excuse that would satisfy her. 'Of course,' he said. 'But I would like to know your motive.'

Lady Aldhurst gave him a bland smile. 'Why do I need a motive? They are newcomers to London, James. That poor girl needs dancing partners who are a little younger than Percy Greville and Arthur Porteous, wouldn't you say? Even in his early years Percy Greville hadn't the least notion how to keep in step, and Porteous was always a dead bore. Surely she deserves better than that piece of inflated self-importance. She has style! I like the look of her! Do go, James!'

Lady Aldhurst was still a respected member of society, and Lady Pendell readily agreed to her request. She brought both Calverleys over to Lady Aldhurst, who received them graciously, smiling benevolently as Sir Henry bowed over her hand.

'And this is your daughter, Sir Henry,' she said, eyeing the girl who was standing demurely at her father's side.

'My daughter, Antonia, ma'am.' Antonia curtsied.

'Charming!' said Lady Aldhurst. 'Quite charming.' She turned round to James, who till now had remained in the background. 'I should like you to meet my grandson. Lord Aldhurst, Sir Henry.'

Miss Calverley stiffened as James took a step forwards. He bowed, and then, smiling ruefully, he said, 'Miss Calverley and I have already met. I'm afraid she has a poor impression of me. I...I mistook her for someone else, and probably disconcerted her. Will you forgive me, ma'am?'

'Certainly,' she said coolly and dismissively. 'But whatever made you think I was disconcerted? Annoyed perhaps, but that was only briefly. Anyone can make a mistake.'

Sir Henry laughed. 'Antonia has no nerves,' he said. 'It would take a great deal to disconcert her.'

James had a brief and unworthy desire to test this out some time in the not-too-distant future, but at that moment Sir Henry put his hand affectionately on his daughter's shoulder...and James froze as he caught sight of the ring the man was wearing on his third finger. It was of heavy gold, set with a black stone. James could clearly make out the initials carved on it—HJC. It was unmistakably the one Holford's son had found in the stream.

After a moment of shock his mind raced. Antonia Calverley *was* the girl who had been with him at Hatherton! That ring proved it beyond all doubt. She had picked it up from the table on that last evening at Hatherton and now here it was on Sir Henry Calverley's finger. Incredible though it was, Sir Henry's daughter was undeniably the girl he had rescued and kept with him at Hatherton! He remembered asking her what her name was and she had begun, 'I'm An...' and stopped. He had called her Anne because of it. But she had been trying to say *Antonia*! *AC* on the purse for Antonia Calverley!

His heart missed a beat, as he realised what else this meant. Antonia Calverley was neither married nor, if Charles Stainforth was to be believed, betrothed. Her ring with that message of love inside it belonged not to a husband, but to her father. His Anne was not only found—she was free to love and to marry where she pleased.

The elation caused by this discovery faded a little as he was faced with the unpalatable truth that her memory had played another trick on her. Unless she was a consummate actress, she was not pretending. Anne had completely forgotten him, along with everything to do with her life at

Hatherton. The love affair that had changed his life simply didn't exist for the girl he loved.

The thought was bitter, and the present situation ironic. In Hatherton she hadn't remembered her previous life. In London she had forgotten Hatherton. 'I couldn't imagine ever forgetting *you*,' she had said on their last evening together. But apparently that was exactly what she had done.

His grandmother's voice broke in on these gloomy thoughts. 'James?' She had finished talking to Sir Henry and was giving him an impatient look.

'Ma'am?'

'James, Miss Calverley tells me she has no partner for the next set of dances.'

Miss Calverley said hastily, 'Lady Aldhurst, you misunderstood me…' But she was no match for James's grandmother. While the ladies exchanged polite denials and excuses, which were met with equally polite counter-suggestions, James had time to come to a rapid decision. He must not do anything at the moment that would betray the young lady who was, and yet was not, his Anne. Antonia Calverley could well lose every scrap of her reputation if it became known that she had just spent a week with him at Hatherton, unchaperoned except for one or two servants. No, he must keep that potentially explosive information strictly to himself for the moment—though he would have given much to know what she had told her family!

One all-important question remained. Was their love affair as dead as he feared? Or were feelings as strong as theirs impossible to destroy completely? He turned to her. She gave him a cool little smile, and began, 'Lady Aldhurst is very kind, but I really don't think—'

But before she could go any further James interrupted with a particularly attractive smile of his own. 'What an excellent idea!' he said. 'Miss Calverley, please! You cannot refuse me. If you do, I shall think you have not forgiven me after all. I am truly sorry to have annoyed you. Please dance with me again.' He held out his hand, challenging her to accept it.

Chapter Twelve

Antonia had never backed down from a challenge in her life, and she was not about to start now. But as she stared at the hand held out in invitation she felt a strong reluctance to take it. He might have smiled when she had been so rude to him a short while ago, but the smile hadn't reached his eyes. He had been very angry. Why was he looking at her now as if he knew and liked everything about her? As if they were old friends? Or was that just part of the infamous Aldhurst charm her aunt had warned her about?

She had seen him as soon as she had first entered the ballroom and had felt straight away that she knew him. Throughout the introductions to various dignitaries that followed, she had continued to look for glimpses of him, trying but failing to remember where she could have met him before.

In the end she asked her hostess. 'That is our famous Lord Aldhurst,' said Lady Carteret. 'He's very handsome, is he not?'

Antonia turned to her with a smile. 'Lord Aldhurst? For a moment I was sure I had met him somewhere, but I don't think I can have. I don't remember the name.'

'Lady Aldhurst is his grandmother. His fondness for her is one of his few redeeming features.'

Antonia laughed. 'Dear me! You are severe, Lady Carteret. What has Lord Aldhurst done to offend you?'

Lady Carteret pursed her lips. 'James Aldhurst is an accomplished flirt and you would be wise to avoid him, Miss Calverley. He has broken the heart of more than one poor young woman.'

'Has he indeed?' said Antonia.

'I dare say one day he will bow to his grandmother's wishes and marry, if only to please her. He is very attached to her. But no other female has held his interest for long. Indeed, the sad truth is that once he is sure of a woman's affection his interest in her fades. He may be handsome, rich, and, of course, extremely eligible, but I would advise you not to risk becoming another victim of his undoubted charm.'

The spite that was evident in Lady Carteret's voice was most unpleasant, and Antonia found her advice impertinent. So she gave the lady one of her cool smiles and said, 'Thank you, ma'am. I'm sure your warning is kindly meant, but it really isn't necessary. I believe I am too sensible to become any sort of victim of any man's "undoubted charm", however rich or eligible he may be.'

Lady Carteret looked slightly taken aback. 'Indeed,' she said a touch coldly. 'Forgive me, I had forgotten. I hear you are an intrepid traveller, and have had all sorts of adventures. You are no doubt well able to take care of yourself. You must tell me about your travels some time, my dear Miss Calverley.' She walked away, and Antonia's aunt came over, shaking her head.

'Antonia, Antonia! What did I tell you? What happened to the prettily demure air I recommended? Débutantes don't tell their hostess she is an interfering busybody, my dear!'

'But she was!'

'That is not relevant. Actually, you probably touched a nerve. Lady Carteret's daughter was one of the foolish girls who thought she was in love with James Aldhurst. He paid no more attention to her than to anyone else, but her own hopes and her mother's ambition persuaded the silly girl that he was in love with her, and she almost went into a decline when it became clear he was not. My sympathies are with him in that particular case. I am quite sure he never encouraged her. The girl is now to marry someone else, but her mother still bears Lord Aldhurst a grudge.' She looked thoughtfully at Antonia. 'All the same, he is dangerous. Look at him now. He has already broken poor Barbara Furness's heart once, and now he appears to be trying to break it all over again.'

James Aldhurst was on the other side of the room talking to a young woman in a green dress. He was looking down at her, with one hand on the pillar behind. Neither his urbane air, nor the elegance of his beautifully cut evening clothes, could disguise the fact that, with his black hair, broad shoulders and long legs, he was all confident male, and Lady Barbara's expression showed how very aware she was of the fact. She laughed when he made some remark that amused her, and with a flash of white teeth he joined in.

Looking at the two of them, Antonia experienced a sudden fit of angry disappointment, which was so intense that it left her trembling. In a moment it had gone again, and she was left dazed and wondering where on earth it had come from.

'I wonder how long it will last this time?' her aunt said, her eyes on the pair across the room. She shook her head and, taking Antonia's hand, said very seriously, 'Antonia, dear, I am not suffering from Lady Carteret's particular spleen, but at the risk of having you bite my head off, I should warn you—Aldhurst is *not* husband material. You are a lovely newcomer, and he is almost bound to try to add you to his list of conquests. That man is far too attractive for any female's peace of mind, so don't let him lead you astray! Please!'

Antonia looked at the couple again. Lady Barbara was now giving Lord Aldhurst an outrageously flirtatious look, and he was laughing again. That dress was only just the right side of respectable—no wonder he looked so interested. How could any man be charmed by such an obvious sort of creature? 'I am surprised you think he could,' she said with unwonted force. 'You may set your mind at rest, Aunt Pendell. I am not at all at risk.'

* * *

But later she had seen him looking at her from the other end of the room, and for a moment she knew she *knew* him and had been filled with delight at seeing him again. She had smiled before she could stop herself. And only then she had realised that he was the infamously charming Lord Aldhurst.

After they had been introduced she had discovered how charming James Aldhurst could be. His dark grey eyes had seemed to hold a special smile for her, what he said seemed to convey a special meaning, and the feeling of his hand on hers had taken her breath away. The man was not just charming—he was lethal! She had been furious with herself and with him for the effect he was having on her, and the waltz that followed had been a disaster. She had finally been unpardonably rude to him. He had smiled, but his eyes had been cold, and they had parted company with relief.

And now here he was inviting her to dance again, apologising for having annoyed her, holding out his hand and challenging her to take it. She could see he was watching her closely. The warmth was back in his dark grey eyes, and again it was almost as if he knew her better than she knew herself. That was nonsense, of course. She would accept his challenge, but this time she knew its extent and would be ready for it. Antonia lifted her chin and gathered up the train of her dress with one hand. 'Very well, Lord Aldhurst,' she said. 'I will.' And she put her other hand firmly in his.

His hand enveloped hers and even through her glove she was achingly conscious of every part of it—flesh, bone, sinew, its warmth, its strength… It was incredibly familiar. She wanted to pull it towards her, feel his body close to hers. She stumbled as she took a step back and snatched her hand away. He caught hold of her.

'Miss Calverley!' he said, putting a steadying arm round her waist. 'Are you not well?' He was looking at her with sympathy…and something else in his eyes. Satisfaction? How dared he feel either! She gathered her wits together and pulled away.

'Perfectly well, thank you!' she said with as much composure as she could muster. 'Shall we dance?'

He led her onto the floor and bowed as the music began. Grateful that it wasn't a waltz, but a set of country dances, Antonia curtsied and they danced down the set together.

Four pairs of eyes watched them with interest. Sir Henry's thought was quite simple. The two made a handsome couple. He would ask his friends about Aldhurst—the fellow might be just the sort of man he wanted for Antonia.

Lady Pendell was worried. She had forgotten how much society loved gossip, and this ballroom was full of it. How much longer was Antonia going to wait before she told her father the truth about her delayed arrival in Upper Grosvenor Street? She looked round the room and was petrified at the thought of the scandal if anyone here ever caught a whisper of those missing days. And as if that wasn't enough, James Aldhurst showed every sign of embarking on a flirtation with her headstrong niece, exposing her to the full force of his dangerous charm.

Lady Aldhurst's expression was inscrutable, but her mind was working overtime. This evening the deep unhappiness that James had tried but failed to hide from her had suddenly disappeared. Why? She could see, even from where she sat, how her grandson, normally so punctilious in his manners, was practically ignoring everyone else in the set to focus his attention on the Calverley girl. There was a mystery here which she found extremely intriguing... Lady Aldhurst began to review her engagements with the aim of inviting the Calverleys to dine.

And at the back of the room, shunned by many who had formerly been only too glad to be seen in his company, was the man who was following Antonia Calverley's progress with a look of bitter hatred. Lord Croxton was making arrangements to leave England in the near future, and he burned with resentment at his downfall, for which he blamed Sir Henry Calverley and his accursed daughter. Why had Briggs and his useless accomplice let her escape? Disaster could have been avoided if only the fools had held on to her. And it would have been a *real* pleasure to see Calverley squirm when he was told that his precious Antonia was in the hands of a man he was trying to destroy and given the terms for her release—her *eventual* release. But Briggs had failed him in that, too....

Another former friend passed him, studiously

avoiding his eye. Croxton muttered a curse and left the ballroom to escape onto the terrace.

At first, tension made Antonia as stiff as she had been before, but she found she could relax as the dance continued. In view of his reputation Lord Aldhurst was behaving surprisingly well—with more circumspection than most of her previous partners, in fact. He seemed almost reluctant to touch her, holding her very lightly, keeping his arm round her waist for no longer than the demands of the dance dictated, and seeing to it that they were never too close.

'London must be new to you, Miss Calverley,' he said after a while. 'I understand you have travelled a great deal abroad.'

It wasn't easy to concentrate when her nerves tingled every time he touched her, but Antonia's long training in difficult situations helped. 'It is new, yes,' she said with a fair degree of composure. 'I haven't yet seen a great deal of it. And I suppose I have travelled quite widely. After my mother died, my father took me with him wherever he went.'

'That must have led to some strange adventures.'

She managed a smile. 'You might say so!'

'Weren't you ever nervous—or frightened even?'

Her moment of ease was over as she had a sudden and vivid vision of the cellar, Lawson's body, the coach. She shut it out. If he really possessed the ability to read her mind he must not see those pictures. They belonged to a part of her life she would rather forget. She bit her lip and said curtly, 'Of course! But I prefer not to think about it, Lord Aldhurst. Especially when I am dancing.'

She had a moment's respite as they started off back down the set, but then he began again, 'Why haven't I seen you before? Have you been in town long?'

Her heart missed a beat, but she said calmly, 'Not nearly long enough, Lord Aldhurst. There is so much to see.' She cast around in her mind for something to say. 'Lady Carteret has found a very pretty way of decorating the ballroom, has she not? The…the way she has…she has arranged the greenery round those arches is particularly effective.'

'Very effective.'

They danced in silence for a few minutes, then

he began again. 'Is your father fully recovered from his illness?'

'Very nearly.'

'I hear his return to London was delayed because of it.'

Why did he have to keep returning to matters she was particularly anxious to avoid? Couldn't he see that she didn't want to talk about them? She forced herself to say quite normally, 'He still tires easily, but I am sure he will soon have his strength back.' Once again she steered the conversation to safer ground. 'The...the orchestra tonight is remarkably good, don't you think?'

'Remarkably. But I am sorry.'

'Whatever for?'

'That your first acquaintance with England was so unfortunate. I suppose your father's weakness forced you to make the journey to London in easy stages? That must have been tedious for you both.'

They were separated once again by the dance. This time Antonia was really angry. He had to be doing this deliberately. There was something of a snap in her voice as she said, 'On the contrary, it gave us an opportunity to admire the scenery!' She lifted her chin, and gave him a bright smile as she continued, 'I had not realised how lovely the English countryside can be, even in spring. We were both enchanted by it. Of course, the weather has been unusually kind.' One more round, she told herself as she whirled away, and this interminable dance would be over. 'Do you think it will hold?' she said when they met for the last time.

The music came to an end with a flourish and with the utmost relief Antonia curtsied to him and made to leave the floor without waiting for an answer. But he caught up with her and took her arm.

'Come, Miss Calverley!' he murmured, looking down at her reproachfully. 'I am disappointed. You can surely do better than that.'

She looked up, astonished. One eyebrow was raised and he had a distinct look of amusement in his eyes.

Antonia stopped and demanded, 'What do you mean, sir?'

The ballroom had warmed up as the evening progressed, and someone had opened more of the windows leading onto the terrace. Now he drew her through the nearest one, but when she resisted he went no farther than the threshold.

'If you don't wish to talk about your journey,' he said softly, 'a young woman who has travelled the world so widely surely ought to find more interesting alternatives than Lady Carteret's decorations, the merits of her orchestra, or, God help us, the weather! Any simpleton can fill the time with such trivialities.'

Antonia's throat was dry. This was more than chance. Lord Aldhurst had somehow heard something about her missing week and was fishing. Always at her best when she felt under attack, Antonia braced herself. 'I am sorry if I bore you,' she managed to say sweetly. 'I thought I was suiting my remarks to my company.'

James laughed out loud. 'Well said, if inaccurate! You don't really mean that. Why don't you want to talk of your return to England?'

Had one of her aunt's servants been talking? Had news of those missing days begun to percolate via London's servants' quarters to the rest of society? A cold shiver went down Antonia's spine—what if people started to put the same questions to her father? She now saw how dangerous it had been to come tonight without having first told him the truth. She said in a low voice, 'You are perfectly right. I do not wish to talk of my return. Why will you not let the subject rest? It was a stressful, *very* stressful, situation, and I do not wish to discuss it.' She clasped her hands together to hide the fact that they were trembling, but try as she might she could not keep her voice entirely even, as she went on, 'You will oblige me by not questioning my father about it, either. He is still not perfectly well, and it will only upset him.'

Till now he had maintained an irritating air of someone with a private source of amusement, but at this he grew quite serious. Taking her hands in his and holding them firmly, he said, 'That is the last thing I want to do. I have no wish to upset either of you.'

She felt strangely comforted. But there it was again—the consciousness of his hands round hers, the feeling that her blood was running faster through her veins because of it… That strange desire to be closer, held in his arms… She must be mad! 'Thank you,' she managed to say, taking her hands away.

'But I should still very much like to hear more about your travels. Do you ride, Miss Calverley?'

'Of course, sir. Though I haven't yet been riding in London.'

'Would you care to ride with me tomorrow morning? I could introduce you to Rotten Row in Hyde Park.'

'Of course I won't! I hardly know you.'

'I'm hoping that time will remedy that. Please come! I promise to behave...impeccably!' He was looking at her still with that little smile in his eyes, and once again she felt a strong pull of attraction. She would be mad to agree.

He was waiting. 'You look as if you are about to refuse,' he said. 'Would you prefer to go for a drive instead? Or...are you afraid, Miss Calverley?'

'Afraid? Of course not! Why should I be afraid? What on earth is there to be afraid of?' She could hear her voice rising and stopped and cleared her throat. She was ready to present him with a perfect excuse, until she looked up at him. How could a man smile and at the same time look so anxious? 'Very well,' she heard herself say. 'Thank you, I should like to ride in Hyde Park. But I have something I must do first. Shall we say noon? And now I should like to rejoin my father, if you please.'

* * *

Croxton heard them walk back into the room. He stood thinking on the terrace for a moment, then left Marchant House without taking his leave of his hostess and went out into the night in search of Briggs.

Sir Henry had always been an early riser, and even after a late night he was up and finishing his breakfast by the time Antonia came downstairs to join him.

'I didn't expect to see you so early, my dear,' he said, rising to greet her with his customary courtesy.

'I couldn't sleep, Papa. And I wanted to see you before my aunt was up.'

Sir Henry laughed. 'She won't be down for some time. Late to bed and late to rise—that was always Frances! What was it you wanted to see me about?'

'Shall we go into the library?'

Sir Henry was still smiling. 'That sounds serious! Very well. As soon as you are ready, the library it is.'

Once in the library Antonia closed the doors carefully, waited until her father was sitting back comfortably in his chair behind his desk and then stood facing him.

'You're looking extremely serious, Toni. What is it? You haven't fallen in love, have you?'

'No, Papa! Nothing like that. I don't intend to become involved with anyone at the moment. I'm not even sure why I agreed to go for a ride in Hyde Park with Lord Aldhurst later this morning.'

'There isn't anything wrong with that, surely? You can't come to any harm in Hyde Park, and Lord Aldhurst has my approval as an escort. The general opinion among my friends seems to be that he is sound. Why don't you want to be involved? I thought that was behind the idea of coming to London.'

Antonia was finding this more difficult than she had thought. 'I...I...have a confession to make. I was waiting until you were quite well again. But it can't wait any longer...' She paused.

'Well, don't keep me waiting—what is it? It can't be anything to do with Croxton—that's all done with. What else can be so important?' said her father patiently.

'It is about what happened in Portsmouth after we left you.'

Sir Henry sat up sharply in his chair and exclaimed in surprise, 'Portsmouth!' Antonia flinched. He looked hard at her, then said gently, 'It can't be as bad as all that, my dear. Sit down and tell me. Whatever it is, we can deal with it together. We always have. But you must tell me what it is!'

Antonia sat twisting her handkerchief in her fingers. After a moment she took a deep breath and began, 'You may remember that when we arrived in Portsmouth you were so ill that you couldn't travel to London straight away, and you stayed with the Turvills. Time was short so we decided it was safe enough for me to go on ahead to London with the papers for the Foreign Office.'

'I remember that. So?'

'We were wrong. Lord Croxton's men were lying in wait for us when we landed, and after Lawson and I had left you at the Turvills they followed us. Lawson held them back for a while, but I knew they would follow me, so I gave Martha the papers and put her on the London coach just before it left.'

'You were taking a big risk trusting a servant with my papers.'

'It was the best we could think of, Papa. When you hear the rest you'll agree I did the right thing. Martha got away safely, and we collected the papers from her last week.'

'How did you escape?'

'I didn't. The men caught me.' She paused and swallowed, then began again. 'They took me to an inn in one of the back streets near the dockyard. I told them I didn't have any papers, but they decided to search me.'

Sir Henry exclaimed and started to get up out of his chair and she said quickly, 'It was all right, Papa! The landlady wouldn't let them. She said it wasn't right—she would search me herself.' Antonia gave a wry smile. 'In return she took my pelisse, my dress and my shoes and gave me a cheap dress and boots to wear in their place. I was so relieved that she had saved me from the hands of those men that I wouldn't have objected, even if I could! I was locked in a cellar for the night and the next day I was put in a coach to be taken to London.'

Sir Henry got up angrily from his chair and came round to her. 'Antonia! I had no idea! Why the devil didn't you tell me this before? I would have seen Croxton hanged for it!'

'Don't, Papa, please! You mustn't get too excited, it isn't good for you. We all came through it safely and the papers were delivered in time.'

'Lawson rescued you?'

'Not...not exactly. The coach took a wrong turning and had an accident. It had turned up a lane off the main road, so Lawson couldn't find it when he came to look for me.'

'An accident?' Sir Henry looked so pale that Antonia hurried along to finish her story.

'That accident made it possible for me to escape. And...and eventually I got here two days after you. They told you I couldn't see you because I had a cold, but in fact I wasn't here.'

'What? But it can't have taken you ten days or more. Where were you all that time?'

There was a silence. Then Antonia said, 'That's really what I have to tell you. I...I don't know. I don't remember anything between running away from that coach after the accident and arriving on the doorstep of this house.' In spite of herself Antonia's lips trembled. 'I have completely forgotten two weeks of my life, Papa!'

Sir Henry took her into his arms and comforted her, thanking God she was safe. Then he walked restlessly up and down, stopping every few minutes to question her, or swear vengeance on Croxton. He called Lady Pendell in and sent for Lawson, and demanded to know why they had kept Antonia's disappearance from him.

Sir Henry eventually calmed down enough to listen to them, but afterwards he and Lady Pendell knew they were threatened with catastrophe. News of Antonia's missing two weeks would be perfect fodder for every scandalmonger in London! Her reputation would be in tatters and her chances of making a good match reduced to nothing. Long after Antonia had reluctantly departed for her ride in Hyde Park, her father sat with his sister in the library, trying to decide what could be done.

Chapter Thirteen

James had returned from the ball at Marchant House full of elated optimism. He had found Anne, but not only that, there was nothing to stop his marrying her—she had no husband, and, as far as he could tell, no other commitment. Compared with those two miracles everything else paled into insignificance. The fact that she had turned out to be London's latest matrimonial prize was irrelevant. He wanted to marry her, whoever she was.

His elation faded a little when he began to consider his next step. It had been a shock to realise that Anne had completely forgotten him, but now he could see that this was perhaps not so very unexpected. Her two worlds—her real identity and the one she had adopted at Hatherton—had somehow become completely separate. At Hatherton she had forgotten Antonia's past life, and in

London she had forgotten Anne's. He called to mind the words of his friend in Guildford. 'The loss of memory is probably temporary. Don't tell her who she is. Let her remember it for herself.' His friend had been right. Anne *had* remembered Antonia, though it was ironic that she had forgotten Anne in the process. Now, he supposed, he must be patient again. He must wait for Antonia to remember Anne.

After a while he began to be intrigued by the situation. He had fallen in love with Anne, and had won her love in return at a time when she had been completely dependent on him. Now it looked as if he would have to win her all over again, this time, no doubt, in the face of some keen competition. He might have started off rather badly, but he had at least persuaded her to ride with him the next morning.

But whatever he decided to do about telling Antonia, he could not keep her family—more particularly her father—in ignorance of where she had been. He must seek an interview with Sir Henry.

James began to plan his campaign with interest.

* * *

Antonia set out that morning to meet Lord Aldhurst, relieved that her father now knew the worst. But on the other hand it had been brought home to her how unlikely it was that her secret could be kept for ever—even a whisper or an unguarded remark would be enough to start rumours flying. Was that why Lord Aldhurst had been so persistent the night before? Had he some reason to suspect her? If only she could remember!

Lawson had saddled her mare and was waiting for her at the stables when she came out. 'The Park should be safe enough, but she's fresh and feeling a bit skittish, Miss Antonia. Don't take any chances with her—you don't know her well enough yet.'

'But she's beautiful. Don't worry—I'll be sensible. When am I not, Lawson? Shall we go?'

But when she saw Lord Aldhurst waiting for her at the gate to the Park she was less sure of her ability to remain sensible. That little leap of the heart wasn't very sensible at all! Nor the feeling of attraction, which was as strong today as it had been the night before. Neither his strange behaviour when they first met, nor her aunt's warning, had apparently cured that treacherous little leap of her heart. Why was she so sure that he would never harm or upset her? And what if she was wrong? But she put these questions behind her as she drew up at the gate and wished him good morning as coolly as she could.

'Good morning,' he replied, giving her a small smile. If she hadn't known him to be supremely self-confident she would have said the smile had an element of relief in it. Relief and something more... He was looking at her as if she was... precious.

'It's—it's—a-a b-beautiful day,' she stammered, trying not to allow that look to affect her. And why was his groom staring at her as if he couldn't believe his eyes?

'It is *now*,' he said. Her eyes widened and she could feel her cheeks growing warm. She had dealt with compliments far more blatant than that without turning a hair—why was she blushing like a sixteen-year-old novice? She bent forwards to pat her horse and said hastily, 'Shall we ride?'

They set off and rode sedately enough down to the Piccadilly end of the park.

'It's almost deserted here this early in the day,' he said, 'but if you were to come here at five in the afternoon you'd hardly be able to move for carriages and horses. This is Rotten Row.'

'I've heard a lot about it,' she said looking down the Row in front of them. 'It looks very tempting at the moment, but my aunt tells me that galloping along it is frowned on?'

'It is. But who is here to see you, Miss Calverley? I won't tell. Nor will Sam, here.'

'All the same, I think I shall be circumspect for the present.'

'Well then, we shall ride circumspectly. And you shall talk to me of places you have been to. I know Portugal, France and Spain quite well, but not many other countries.'

'Were you in Spain with the Duke of Wellington?'

They rode up the Row at a respectable pace, talking of Spain and France, and had almost reached the far end of it before they noticed it. When he chose, Lord Aldhurst could clearly talk interestingly with no nonsense, no flirtatious double meanings, and Antonia enjoyed listening to him. In fact, she was quite in charity with him by the time they came back to the gates, so much so that when he suggested another ride the next morning at the same time she readily agreed.

He escorted her back to Upper Grosvenor Street

and helped her dismount. Lawson led her horse away and she held out her hand.

'Thank you,' she said. 'I enjoyed the ride. I look forward to tomorrow.'

'Will you be at Lady Fenwick's tonight?'

'No, my father is still living rather quietly at the moment. He mustn't overtire himself, so he is staying at home and my aunt and I are going to a concert.'

'May I escort you there?'

Antonia shook her head. 'Thank you, but Lord William Chatteris has already offered.'

He frowned, then nodded and said, 'In that case I shall see you tomorrow morning. Goodbye, Miss Calverley.'

Antonia went in, wondering how to explain to her aunt that she had agreed to go riding again with Lord Aldhurst. But, she decided, of all the men she had met in London he was by far the most interesting. She had enjoyed her ride, and would not be put off from another one by any warnings of danger from her aunt. She had often lived with danger in her travels. It added zest to life.

Sir Henry spent the afternoon at the Foreign Office, but his mind was not on his work—it was full of bitter recrimination. He should never have put Antonia in such danger. Although she was safe and Croxton had been disgraced, his worries were far from over. He had made such plans for this visit to London with his beautiful daughter. After years of wandering the world, they should at last be able to find a suitable match for her, someone with whom she would be happy, and he would be able to settle down on an estate in the country and enjoy a peaceful retirement. He had planned to write... But now it might be better to take her abroad again. They would always be waiting for the scandal to break if they stayed here. Someone knew her secret. Someone somewhere must know where she had been!

Later that evening Sir Henry was sitting alone in his library, still debating the options available and finding little comfort in them, when Blandish came in with a card.

'Lord Aldhurst? I can't see him tonight. Ask him to come some other time.'

'His lordship was quite pressing, sir. He said the matter was urgent and private.'

Antonia had been out with Aldhurst earlier in

the day. What could the man possibly want? Sir Henry sighed and said, 'Very well. You'd better show his lordship in, Blandish. The ladies are out at a concert tonight, are they not?'

'Yes, sir. They left half an hour ago.'

'You can bring in some wine. Or brandy might be better. Whatever Lord Aldhurst wants.'

James came in, refused an invitation to sit down, but accepted a glass of Sir Henry's finest brandy. He was perfectly at ease, but not altogether sure where to start.

'How can I help you, sir?' asked Sir Henry after a pause.

James put his glass down and said abruptly, 'I would like to have your permission to pay my addresses to your daughter, Sir Henry.'

Whatever Sir Henry had expected it was not this! He began to wonder what other shocks the day might have in store for him. He said cautiously, 'This is a surprise. You hardly know her!'

'Would you object otherwise?'

'I don't think so. I can't claim to know *you* any better than *you* know my daughter, but from what I've heard you're a man of character. You're certainly very eligible. The world would think she was making an excellent match. No, I would have no objection. I can't answer for my daughter, of course. You may have perhaps noticed, Aldhurst, that she's a young lady who knows her own mind.'

'Indeed! And if I were to ask her at the moment she would very possibly refuse me. I would like to…to wait until she feels she knows me well enough. But I have hopes—' He stopped, then after a moment's pause he said slowly, 'I have something to tell you, Sir Henry. But before I begin I would like you to promise me you will keep it from your daughter. In return I will assure you of my own silence, whether she accepts my proposal or not.' In response to a slight frown he went on, 'It sounds mysterious, I know, but you will understand what I mean when you've heard what I have to say.'

Even in his present state of distress Sir Henry found this amusing. Today seemed to be a day for confidences. He wondered what the devil Aldhurst had to say. He nodded and again invited his guest to sit, hoping that, whatever it was, it would be less sensationally unpleasant than what he had heard that morning.

James sat down, took a gold chain out of his pocket, and laid it on the table between them.

'I believe your daughter was recently involved in an accident. Has she…has she told you about it?'

Sir Henry examined the chain and looked up with a frown. 'Of course she has! But what do *you* know about it, sir? And where did you get this chain?'

James smiled and shook his head. 'Believe me, Sir Henry, I mean no harm. It was found at the scene and brought to me by the person who found it. It was knotted round the ring you are wearing on your finger.'

He paused, but there was no reaction. Sir Henry's face was totally without expression. 'Really?' he said.

'You said that I hardly know your daughter, but you were mistaken. I love her, and more than anything in the world, I want to make her my wife.' He paused again but when Sir Henry remained silent James went on, 'The accident took place some time ago now. Do you know what happened afterwards?'

There was a silence. Then Sir Henry shook his head in resignation. 'I had hoped the world need never learn of it,' he said heavily. 'But you obviously know or have heard something.' He paused again then said, 'Antonia has no memory of what happened to her between the accident to the coach and the day she arrived in London. If you know any more, I should like to hear it.'

'The accident took place not far from my grand-mother's house at Hatherton. Miss Calverley escaped from the coach and was given shelter there until she was strong enough to set off for London.'

Sir Henry lost his mandarin-like composure. 'What?' he exclaimed. Then he gathered himself together and said coldly, 'If what you say is true, I am surprised that Lady Aldhurst did not see fit to tell us.'

'My grandmother didn't know. She wasn't there. Apart from the servants Miss Calverley and I were alone.'

Sir Henry rose to his feet. 'I don't believe you!' James also stood up. 'It is true, sir.'

'The two of you? Alone? Together? Are you telling me, that you kept her with you for all that time without a word to her family?' Sir Henry spoke quietly, but his voice trembled with rage. 'And now you come here tonight proposing to put it right by offering to marry her?' He walked away, then turned and said icily, 'I was wrong about you. I considered you a gentleman, a man of honour!'

James said steadily, 'And so I am.'

'You must allow me to tell you, sir, that I think you are neither! Can you explain why the devil you didn't restore a decent girl straight away to her family, why you didn't even bother to let them know where she was? I can't believe she was seduced into staying with you willingly! Come, sir! I would very much like to hear your reasons for behaving so...so dishonourably.'

James was pale, but he continued calmly enough, 'You're very naturally concerned for your daughter. But before you insult me any further, let me tell you that I *am* a man of honour, Sir Henry, and have treated Miss Calverley with all the respect and care she deserves. I want to marry her because I love her and for no other reason. But I'm not a miracle worker.'

'What am I to understand by that?' demanded Sir Henry.

'We couldn't restore her to her family because she couldn't tell us who she was! We found her lying unconscious on the drive of my grandmother's house. When we carried her inside it soon became obvious she had been running away from someone who had held her against her will, and that she had met with some sort of accident on the way. But she was quite unable to remember her name or how she came to be lying on the drive. She was obviously very unwell, so we kept her at Hatherton, where she was cared for by my grandmother's housekeeper.'

'But how could she have forgotten so completely?'

'We think it happened when she fell and hit her head.' James smiled wryly. 'It is not the only trick her memory has played. Since she came back to London she has forgotten everything about her stay at Hatherton. Including me. I…I fell in love with her when she was there with me, and I thought…I was *sure* she loved me in return. It's…hard for me to understand that she doesn't remember anything of that.'

'I see…'

'She left Hatherton last week, suddenly and without my knowledge. I set out at once to search for her, and could hardly believe my eyes when I saw her last night at Lady Carteret's ball. As I said, for the moment she doesn't remember anything at all about me or her time at Hatherton.'

Sir Henry looked at him searchingly. 'Are you sure she *wants* to?'

'I think she still loves me. I hope she does.'

'You must ask her, Aldhurst. Tell her the truth.'

'Believe me, there's nothing I should like to do more. But while she was with us at Hatherton, I took medical advice on cases such as hers. I was strongly recommended to let her memory recover by itself, and now I suppose the same applies.'

Sir Henry said thoughtfully, 'It was good advice. I remember now there was a case in Vienna... The specialists there recommended much the same treatment...' He shook his head ruefully. 'I can see it must be hard for you.'

After a silence he went on, 'I apologise. I spoke too hastily before. You obviously did what you could for Antonia and I'm grateful. But...how can you be so sure she loves you? A week is hardly long enough to form any lasting passion.'

'I think now a day was long enough for me,' said James with another wry smile.

'Hmm.' Sir Henry sat down again. 'So, what do you suggest we do now?'

'If you approve, I should like to try to win Antonia's love as I won Anne's.'

'Anne?'

'It's all she could remember of her name, so that is what I called her.'

'Curious. Anne was her mother's name. Well, I won't stand in your way. But I told you—Antonia makes up her own mind.'

James grinned. 'I wouldn't have her any other way, sir. She was lost and fragile when she was at Hatherton, but still full of spirit.'

Sir Henry nodded with a smile and gestured towards a chair. James sat down and asked, 'Do you know how she fell into the hands of the two men who had abducted her? Now that I know her background, I suspect it was Croxton's work. Am I right?'

Sir Henry told James the story he had heard just that morning from Antonia herself. At the end of it James paused, then asked, 'Do you believe she is still in any danger?'

'I hardly think so. Croxton is a spent force. He's lost his power over the Prince and I think he is soon to leave England for good. The damage to his career has already been done—what can he gain by hurting me or mine?'

'Satisfaction? He lost a great deal through you. I wouldn't say I know the man well, but from what I've seen and heard he isn't likely to forgive or forget very easily.'

Sir Henry smiled. 'I think you'll have worries enough with Antonia without borrowing any more, Aldhurst. Croxton's claws have been well and truly clipped, and Lawson will see that Antonia is safe. Well, I have to say I am easier in my mind than I was when you arrived. I hope you'll forget my harsh words earlier. But now I'd like you to tell me about my daughter's stay at Hatherton, if you will.'

James's account of Antonia's life at Hatherton was of necessity not complete in every detail, but it reassured Sir Henry. This was no trifling affair. James Aldhurst really loved the girl he had rescued in the storm. He said at the end, 'My daughter was lucky in her rescuer in more ways than one. You kept her safe for me, and...' he smiled '...I would be more than happy if you looked after her for the rest of her life. I hope she will let you, Aldhurst. Will you drink to that?'

After the two men had spent an hour in a conversation that ranged widely over Sir Henry's work, James's service with Wellington in the

French wars, the situation in Europe, Sir Henry was impressed and very relieved. There was more to James Aldhurst than he would have suspected. Beneath his amusing conversation and delightful manners he had a serious and well-informed interest in the world and its politics. In other words, he was exactly the sort of son-in-law Sir Henry would have chosen.

James found that his host had a lively, if ironic, sense of humour, very similar to Antonia's. In fact, much of what appealed to him in Antonia's character could be seen in her father, too. Time passed quickly until James finally announced that he had to go. 'The ladies will soon return,' he said. 'The last thing I want is that Antonia should see me here tonight. By the way, sir, I've asked her to ride with me again tomorrow. In fact, I'd like to make it a regular engagement.'

'Did she accept the invitation?'

'She did, but I'm not sure she would commit herself to more than one. I hope to persuade her, however.'

'My dear fellow, if you are able to persuade my daughter to do something she is not sure she wants to do, then your success is guaranteed. You're as good as married! And you have my word. I shall say nothing of what you have told me tonight to her or anyone else.'

The next day Lady Pendell came in to Antonia's room, carrying a basket of late spring flowers. 'These are for you. Aren't they lovely, my dear! I wonder if William Chatteris has sent them. He seems much taken with you.'

She was less pleased when Antonia handed her the card which had come with them. 'Lord Aldhurst! Oh, Antonia! I knew no good would come of these rides with him!' Antonia tried to reassure her.

'Truly, Aunt Pendell, Lord Aldhurst has been very correct and not at all…not at all flirtatious. I've really enjoyed talking to him—he knows a lot about the places Papa and I visited. He is amusing, of course, but he can be quite serious.'

'That's just his way,' said Lady Pendell bitterly. 'Oh, he's so clever! He can see you are not to be cozened with sweet words and compliments, so he flatters you by appealing to your intelligence. Don't be misled, Antonia!'

'These aren't meant to appeal to my intelligence, ma'am,' said Antonia, sniffing the offending flowers. 'They definitely appeal to the senses.

They bring to mind gardens full of bright colours, sheltered from the harsh winds of winter...'

The scent of the flowers was quite strong. She suddenly saw a walled garden full of flowers. And a path leading to a shadowy figure on a bench... She had to see who it was...

'Antonia! Antonia!' Her aunt's voice broke into the vision and it was gone. The scent of flowers was all that was left. She sighed, braced herself and said firmly, 'Really, Aunt Pendell, you can surely trust me not to be bowled over by a few flowers! Gentlemen have sent me bouquets before—it's quite customary abroad. And these are lovely, as you said. I hope you aren't going to suggest I don't ride any more with Lord Aldhurst. Please don't forbid it—I enjoyed yesterday's ride so much!'

'That is exactly what worries me!' Lady Pendell was *so* worried that she spoke to her brother about it. But he was quite clearly in favour of Antonia's excursions, and Lady Pendell gave up. She did not comment when a small bunch of sweet-smelling violets arrived after Antonia's next outing with Lord Aldhurst, but was unhappy to see Antonia take them up to her room, and would have been even unhappier if she had seen Antonia arrang-

ing them next to the mirror on her dressing table
with a secret little smile.

In fact, poor Lady Pendell remained unhappy
until a note arrived from Lady Aldhurst inviting
the Calverley family to dine with her the following week. Then, for the first time, she began to
wonder if James Aldhurst might be more serious than she had assumed. His grandmother was
not the sort of woman to let herself be used in
a casual flirtation. As far as she knew, none of
the young women whose names had previously
been linked with Lord Aldhurst had been invited
to dine with her! Had Antonia succeeded where
London's débutantes had so often failed?

Chapter Fourteen

Antonia would not have liked her aunt to know just how much she looked forward to her morning rides. She found James Aldhurst by far the most stimulating and amusing person she had yet met in London. He took care not to make her feel at all uneasy or threatened in his company, though just occasionally, when he held her hand or helped her to dismount, there would be a moment when her heart would race and she found herself short of breath. But she could hardly blame him for that.

But one morning when she was feeling relaxed and happy, even laughing at some remark he had just made, a huge dog suddenly burst out of the bushes at the side of the Row and made for them, teeth bared in a terrifying snarl. The unexpected attack startled Antonia's horse, which reared up and took off down the track at full gallop. Antonia was taken by surprise, and wondered briefly whether she was going to keep her seat. But much to her relief, after a few hair-raising seconds she was once again firmly in the saddle with the reins tightly in her hands. For the next few minutes she had to use all her skill and strength to hold the mare steady until the frightened animal slowly began to respond and finally came to a panting halt not far from a clump of trees. Lord Aldhurst came racing up towards her, threw himself off his horse and was at her side all in a single movement. She stayed where she was for a moment, not quite sure whether her legs would hold her if she tried to get down.

'Don't worry,' he said, looking up at her. 'I'll catch you.'

'I…I'm perfectly all right,' she said. 'You needn't—'

'Antonia, my love,' he said softly. 'Come down! Now!'

She was only vaguely aware of his words. Reaction had set in, and she was shaking when she slid obediently from her horse into his arms, noticing with surprise that he too was trembling. He didn't release her immediately, but with a smothered exclamation lifted her up like a child and cradled her, his face close to hers. Her frightening experience was forgotten and she felt secure, cherished. Their eyes met, grey eyes looked deep into blue, and Antonia was sure he was about to kiss her... She wanted him to... She longed for it... But then the moment passed and she was suddenly confused and ashamed. 'P-please!' she said desperately. 'You must put me down, Lord Aldhurst. This instant!'

His look of intense disappointment took her by surprise and she thought for a moment he was going to protest. But then he took a deep breath and he said calmly enough as he set her carefully on the ground, 'Of course, I'm sorry. I was still recovering from that mad gallop myself. I...I expected to see you come off at any moment. Are you sure you are not hurt?'

Lawson arrived, he and his horse both out of breath. 'Miss Antonia,' he said, 'are you all right? I thought you'd be safe now the Croxton business is finished, but—'

Antonia was shaken but at this she pulled herself together and threw him a warning glance. 'Nonsense—that dog appeared from nowhere.'

Lawson was still shaken, out of his usual discretion. 'I'm not so sure, not with Croxton still about. Your father trusts me to keep you safe. After what happened in Portsmouth…'

'You're not to worry the master any further, Lawson. There's no need to tell him anything about this. Where is the dog now? It should be caught.'

But there was no sign of the dog or of anything else. Lawson was still unconvinced. 'It could have been a stray,' he said doubtfully, 'but it looked a bit too well fed for that. What's more, I think I've seen it before.' He turned to the others. 'My lord, did you or your groom happen to see anyone nearby?'

Antonia was exasperated. 'I've told you! There was no one. It was a stray!'

Lord Aldhurst's groom looked as if he was about to say something, but stayed silent when his master gave him a brief shake of the head.

Lord Aldhurst turned to Antonia. 'Do you feel better? Shall we go back?'

'Of course.' Antonia forced a laugh. 'At least I had my gallop,' she said gaily, 'though it wasn't quite what I had expected!'

'So you did. And what a magnificent piece of horsemanship it was, too! I am impressed. We must go somewhere soon where you can enjoy a genuine run. Just a few miles out of London there are some wonderful runs on the Downs.'

'I'd like that. Thank you.' In spite of these brave words she was still shaken as they set off back towards the gates. But here they were accosted by an army officer who was escorting a young lady on a magnificent grey. Antonia had last seen her at Lady Carteret's ball talking to Lord Aldhurst. Or rather, to be more precise, flirting with Lord Aldhurst.

'Good Lord, James, I thought *we* were out early. You must have been up with the lark,' said the officer, drawing up and eyeing Antonia with open admiration.

'Miss Calverley, may I introduce you to my friends? Lady Barbara Furness and Captain Harry Barcombe. Captain Barcombe and I served together in the army, and Lady Barbara is a family friend.'

Dressed in a green riding habit made à la Hussar, and wearing a very stylish hat, Lady Barbara surveyed Antonia from head to toe. Antonia was battling with certain chaotic feelings of her own but, under the gaze of those critical green eyes, she was aware that she must look unbecomingly flushed after her mad gallop, that some of her hair had come out of its neat bun and was lying halfway down her back, and that her old slate-grey riding dress, which had seemed so suitable for an early morning ride in the park, was very plain, and might even be called dowdy.

Though she felt at a distinct disadvantage, Antonia straightened up and surveyed Lady Barbara with equal deliberation. Then she gave each of them a cool nod.

'I'm dashed glad to make your acquaintance, Miss Calverley,' said Captain Barcombe. 'I've heard so much about you!'

His enthusiasm had apparently displeased his companion. 'I, too, am delighted to meet you, Miss Calverley!' said Lady Barbara with a touch of acid. 'But I think you must have been having a race in the Park? How daring of you to challenge the ways of our world! Or was it James who led you astray?'

'Neither,' said Antonia, who was not going to admit that her horse had taken off with no encouragement from her. 'I have still to learn the ways of your world before I can challenge them, Lady Barbara. That shouldn't take long—it's quite a small world. But I assure you I am not very easily led astray.'

'Babs! You're the last person who should comment on anyone's behaviour,' said Captain Barcombe affectionately. 'What about the scolding you got from Lady Sefton when I raced you up Rotten Row? She was furious with you.'

'And you seem to have forgotten your bet with John to drive his curricle up Pall Mall!' Lord Aldhurst turned to Antonia. 'Now that was far worse than riding a little fast in the Park, Miss Calverley, and I'm sure you wouldn't dream of doing anything so improper. Incidentally, Barbara, Miss Calverley's horse was attacked by a mad dog. I doubt even you could have stopped it from bolting.'

Lady Barbara looked put out, but then shook her head and laughed. 'Miss Calverley, I apologise. But why is it that our dearest friends are so ready to remind us of past indiscretions? That race was years ago and so was the drive in the curricle. I hope I know better now.' She gave James a malicious look and then drawled, 'But since we are talking of indiscretions, James, does Lady Aldhurst know that you had a *chère amie* staying with you at Hatherton recently? And don't tell me it was Mrs Culver!'

Antonia's eyes happened to be on James Aldhurst. His look of angry consternation had come and gone in a flash before either of the others had noticed it, and he was once again smiling his lazy smile. 'I don't propose to tell you anything, Barbara!'

Captain Barcombe stared in astonishment at Lady Barbara, then turned to grin at his friend. 'James! You sly dog! I thought you had gone there to work! Is it true?'

'Of course it's true!' Lady Barbara said. 'The Fanshawes were staying nearby. They tell me they saw James riding up towards Roade with a lady in a green riding habit at his side. They thought I was the lady, and were shocked, until I told them I was in Scotland at the time. How fortunate they didn't join you, James! It might have spoiled your little idyll.'

'Barbara, I don't think your mother would approve of your present conduct. If I *was* committing an indiscretion, it would be highly improper of you to question me about it.'

'You can't put me off like that, James! You've

just reminded me of how improperly I can behave when I choose. So who was this lady?'

'Do you really believe that I should take any female to Hatherton while Mrs Culver was there? I thought you had more sense. She wouldn't tolerate it for one second—I wouldn't even dare suggest it. Your friends are wrong. Like many people here in London, they invent scandal because they're bored, I'll swear!'

'But they *did* see a lady. They didn't invent her. Who was she?'

'Why are you so interested?'

'James! Stop prevaricating! I demand an answer!'

He shrugged his shoulders. 'You'll find it very dull. I think it might have been Mildred Pettifer. I took her up to Roade one day to give me advice on some plantings there.' He turned to Antonia. 'You must find this conversation very tedious, Miss Calverley. I don't know why Lady Barbara is pursuing it. Mrs Culver is my grandmother's highly respectable housekeeper at Hatherton, and Mrs Pettifer is a widow who lives in the village nearby. She is a considerable expert on all kinds of plants.'

'Mrs Pettifer! A middle-aged widow of the

utmost respectability and sobriety wearing a dashing green riding habit, James? I can hardly believe that!'

'You're becoming a bore, Barbara! I don't remember what she was wearing. You must ask your friends. Should I confess that she called in at Hatherton, too—to talk to Mrs Culver and collect some seedlings!' He took up his horse's reins with decision and nodded. 'And now that's enough of my dissipated ways. You'll give Miss Calverley an even poorer opinion of me than she already has. I must take her home before she refuses to have anything more to do with me.'

Lady Barbara was clearly unconvinced, but she abandoned the topic. 'You *do* remember that you are coming to Mama's soirée at the end of the month, don't you? It just might be a special occasion and I want you to be there. I believe you and Lady Pendell and Sir Henry are invited, too, Miss Calverley.'

'Might be special? Then I shall certainly be there,' said Lord Aldhurst with a brief smile. 'But I can't answer for Miss Calverley. I shouldn't be surprised if you've put her off all of us.' He went on briskly, 'But for now you'll have to excuse us. Goodbye!'

* * *

James was frowning as they rode back up Park Lane. Antonia was not surprised. Lady Barbara's question had shaken him, almost as much as it had shaken her, and she guessed that he was busily debating what to do about it if it should come up again. Unhappily for her, she did not believe, any more than his friends had, that the lady in the green riding habit was Mildred Pettifer. But apparently a dragon of a housekeeper had been there, too, which would make it an unlikely setting for a love idyll. Perhaps there was an innocent explanation for the lady's presence, which he was not prepared to share? Antonia wanted to believe this more than anything in her life before.

They had reached the turning into Upper Grosvenor Street, but had to wait while a carter loaded something onto his wagon. Antonia looked round. 'I...I came up here,' she said suddenly. 'Mr...Mr Cobden brought me...'

'Yes?' said James, suddenly alert. 'Yes?'

Antonia was startled. He couldn't possibly know the significance of what she had said. But once again the image had come and gone before she could take hold of it. 'Nothing,' she said, with a sigh of frustration. 'It was nothing.'

'Who is Mr Cobden?'

Antonia frowned. 'Who?'

'The person you said brought you.'

He was looking at her closely. Antonia pulled herself together. 'I really cannot remember,' she said lightly. 'It must have been when I was a child. We visited London quite often when my mother was still alive.'

The way was clear again and they turned towards Grosvenor Square and stopped and dismounted in front of Antonia's house. She held out her hand. 'It has been a…more interesting morning than usual, sir. And I wasn't at all bored by your friends.' She was quite unable to stop herself from adding, 'Lady Barbara seems to be taking a proprietary interest in you?'

That smile was back in his eyes as he shook his head at her. 'Not so, Miss Calverley, Lady Barbara and I are old friends, never anything more. I have a suspicion that she is about to accept Harry at long last. It's high time she did, though what sort of marriage that will be I cannot imagine. Not the one I should ever contemplate.'

'Oh? What sort of marriage would *you* contemplate, Lord Aldhurst? From what I've heard you are a sworn bachelor.'

'You're wrong. But when I do marry I shall look for an equal partnership, not one where one partner always does the kissing and the other waits to be kissed.'

Antonia couldn't stop herself. 'Perhaps you are considering the lady in the green riding habit?'

After an appreciable pause he said soberly, 'If you are asking a question, Miss Calverley then I'm afraid I can't answer it. Not at the moment. There are…difficulties.'

He hadn't denied it. Antonia had suffered a blow but she managed to give him a mocking smile and say, 'Will you accept a piece of advice? It comes from someone with long experience in the diplomatic world…'

'Of course! What is it?'

Blandish was holding the door open. She turned on the step. 'If you're inventing a story, it's better to keep details to a minimum. It is less easily disputed.'

With a small grin he said, 'So you weren't convinced by Mrs Pettifer and her plants?'

'No. Nor were the others. But it really isn't my business.'

His expression changed and he took her hand and kept it in his as he said, quite seriously, 'Strangely enough, I think it is. And I'd like you to believe me when I say that there is nothing dishonourable in the real story of that lady in green. One day I'll explain to you.'

He held her hand to his lips, but she took it away and said coolly, 'You sound very mysterious, but there's really no reason why you should explain anything to me, I assure you.'

He shook his head, but simply asked, 'Will you still ride with me tomorrow morning? It isn't often as dangerous as it was today. I don't know where that dog came from. The park rangers are usually careful to collect strays. Will you come?'

She hesitated. She was not afraid of the danger from stray dogs. This morning her eyes had been opened to danger of a very different kind. It might be better for her peace of mind to avoid his company in future. 'I'm not sure...' she said at last.

He seemed to sense she was about to refuse. 'No!' he said. 'Don't answer me now. Wait till you are feeling better. You can tell me this evening.'

'This evening?'

'I believe that your father is once again to be a

guest of honour—this time at Lady Atheridge's ball.'

'Yes, yes, he is,' said Antonia. 'No doubt I shall see you there.'

'You must save me at least one dance, and you can tell me then if you are willing to risk another ride with me.' He smiled at her so warmly that her heart turned over. The outright refusal she had intended died on her lips.

'Till tonight, then,' she stammered. 'Goodbye, Lord Aldhurst.'

James waited until Antonia had gone in before turning towards Brook Street, and Sam caught up with him after a few minutes.

'What is it, Sam?'

'I've been round at the mews having a word with Miss Calverley's man. He seems sound, but he's not sure what to do. Miss Anne—' He checked himself. 'Miss Calverley, I should say, told him not to say anything to his master about what happened today when her mare bolted.'

'Quite right. That's perfectly understandable— Sir Henry is still not strong, and Miss Calverley prefers not to worry him without good cause. I hope you're not suggesting we interfere?'

'But that's just it, Master James! Mr Lawson and I think there *is* good cause. Very good cause.'

James stopped. 'Tell me, Sam.'

'Mr Lawson thinks he recognised the dog. It isn't a stray, it belongs to a man called Briggs.'

'Who is Briggs?'

'He's one of them villains that took Miss Calverley in Portsmouth. When Mr Lawson tracked them down in Putney, he had what you might call "a chat" with them. That dog was with them there. He's an ugly-looking brute, not the sort you'd forget. Mr Lawson is sure that Briggs deliberately set that dog on to your lady's horse!'

'Hoping she would have another "accident"?'

Sam nodded. 'If she hadn't been such a good rider, she would have, too.'

James stared at him. After a minute he said, 'We can't stand in the street discussing something as important as this. You'd better tell me again when we're inside the house. Come.'

Once inside in James's rooms, Sam repeated what Lawson had told him, and then added, 'You can see Mr Lawson's dilemma, can't you, sir?'

'I can indeed. And I think we must deal with this Briggs. He has to be stopped—and so has his master!'

* * *

After Sam had gone James was unable to rest. He was now seriously afraid for Antonia. He had been right to think that Croxton would not leave tamely for the West Indies without taking revenge for his downfall, and Sir Henry's most vulnerable spot was his daughter. This was his first attempt, and it had failed—what else might he try? Croxton couldn't have much confidence left in Briggs, so what would his next move be?

He sent again for Sam, and it was arranged that he and Lawson would descend on Briggs that evening and use what skills they possessed to persuade him to talk. Meanwhile they would all keep a careful eye on Lord Croxton.

As soon as she was inside the house Antonia escaped to her room. There she sat unseeing at the window, while she faced the truth. She had come back to England fully intending to please her father by finding a husband. She had never expected to fall in love, had never regarded herself as a romantic, and would have been quite content to share her life with someone agreeable, someone who had similar interests, perhaps one of her father's young colleagues. But because of the mystery of her disappearance her father's plans had received a severe setback. She could hardly accept an offer of marriage without confessing that she had no idea where—and with whom— she had spent more than a week of her life, and it would be a rare man indeed who would be content to take such a woman to wife. It had seemed at the time to be a disaster.

But now all this no longer seemed to matter. For, however irrational it was, she had discovered today that she had fallen in love with Lord Aldhurst, had known that he was the only man she would ever consider marrying. But, ironically, in a bitter twist of fate, she had learnt almost immediately afterwards that he was already in love with someone else.

How could she have been so blind? She had thought she could ignore all the warnings, had been so sure that she was safe, sensible. She had imagined she could find his conversation interesting, his wit amusing, without falling into the trap of love. But today in the park she had discovered how woefully wrong she had been.

She sat for a while, reliving the moments in his arms after her horse had bolted, the certainty that this was where she wanted to be, where she *belonged...* She had longed for him to kiss her. She would give anything to live those moments again, to feel the delight, the exhilaration of being held by him, his face, his lips, so close to hers. For a moment she had been sure that he loved her...

The delight had lasted such a short time—too soon afterwards she had heard about the mysterious lady in the green riding habit. And she had known immediately that this was the one he really loved. Antonia Calverley was just another stupid victim of the famous Aldhurst charm.

A sob escaped her and she felt a tear rolling down her cheek... But then she jumped up and started to walk impatiently round the room. This would not do! Antonia Calverley had always been a fighter, and she was not about to sink into a decline merely because she had thought she had seen a special look in a man's eyes, a special smile that had seemed to be just for her... How stupid could you be? All those other girls had probably felt exactly the same! But she would rid herself of this feeling if it killed her! And she would start working on it tonight.

Chapter Fifteen

London society already approved of Miss Calverley's charming manners and elegant looks, but that night it watched in admiration as she dazzled everyone with her wit and gaiety. She was besieged by young men crowding round to claim a dance, and enchanted those who succeeded with her lively conversation and laughter. Chief among them was Lord William Chatteris, and the gossips observed how happy she seemed in his company, how much time the two spent together. And they looked knowledgeable and reminded one another that Lord William was the son of the third Earl of Denton and one of the rising stars in the Foreign Office... Such a suitable match! Miss Calverley could do a lot worse for herself.

James arrived late at the ball, having first waited to hear what Sam and Lawson had to say about their visit to Briggs. He looked for Antonia as soon as he came into the ballroom, but saw she was dancing with William Chatteris in a set of country dances, and went to find some refreshment. He looked for her again when he returned to the ballroom, but, though he was sure she saw him, she turned away and nodded to one of the young men surrounding her. In no time she was away again with her new partner down to the other end of the room. James waited patiently until the dance was nearly over, then started off to meet her. But he was too late. She had already taken to the floor, for the second time, with William Chatteris. To all appearances she was clearly enjoying herself, perfectly at ease with her partner, laughing with him as he guided her through the steps of the quadrille. James stopped where he was, and made an effort to control his temper. What was Antonia up to? Earlier in the day he had thought they had reached an understanding…

'Lovely to watch, aren't they?' commented Sir Charles Stainforth, who had come to join him. 'They're putting bets on young William's chances, though I wouldn't rate them overhigh myself.'

'Chances of what?'

Sir Charles gazed at him in astonishment. 'Chances of winning the young lady, my dear boy! What else would they be? Everyone knows her father is looking for a husband for her.'

'You mean...people think that An— Miss Calverley might... But she—' James stopped abruptly, and hoped that the town's most notorious gossip had not seen how disconcerted he was. He managed to say casually, 'What makes you think Chatteris would have any chance at all?'

Sir Charles looked surprised. 'Why not? Chatteris is eminently eligible and has the same diplomatic background as her father—they'd have plenty to talk about. But I wouldn't put my money on him. He's pleasant enough, but a touch too staid. I'd say he's just not up to her weight. There are others who would make far more interesting partners for life for her. And, judging by tonight, he'll have plenty of competition. She was her mother's heiress, you know, and there are any number of eligible young men who would be tempted by Miss Calverley *and* her fortune.'

They watched the dancers in silence for a while, then James asked, 'What about the lady herself? What has she to say to all this?'

'She doesn't seem to prefer anyone as yet.' Sir Charles gave him a sly glance and laughed. 'I shouldn't think you'd be in the running, Aldhurst! She didn't seem to like you much at the Carterets'.'

The quadrille had ended some minutes ago, but Antonia and Chatteris were still carrying on an animated conversation. What on earth could they be talking about all this time? James forced himself to smile and say, 'Oh, that's all in the past, Stainforth! Miss Calverley and I have since become quite good friends. In fact, if you'll excuse me, I'll just have a word with her now…'

He nodded to Sir Charles, who was now looking very interested, and crossed the room to where she was standing. As he approached he saw her look teasingly at Chatteris with laughter in her eyes. That look was achingly familiar… It belonged to him! What the devil was she doing directing it at Chatteris? It had to stop!

He reached the couple, said politely but firmly, 'Good evening, Miss Calverley,' and nodded at her partner. 'Chatteris.'

Antonia turned. 'Lord Aldhurst!' Her smile faded, and her manner became markedly cooler.

'Are you engaged for the next dance?' he

demanded. She stiffened and James was conscious that the question had lacked the cool elegance for which he was famous. He tried to improve it with a smile. But it didn't work. Antonia said coolly, 'I'm afraid I am.'

'The next, then, perhaps?' he said in a more conciliatory tone.

Antonia paused, took a breath then, said very firmly, 'I'm so sorry. But I'm afraid my card is quite full for the rest of the evening.'

James studied her. In the face of such a snub any gentleman would bow and leave. He stayed. 'You promised to save me a dance,' he said. 'After our ride this morning.' Antonia's colour rose.

'No, Lord Aldhurst,' she said stiffly. 'I did not promise. You *told* me to save you one.'

Chatteris looked as if he was about to intervene, but James silenced him with a glance. 'Excuse me, Chatteris. May I?' he asked, and without waiting for a reply took Antonia's arm and led her away. 'What is this nonsense?'

'Take your hands off me, Lord Aldhurst!' she whispered. 'Do you want every gossip in the room to start talking?'

'I don't care about them. Tell me what I've done to make you angry.'

'Nothing, I assure you. Why should I be angry with you?'

James marched her out on to the balcony. Here he stopped and turned her to face him. 'Tell me why you've been ignoring me? Why you won't dance with me. And why you're flirting with young Chatteris? He's not for you.'

Colour flamed in her cheeks. 'What right have you, Lord Aldhurst, to censure or even comment on anything I choose to do? I was not flirting! And why should you care if I was?'

He began, 'The right of a man who—' He stopped. 'A man who doesn't like to see you wasting your time on Chatteris. Or indeed, on anyone who would assuredly bore you within a week, however eligible and worthy they might be.'

'I was not wasting my time! Lord William is not a bore! And I was not flirting with him. In fact, I was enjoying a conversation with a friend, whose manners are considerably better than yours! And now I shall go back to him.'

She turned to go, but James put a hand on her arm to stop her. 'Don't go, Antonia! Were you angry with me because I was late?'

'Really, my lord, supposing I even noticed you were, why on earth should it affect me?'

He took her hands in his. 'No reason. I suppose I just hoped it would.'

She looked down. He said softly, 'But whatever it is that I've done to offend you, I hope you'll forgive me for it.' He lifted her chin with a finger and made her look at him. 'Dance with me now. It sounded to me this morning as if you *did* promise, you know. It meant something.' For a moment it looked as if she would refuse. But he held her eyes with his own, and after a moment she gave a resigned little shrug. 'Very well. Shall we go back into the ballroom?'

It was, of course, a waltz and as he put his hand on her waist he heard her give a small sigh and follow his lead onto the floor. They danced for the most part in silence. The temptation to hold her as closely, as lovingly, as he had held her at Roade was very strong, but, aware of the many curious eyes on them, he resisted it. Just once, when a turn brought their bodies into closer contact, Antonia drew in her breath and faltered and he held her more tightly until she had recovered. But if he had hoped she would spend more time with him after this he was wrong. At the end of the dance she curtsied and was off again with yet another partner.

* * *

She had been resolute in refusing to dance with him again. For the rest of the evening James had to watch from the side of the room, or take a frustrated walk round Lady Atheridge's conservatory. He did not ask anyone else to dance with him. After that waltz, the idea of holding anyone else in his arms was totally unappealing. Antonia, he thought bitterly, did not appear to have the same difficulty. She continued to be besieged on every side by willing partners and she danced every dance, though he did notice that some of her sparkle had gone. In the end he could bear it no longer and went to have a quiet word with Sir Henry. The next time Antonia came off the floor he was ready for her. 'I believe Lady Pendell is looking for you, Miss Calverley,' he said. 'She thinks Sir Henry is getting tired and needs an excuse to leave. May I take you to her?'

Antonia must have been weary, for she went with him without comment. Before he left her he reminded her that he would see her the next morning.

She shook her head, and said in a low voice, 'I don't think I can ride tomorrow. I...I'm very tired. Goodnight, Lord Aldhurst.' And she was gone, leaving him with the uneasy feeling that unless he acted quickly he was in danger of losing her, after all.

Tired though she was, Antonia could not rest. Tonight had proved to her how impossible it was to forget her feelings for James Aldhurst. He had only to smile at her and take her hands in his, and she had found it impossible to refuse him. After that waltz the rest of the evening had been a wasteland. She got up and paced about the room, and after a struggle decided that, even if it eventually led to heartbreak, she would be happier for the present enjoying his company, talking to him, riding, dancing. She would even listen to his explanation of his green lady if he wished! And afterwards, when he finally went back to this 'green lady', she would ask her father to take her abroad again.

The decision made, she went back to bed, pausing on her way to pick up the posy of violets and hold them for a moment under her nose. The scent was still fresh, bringing solace to her bruised heart, and it lingered in the air as she eventually fell asleep. Pictures floated in and out of her dreams without logic or reason—images of an old house with a garden surrounded by a wall, of flickering firelight in a book-lined room, a chequerboard pattern of black and white, sunshine and shade on a long path and a graceful white house at the end of it...and a shadowy figure in the background. But when she tried to see it all more clearly it faded and dissolved.

She woke early and lay thinking. She must have seen those houses at some time or other—they had been very real. Antonia forgot her heartache as she wrestled with her memory. Where had she seen them? *Had it been during those missing days?* She attempted to visualise the houses again, to remember anything about them that could help her link what she knew with what she had forgotten. But it was like trying to take hold of floating mist. The harder she tried, the further away the images drifted. She buried her face in her hands with a cry of despair. *What was wrong with her? Why couldn't she remember?*

Antonia was pale and heavy-eyed when she came down later that morning. But to her surprise Blandish informed her that Lord Aldhurst had called and was asking to see her.

'Lord Aldhurst? To see me? I don't think I—'

'Sir Henry has had a word with his lordship, and has left him in the library, Miss Calverley.'

Antonia wondered if James had come to talk about the incident in the park. It was unlikely— he knew she didn't want her father to be told—but why else would he call? She followed Blandish to the library.

James was standing with his back to the window, but she could see that he looked serious. 'You look pale,' were his first words. 'Are you ill? Was it yesterday's fright? Or have you been doing too much?'

'No,' she said cautiously. There was a silence. 'Is that what you came for? To ask about my health?' she asked finally. 'You needn't have. I'm stronger than I look.'

He shook his head, then said with a rueful laugh, 'No, that isn't it. That isn't it at all! I had planned so carefully what I was going to say, but when you came in just now I was reminded of how you looked when I first—' He stopped and started again. 'The fact is, Miss Calverley, that I very much hope you will agree to marry me.'

'M-marry you?' she faltered. His words were so far from what she had expected to hear that she had to clutch the back of a chair in a chaotic mixture of shock and incredulity, delight and doubt. What did his proposal mean? She thought…no, she was *sure* that he was in love with someone else, so what did this mean? He was looking at her, waiting for her answer. She must say something, play for time. She said again, 'Marry you? But…but we hardly know one another!'

He seemed to be choosing his words carefully as he said, 'Do you think so? I feel that we know one another better than these past days would lead you to expect. Do you…have you not felt the same?'

Antonia still could hardly believe she had heard him properly. Holding on to the chair for dear life she stammered, 'Does…does my father know about this?'

'Of course,' he said. He smiled at her. 'Don't look so surprised—I am really a very conventional man. I have your father's approval. But…I need yours, too.' He came over to her, and took her hands in his. 'Could you…like me enough to marry me?'

Shock and doubt gave way to longing. The temptation to put her arms around his neck was almost too strong, to pull his face down to hers, to have him hold her closely, so closely that she wouldn't be able to breathe. The tension mounted between them, and he leaned forwards and bent his head. He was going to kiss her and she would be lost...

'No!' she said, pulling away. 'No, I can't! I mustn't.'

He was breathing rather quickly, but let her go. 'Why...not?'

Antonia would have given anything she had to say she would. Green lady or not, she loved him and would be prepared to take whatever he had to offer. But how could she promise to marry any man she loved, while the threat of scandalous exposure hung over her like a cloud? 'I...I can't,' she repeated.

He looked closely at her. 'You haven't said you don't like me enough,' he said slowly. 'In fact, I think you do.' His face cleared and he smiled as he pulled her back again. 'You do, don't you?' His face was so close to hers...

'Whether I do or not, I still can't marry you,' she said in a whisper.

He was still for a moment. Then he smiled and nodded his head. His hand came up and caressed her cheek. 'Antonia, you will marry me,' he said softly. 'I think I know why you're saying you can't, and, I promise you, it doesn't matter at all. I know.'

'What? What do you know?'

'I know about that gap in your life. And it doesn't make the slightest bit of difference. Trust me.'

'How do you know? Who told you?'

He hesitated. After a pause he said carefully, 'Your father and I talked about it. He told me what had happened to you in Portsmouth and how you lost your memory after the accident. You can't remember anything about the time that followed. Is that right?'

She nodded. 'How can I marry anyone when my life has such a mystery about it?' she said miserably.

Now both hands were holding her face while he looked into her eyes. 'I am not *anyone*, Antonia. And I want to marry you. I intended to wait a little longer before I asked you, but after that business in the Park yesterday, and…one or two other things, I've changed my mind. You're…important to me. I want to be sure you're safe.'

'Safe?'

'Your father doesn't seem to think that Croxton

is much of a threat, but I believe he is. Lawson confirmed last night that yesterday's attack by the dog wasn't just a matter of chance. This man Briggs set him on to your horse quite deliberately. You could have been killed. I...I thought for a moment that you would be.'

'You haven't told my father about it, have you?' said Antonia instantly anxious. 'He mustn't be worried.'

'No, I haven't. But Lawson and I are worried and so should you! Croxton wants revenge.'

'What do you suggest we do about him?'

He shook his head. 'First things first, Antonia! I'm still waiting for your answer. Are you going to say you'll marry me or not?'

She studied him, still unable to believe he meant it, not quite daring to ask him about the lady in the green riding habit. 'Tell me why you want me to.'

He looked at her with a hint of amusement in his eyes. 'Why do you think? The usual reasons, of course!' After a pause he added more seriously, 'I want to protect you.'

'Is that all?'

Lord Aldhurst was no longer amused. Almost angrily he said, 'Oh, Antonia, how can you be so blind?' Then he pulled her into his arms, quite roughly. 'This is why I asked you!' he said, kissing her hard. Then he muttered something and kissed her again more passionately, pulling her closer, moulding her to his long, powerful body.

For a delirious moment of madness she revelled in the feelings aroused by the touch of his lips on hers, the strength of the arms around her, but then she pulled away, and exclaimed angrily, 'Lord Aldhurst!' Shocked and ashamed, she was even angrier with herself than with him. She could not remember ever having been kissed with such intensity before, and her own passionate desire to respond was almost frightening. Properly brought-up young ladies simply did not have such feelings—or if they had they didn't admit to them.

They looked at one another in silence. He seemed to be waiting for something, some further reaction from her, but when it didn't come he looked...disappointed. Antonia was asking herself what had happened to her. She had prided herself till now on her ability to remain coolheaded, in command of herself in any situation, however difficult. But now she saw that before meeting James Aldhurst she had never come across real temptation. When he kissed her she was lost in a sea of emotion, tempted to abandon years of self-control, to forget all her pride. Her blood was still racing, her heart still pounding at the memory of what she had felt in his arms. She stared up at the man who had brought it about, with something like fear in her eyes.

'How is it that you have such an effect on me?' she whispered.

He said unsteadily, 'If I were to tell you—' Then he stopped abruptly and shook his head. After a moment he began again. 'I'm James Aldhurst, who…wants only the best for you. I'm sorry if I frightened you.'

'You didn't frighten me. It was more…more that I shocked myself with what I felt.'

'You mustn't be shocked,' he said swiftly. 'Marry me, and I promise you that I will take care of you, and do everything I can to keep you safe and happy as long as I live. Always. Trust me, Antonia. Please trust me.'

She believed he meant what he said, that he would take care of her and try to make her happy… But he hadn't actually said he loved her. How could he? He loved someone else. She had to know. She took a breath and took the plunge. 'Tell me first about the lady in green!'

He didn't reply immediately and her heart sank. She shouldn't have asked—he was not going to tell her! But then he caught her hands in his and said, 'Look at me, Antonia.' When she obeyed, he said slowly, choosing his words with care, 'I can't explain about her at the moment. I wish to heaven I could. But I swear to you that her story will do you no harm, nor affect my love for you. Do you believe me?'

She had to! She wanted to marry him more than anything in the world. And he had mentioned a sort of love. 'Yes,' she said. 'I do believe you. And I will marry you.' He took a step towards her and she went on quickly, 'But give me time to get used to the idea. I still can't quite take it in—it has all happened so fast. I need time.'

He brought her hand to his lips and kissed it. 'You shall have it,' he said. 'But I think your family should be told. And I'd like my grandmother to know tonight before dinner. They'll all keep it to themselves if we ask them to.' She nodded and he said, 'Antonia, I still think Croxton is a threat, and I'd like to engage an extra groom to help Lawson to look after you. Agreed?' When she nodded again, he smiled and said, 'Then shall we call your father in, Antonia?'

James had a word with his grandmother before he took Antonia along to see her. She was not at all surprised at what he had to say. 'An...tonia Calverley! I suspected as much when I first saw her.' She started to laugh. 'So you've found the right woman at last, James? Didn't I tell you before you even went to Hatherton that Sir Henry Calverley's débutante daughter might be just the one for you? If I remember, you were very sure she wouldn't be!'

'I was wrong, ma'am. But we are not quite out of the wood yet. The last piece of the puzzle has still to fall into place.'

'You're sure you're doing the right thing in not telling her the truth?'

'No. But more experienced people say that her memory will be more completely restored if it returns unaided, and I have to go by that. I don't deny it's devilishly difficult not to say something to her, especially when—' He broke off and his grandmother nodded sympathetically.

Lady Aldhurst was at her most gracious when she met Antonia. She offered her cheek for a kiss and said, 'I'm very happy to welcome you, Miss Calverley. It's high time James found someone he could bear to live with. I think you'll do very well. Perhaps you can persuade my grandson to open up the family mansion and live in it. With you to help him he might not dislike the place so much. Roade should be occupied again.' She turned to James and said with a wicked look, 'You might like to take Miss Calverley to Hatherton—quite soon, perhaps?'

Conversation at dinner flowed freely, and by the end of it the two most important ladies in James's life had decided that they liked each other. Lady Aldhurst was so relieved that James was at last going to marry that she would have tried to approve of any girl he chose. But she soon saw that Antonia Calverley had just the sort of qualities she had hoped for—exquisite manners, independent enough to be interesting, well informed but with too strong a sense of humour to be a bore... and in love with James.

After dinner, James suggested that Antonia should play for them. She shook her head at her father's claims for her, but sat down readily enough at the piano and asked, 'What would you like?'

After she had played one or two requests from her father and Lady Aldhurst, James pointed at some sheets of music that were lying on the piano. 'What about these, Miss Calverley?'

Antonia smiled and took the first one. It was a little waltz which she already knew by heart. She began to play… Never before had she found it so enchanting. James's eyes were on her and she felt as if she was being drawn into his arms, the music taking her swirling into an empty ballroom, she was dancing, dancing… Such joy, such delight… Such heartbreak… Why was there heartbreak? She was about to lose James! She gave a cry and her hands landed on the keys with a crash. She swayed and almost fell, but James caught and held her, reassuring her, stroking her hair, while the rest of the party looked on in concern.

Lady Pendell came over, but Antonia was already freeing herself from James's arms. 'I…I don't know what happened,' she said, looking at James. 'I felt as if I was dancing and got dizzy. For a moment I thought I—' She stopped and tried to smile. 'Forgive me. You must think me very foolish. Let me play something else. A march or one of the Haydn pieces, perhaps?'

'If Lady Aldhurst will excuse us, I think we should take you home,' Lady Pendell said. 'You've been doing too much, Antonia.'

James had been standing in the shadows, but now he came forwards. He looked pale. 'It's my fault,' he said. 'I asked too much of her. And on our ride yesterday—'

'Oh, but I have loved our rides!' Antonia cried. 'James, you promised to take me to Richmond. Let's go there tomorrow! The fresh air will do me good. In fact, all I need is a little fresh air. Do say you'll take me!'

After some discussion Lady Pendell was persuaded that her niece would not suffer if she went out to Richmond the following day, and the party broke up with an arrangement that James would collect Antonia at eleven.

After everyone had gone Lady Aldhurst sat back and considered the situation. She found it highly intriguing. It was clear that James was very much in love with Antonia Calverley, his 'Anne'. The girl herself was charming, but there had been something about that waltz... James seemed to blame himself for what happened. Had he been attempting to stir her memory? She frowned as she wondered how Antonia would react when she finally knew the truth. James was being very patient, but was he being wise in not telling her everything? He meant it for her own good, but the situation would have to be handled with the utmost care, if she were not to feel betrayed by his deception.

And then, since she had as strong a sense of humour as either James or Antonia, she amused herself by picturing the scene when James took his new bride to Hatherton to be introduced to Mrs Culver. That would be something worth witnessing! She must do her best to be present!

Chapter Sixteen

James reproached himself bitterly for the effect of that waltz on Antonia. He had hoped perhaps to stir her memory by asking her to play it, but he had succeeded only in causing her confusion and distress. He told himself he must be patient, must do his best to build up Antonia's confidence in him, her trust and love, without trying to remind her of their time at Hatherton. To that end he took her riding in Richmond Park, danced with her at the Porteouses' ball, and wooed her as carefully, as cautiously as he knew. It wasn't easy. James was a man deeply, passionately in love for the first time in his life, and, because of the extraordinary circumstances at Hatherton, he had been closer to Anne than normal society would ever have allowed. It wasn't easy to behave with conventional restraint towards Miss Calverley of Upper Grosvenor Street when his mind was filled with memories of sitting with her through the night, comforting her, cherishing her, coaxing her out of her despair, and in the end loving her. But he did not forget the fear in her eyes on the one occasion his feelings had got the better of him. 'Who are you?' she had whispered. 'How do you have such power over me?' He had come so close to telling her then, and instinct, as well as the words of his friend, told him now that that would have been a mistake.

His patience was rewarded. Antonia was soon herself again, witty, full of vitality and humour, and beginning to look on him as her trusted friend and companion. He was encouraged to believe that her memory would return before very long when, more and more frequently, she interrupted herself, looking bewildered. She would soon carry on as if nothing had happened, but he was sure something she had seen or heard had reminded her of that recent past. In Richmond Park she saw White Lodge in the distance and started towards it, exclaiming joyfully, 'There it is…the white house…' Then she stopped and shook her head. There was desolation in her voice as she said, 'No, that isn't it, after all.' But she turned to him with a determined smile and in a moment he had her laughing at a scandalous story about the occupants of the house.

While James was carefully building up his relationship with Antonia Calverley, Lord Croxton was brooding on ways to avenge himself on her father, the man responsible for his ruin and coming exile. The former all-powerful favourite of the Prince Regent knew it wouldn't be easy—Briggs's attempts so far had both failed. It would be safer—and much more satisfying—to destroy the Calverleys as they had destroyed him: by ruining their reputation. That wouldn't be easy, either—the Calverleys were highly regarded, and the daughter was one of the Season's successes. But they must have a weak spot somewhere—anyone, thought Lord Croxton cynically, anyone who claimed to be so respectable *must* have something to hide. Then fate in the person of Lady Barbara Furness gave him an idea…

Lady Barbara had not for one moment believed James's explanation of the lady in the green riding habit, and was annoyed at his refusal to discuss it. Spurred on by her love of mischief, she told one or two of their friends, hoping to cause him embarrassment. But even she was surprised at the consequence. The story was slight and, in view of James Aldhurst's reputation, not all that shocking, but it came at a point when the polite world was short of gossip. The tale spread, and soon the identity of 'the lady in green' was the subject of the liveliest speculation. Everyone demanded to know who she could be.

So the story came to Lord Croxton's attention, and it roused his curiosity. It had never before occurred to him to question how Antonia Calverley had got back to London after the accident with the coach, but the Aldhurst estate was only a mile or so from the Portsmouth Road, very near where Briggs had lost her. Had she returned to Portsmouth to join her father? Or was it possible that she had taken refuge nearby—perhaps at Hatherton? Could Miss Antonia Calverley possibly be the mysterious lady in green? Lord Croxton decided it was worth investigating and he sent Portman, his valet, to make discreet enquiries at the Calverleys' house in Grosvenor Street. Portman was a silver-tongued rogue and an accomplished liar, and what he learned from Lady

Pendell's servants was potentially so interesting that his master dispatched him the next day down the Portsmouth Road to Lady Aldhurst's house.

At Hatherton, Mr Portman carefully avoided any contact with Lady Aldhurst's formidable house-keeper, but the other servants saw no reason to be on their guard with him. Now that Miss Anne had gone, surely the need for caution had gone, too! Out of earshot of Mrs Culver they talked quite freely to a man who said he was looking for a little girl, not a grown woman.

'I'm really very sorry we can't help you, Mr Portman,' said Rose, as they walked back from the village. 'It must be such a worry for you. But Miss Anne was much older than your niece, and she had dark hair, not blonde. She never did re-member who she was, though I'm sure she was a lady. His lordship spent a lot of time with her—I think he'd have kept her here, but Mrs Culver wouldn't allow it.'

'Strict, is she?' said Mr Portman with a sympa-thetic grin.

'Oh, she isn't so bad. But she didn't like it when she saw that his lordship was getting sweet on Miss Anne.'

When he saw that Rose had nothing more for him, Mr Portman went on up to Roade, where he was fortunate enough to meet the caretaker's wife. Mrs Agnew was more than ready to gossip.

'You're quite right, Mr Portman! The last time his lordship came here he brought someone with him, but it wasn't a child! Goodness me, no!'

'Ah! I think I know who you mean, Mrs Agnew. Would that be a lady in green?'

'That's right! Miss Anne's riding dress was green. Lovely she looked in it, too. I don't blame his lordship for being so taken with her, but you should have seen the way they kissed, Mr Portman…! In broad daylight, too. I'm not often shocked, but that *shocked* me, I can tell you.'

Lord Croxton was delighted with the story Portman brought back with him, and debated for a while how best to use it. It didn't worry him that people might ask how Antonia Calverley had come to be halfway up the Portsmouth Road in a wrecked coach in the first place. He would be safely clear of England and on the high seas, bound for the West Indies, before anyone worked that out. No, the story was too good to waste. It was scandalous enough that Antonia Calverley had spent a week with any man unchaperoned. But that she had spent it with such a well-known rake as James Aldhurst was more than enough to blow her reputation to the four winds, and to destroy her father's hopes for ever! He gloated as he waited for the right moment to use it.

By a fortunate coincidence Lady Furness had not withdrawn his invitation to her soirée, and that was where he would strike. Henry Calverley had ruined him. In return, before his departure into exile, he would ruin Henry Calverley's daughter.

Antonia was not as perfectly happy as she tried to appear to be to James. He would have been astonished at how much she longed for him to kiss her again with even half the passion he had shown her on the day he had asked her to marry him. But though he was attentive, kind, amusing, he seemed to have drawn back from her since that day, as if he had some secret that he didn't wish to share. She occasionally wondered whether he even loved her—he had never said so, not in so many words. She kept telling herself that it didn't matter. James was honourable, and she loved and trusted him, but the odd feeling persisted. And when stories about the girl in a green riding dress began to circulate all round London, her fears were roused again. James liked her and wanted to marry her, but, as she had known ever since the day in the Park, the one he really loved was the mysterious woman in green.

Antonia's dreams had always been full of images of people and places. Now, this feeling of insecurity gave rise almost every night to dreams in which mocking crowds surrounded her, pointing their fingers in scorn, or turning away in contempt. Though she herself remained in ignorance, she knew they had discovered where she had been and what she had been doing while she was missing and, whatever it was, it was shameful. And now, James was always in the background of these nightmares. She could see him bending over a girl in green, looking so protective, so tenderly possessive while she stood lost and alone, and in her dream Antonia knew she was about to lose him.…

When the Calverleys arrived at Lady Furness's soirée the rooms were already filled with Lady Barbara's friends, who knew that this would be a special occasion and were eager to take part.

Sure enough, halfway through the evening, Lord Furness announced, as expected, that his daughter Barbara was to marry Captain Harry Barcombe. James and Antonia were among those who quickly surrounded Lady Barbara and her fiancé.

Lady Barbara, looking flushed and happy, spoke for once quite genuinely. 'I owe you an apology, James. I think I might have done more harm than I intended with this stupid story of the green lady. I wish now I had kept it to myself.'

'So do I!' said James, a touch grimly. 'But I'm hoping Harry will keep you in order in the future. Try to make him happy, Barbara!' He bent forwards and kissed her on the cheek.

A couple of Harry's army friends at the other end of the room were observing the scene with a doubtful eye.

'I hope Harry knows what he's doing,' said one. 'Barbara Furness isn't a woman for the faint-hearted. I must say, I always thought she'd have Aldhurst in the end. He would have a better idea of how to deal with her tricks. But it looks now as if he's interested in the Calverley girl.'

The other gave a snort of laughter. 'How the devil does James Aldhurst do it? Here in London he cultivates the latest star of society and at the same time makes love to another lady kept discreetly in the country. You know, I'd give a guinea to know who that woman in green really is!'

Lord Croxton had been standing behind them. He raised his voice as he said, 'Would you really like to know, Carstairs? I could tell you who she is, if you wish...' He examined the group of people round him, who had all turned to listen. 'Good heavens!' he exclaimed. 'How you're all staring at me! It's the first time in weeks that most of you have noticed me at all! But now you all want to know the name of Aldhurst's mistress! Well, I think I shall tell you. And how astonished you will be! Astonished... Indeed, I think you will all be outraged!'

The buzz of conversation ceased and there was a sudden silence. James, looking murderous, started pushing his way through the crowds towards Croxton. Sir Henry called threateningly, 'Croxton! Why don't you leave before you make the biggest mistake of your miserable life? We can still change our minds about what to do with you. There are still laws—'

Something about Sir Henry, perhaps the underlying contempt in his voice, infuriated Croxton so much that he forgot caution.

'I don't give a damn for your laws!' he shouted, shaking with a mixture of triumph and rage. 'The world ought to know the sort of girl you've brought to London, you smug hypocrite! Your precious daughter isn't the model of virtue you've led us all to believe. Far from it! Before she joined you in London she spent a week alone with Aldhurst at his grandmothers' place. We can all imagine what they got up to there, can't we!' He turned to the crowd. 'You want to know who the lady in green is?' He thrust out an arm and pointed at Antonia. 'It's her! That one there! The lovely and not-so-innocent Antonia Calverley!'

James broke through the crowds and, before anyone could stop him, had knocked Croxton to the floor and was standing over him, ready to strike again if he attempted to get up. 'You'll apologise before you so much as lift a hair of your damned head again, Croxton,' he said between his teeth. 'I'm waiting!'

Croxton's moment of uncontrolled anger was over, and he was now regretting his public outburst. He had intended to drip the information insidiously into a few carefully chosen ears, not shout it out and provoke a challenge—he was no hero. And now Aldhurst was leaning over him, looking so dangerous that he cowered on the floor and muttered, 'I...I'm sorry! I apologise, I apologise!'

James wasn't appeased. 'Not loud enough, my lord! Let *everyone* hear!' he said, hauling him up and twisting him round to face the rest of the company. 'You've told them half the story. Now tell them the rest! Tell them how she had to be rescued from the men you had sent to abduct her. Tell them how she nearly drowned, how she nearly *died* the night I found her! Tell them how ill she was during her week at Hatherton!' James lifted the man up and shook him like a dog. *'Tell them!'*

'I apologise, damn you!' Lord Croxton shouted into the murmur of horror and condemnation coming from all round the room. 'I didn't know she was ill, I swear. I must have been misinformed. Of course it was all innocent, and I was wrong. But you can't prove I had anything to do with her abduction!' He stared at the sea of accusing faces all round, and muttered, 'Let me go, damn you! Let me go and I'll leave here straight away.'

'Yes, let him go, Aldhurst,' said Sir Henry disgustedly. 'He's probably covered his tracks too well. We won't be able to prove anything—not without a great deal of trouble. No one will believe his slanders. Look at him—he really isn't worth bothering about. Let him go.'

James looked at the man cowering in front of him and, with an exclamation of disgust, thrust him away so hard that he stumbled and nearly fell. After casting a look of burning hatred at James he went out. Sir Henry looked round at the crowd, and said calmly, 'Lady Furness, I hope you and your guests will forgive me if I take a moment of your time. Lord Croxton's desire for revenge has unhinged his mind. I don't know where or how he acquired his information, but he is quite wrong.'

He looked round and continued, 'In fact, my daughter has been engaged to Lord Aldhurst for some time. I knew what Croxton had done long before tonight, and was happy to discover that she was safe, thanks to Lord Aldhurst here. I shall be proud to call him my son-in-law.' He bowed to James. 'And that is all I have to say, except that Lady Barbara and Captain Barcombe deserve to have your wholehearted wishes for their happiness without any further distractions. Thank you.'

Lady Furness, who had been standing frozen

to the spot during the drama, hurried to find her butler to order him to serve more wine, and in a surprisingly short time the room returned to at least the appearance of normal, though the buzz of conversation was a lot louder.

But Antonia was looking like a ghost. James came over to join her, took her hands in his and saluted her lightly on the cheek. 'Smile, Antonia,' he said in her ear. 'I know it's been a shock, but pretend you knew. Please smile!'

'I can't stay here,' she said in a shaking voice. 'I want to leave.'

'You can't. If you go now, you'll undo all your father's good work. You must stay here and look as if you're pleased that the world at last knows of our engagement.'

'Why didn't you tell me?' she whispered, her lips barely moving.

'I'll explain everything later, but, for now, put a smile on your face and look ready to accept everyone's good wishes. Here they come! Be brave, my love!' He looked at her set white face and added under his breath, 'And forgive me.'

Antonia needed all her famous training and strength of character to cope with the rest of the evening. It was as if a different Antonia took over. She laughed, she blushed modestly, she even dealt with one or two less kindly comments with poise and dignity. But, inside, she was numb with shock, unable to feel anything at all, waiting for the moment when she could escape from this sea of well-meaning faces, the noise, the heat— and James. He was always at her side, supporting her and prompting her when she couldn't think of what to say. For the truth, the nightmare, was that at the moment her mind was still a complete blank. She had now been told where she had spent those missing days, but she still had not the slightest recollection of anything about them.

Finally she could take no more, and said, with a charmingly apologetic smile at her hostess, 'Lady Furness, I hope our unexpected announcement didn't spoil what should have been an evening of great pleasure for your daughter and Captain Barcombe. I am sure they will be very happy together. But now I hope you'll understand if I ask my father to take me home. People have been so very kind, but Lord Croxton's malice was... distressing, and I think I need to rest to recover from the shock.'

'Your father, Miss Calverley? Surely it is now

your fiancé's privilege to see you safely home?' said Lady Furness archly.

'Of course it is!' James took Antonia's arm. 'You'll have to forgive her, ma'am. Miss Calverley is not yet used to the idea that we no longer have to keep our engagement a secret!' Antonia turned to make an objection, but he forestalled her. 'All the same,' he continued, 'if you permit me, I think I shall fetch her father, too. After tonight's experience she probably needs his presence as well as mine.' Upon that he thanked his hostess for a delightfully memorable evening and ushered Antonia out of the room.

Soon they were back in the study at Upper Grosvenor Street. Sir Henry sat in his armchair, James was by the window and Antonia stood with her head bent, refusing to look at either of them. James gazed at her steadily as he said, 'Well, Antonia? Now you know the truth.'

'I do. At last.'

'Won't you look at me?'

She looked round, and he saw that her eyes were blazing with anger. 'Look at you? I suppose I must. I have to see now for myself what a real traitor looks like.'

'Antonia! I'm no traitor. I love you! You must know that everything I did, everything I said, was always meant to protect you.'

'Protect me? You *betrayed* me! Everything you did, everything you said was a lie! You knew the first time you saw me at that ball that I had spent that missing week with you, and you have never, *never* made the slightest attempt to remind me! Did it amuse you to keep me in the dark? Were you laughing when I confessed that I didn't know where I had been for a week of my life? "It doesn't make the slightest bit of difference," you said, and I thought you were being noble. But *of course* it didn't make a difference! You knew I had been with you!' She caught back a sob. 'How long was it before you realised you were going to have to offer to marry me? Did one of your servants warn you that Croxton had been asking questions? Was that the reason you came round here in such a hurry to put things right? Or was it because of the rumours spread by your friend Lady Barbara?'

He stared at her. 'I don't understand you. This is nonsense! Don't you remember how I loved you, wanted to marry you when we were at Hatherton, before I even knew who you were?'

'No, I don't!' she said desperately. 'I don't remember anything at all about Hatherton. All I know is that Lord Aldhurst is a…a creature I met for the first time at Marchant House, and he has lied to me, pretended, secretly laughed at me ever since…' Her breath caught in a sob. 'For all I know there could be truth in Lord Croxton's foul insinuations. *Was* I your mistress at Hatherton? Is *that* why you were in such a hurry to make your offer?'

'*Antonia!*'

'Yes, Father?'

'Apologise at once! Lord Aldhurst doesn't deserve such an accusation!'

'How do you know? Were you there, too?'

'Antonia!' Sir Henry stood up. 'My child, you're not yourself,' he said severely. 'You couldn't talk like this if you were. No, I wasn't there, but if *you* don't believe that Lord Aldhurst would always behave honourably to someone who was so entirely dependent on him, then *I* do!'

James had been standing absolutely still like a man who has just suffered a mortal blow. At last he said, 'I never intended you to learn the truth so brutally. I was waiting for your memory to come back of itself. But now…I can hardly believe it!

You mean you really don't remember anything of our time together at Hatherton? Even now?'

'No, I don't! I keep telling you I don't! And I don't want to!'

James came towards her, but she drew away from him. 'Antonia, please!' he said. 'I did what I thought was best. If I was mistaken, you must forgive me. I love you! Come here!'

Antonia's voice rose hysterically. 'No! Don't touch me! I want you to go away! Go away! I can hardly bear to look at you! Go away!'

Lady Pendell came in. 'I heard voices,' she said. 'You must forgive me, Lord Aldhurst, but you'll have to leave this till tomorrow. I don't know what it's all about, but Antonia is obviously not herself. She needs rest and quiet, and I'm taking to her bed immediately. You may call tomorrow if you wish to see how she is. Goodnight.'

She put her arm round Antonia's shoulders and led her out, before either of the men could say or do anything.

After the door had closed behind them there was a silence, then Sir Henry poured out two glasses of brandy and handed one to James. They sank into the armchairs and gazed at one another wordlessly. The silence was broken by Sir Henry.

'God damn Croxton to hell!' he said suddenly. This was so totally unlike the sober diplomat that James was surprised into a laugh. But the laugh was bitter and he recovered instantly.

'No doubt he'll find his way there sooner or later,' he said, and drank. 'But he seems to have taken me down with him.'

'You thought it was for the best. Don't think I don't appreciate the strain it must have put you under. After she had agreed to marry you it can't have been easy to keep up the pretence that you had only known her such a short time.'

'It was...quite a strain. I was tempted so often to remind her of how we—' He stopped. 'How much we really meant to one another...' James saw Antonia's father regarding him with just a hint of a question in his eyes. He shook his head. 'You were right. Antonia was quite safe with me at Hatherton. But I can't deny that there were moments when it came close...'

'Good! It's a comfort to know there's a perfectly normal young male underneath all that gentlemanly honour! Though I'm glad, of course, that you managed to keep him under control. Then and now.'

'I kept hoping she would remember...' James shrugged his shoulders. 'Well, that's past history now.' He drank up his brandy and Sir Henry refilled it without asking. James went on, 'I'm damned if I know what to do.'

Sir Henry gazed into the depths of his own glass for a moment. Then he said slowly, 'Antonia had always been very cool in her attitude to young men. She talks to them quite freely, but I have never known her to permit the slightest of intimacies from any of them. Until now. From what you've said—' He stopped and smiled. 'And even more from what you *haven't*, I would say that Antonia does love you. But she suffered an enormous shock tonight, and she's worried and confused. My sister is right. She needs peace and quiet. She'll be better able to think sensibly after a good night's rest.'

'I hope so. I really hope so. It's a devil of a coil if she can't. I meant what I said, Sir Henry. I love Antonia, but how can we continue with our engagement if she refuses to trust me? On the other hand, how can either of us be released from it? Now that the secret of her sojourn at Hatherton is out, *I* owe her the protection of my name, and *she* must accept it!'

Sir Henry shook his head. 'Leave it to the morning, Aldhurst. I am sorry about tonight, but I'm sure those who were there believed what we said. Any gossip will soon die down. And at least we are now rid of Croxton. We still have to repair some damage with my daughter, but I'm sure you'll be able to do that.'

Antonia slept heavily, largely because of the sleeping draught that Lady Pendell persuaded her to take. But towards morning she became restless, disturbed by nightmares. James was in them, James at Lady Marchant's ball, James in Hyde Park, James in her father's study asking her to marry him… This time his face was perfectly clear. He came towards her and she was filled with delight when she realised he was going to kiss her. But when he came close she could see he was wearing a mask. She pulled it away…and shrank back in horror, as she saw that the face behind the mask had no features at all. It was as smooth, as white, and as blank as that of an unfinished puppet. She woke up in a panic, her heart pounding, afraid of falling asleep again.

She lay wide awake till daylight, turning the previous night's events over and over in her mind.

Her aunt gave her breakfast in her room, and her father was waiting in his study when she eventually came downstairs. He came over and kissed her.

'Antonia, I'm glad to see you. Did you sleep well?' He looked at her pale face and heavy eyes. 'Not very well.'

'I had bad dreams, Papa. But that's all.'

'Then sit down and we'll have a talk.'

'There's certainly a great deal to talk about,' said Antonia. 'For instance, Papa, I'd like to know how long *you've* known that I was with Lord Aldhurst during that week. And why you didn't tell me.'

'I'm not sure you're yet in the right frame of mind to listen. But it will help if I begin by answering your second question first. Lord Aldhurst took expert advice about your loss of memory, and was told that you should be given as long as possible to remember without any prompting. I had heard much the same in Vienna, and that is what we have both tried to do.'

'How long have you known?' she repeated.

'Since the day after Lady Carteret's ball. He found out who you were at the ball, and came to see me as soon as he could. Do you…do you remember what happened, now that you've had time to recover?'

'No, Papa. I'd like you to tell me, please.'

'I think Lord Aldhurst should tell you that. He'll be here later.'

'I don't wish to see him.'

'Antonia, you must! The man is in love with you. He has acted throughout with honour and in what he thought were your best interests. In all fairness—'

'I don't wish to be fair! He may have done and been all you say, but I feel *betrayed.* I understand now why he sometimes looked at me as if he knew more about me than I did myself. He did! And when he k-kissed me, I could never understand why his kisses had such an effect on me. But *he* did! It must have amused him enormously!'

'I don't think he ever found the situation amusing, my dear. He loves you. If you loved him half as much, you would understand.'

'But I do! I love him, Papa. But I don't remember the other Lord Aldhurst, the one at Hatherton, the one who knows so much about me. How can

I love one without *knowing* the other? How can I trust either of them? How can I marry him?'

Sir Henry began to lose patience with her. He said forcibly, 'I suppose you must have had tantrums when you were a child, but I don't remember them. I've always been so proud of your ability to think in a rational, civilised manner. Now you must take control of your emotions and listen to me! James Aldhurst is an honourable and respected member of the most critical society in the world. Whatever your feelings may be at the moment, you must not let him down. If you refuse to see him, or try to break off your engagement, the world will begin to think that Croxton's version of events was not so far from the truth. James Aldhurst deserves a lot more of you than that.'

'But—'

'No, Antonia, I won't listen to you. You must see Lord Aldhurst and agree to keep up at least the pretence of an engagement until the gossip has had time to die down. After that you can sort things out as you think best. Though if I were you I shouldn't discard a man of Aldhurst's calibre without serious thought. You won't find many others like him.'

Chapter Seventeen

James had been deeply hurt by Antonia's words. Ever since he had found her lying on the drive to Hatherton he had worked hard to protect and cherish her. He had ignored his own feelings in order to do what he thought was best, and had held back with difficulty on many occasions when it would have been easier to tell her the truth. He came to see her the following morning, sure that she would realise how monstrously unjust she had been to him, and be willing to accept his reasons for keeping the truth from her. And he was ready to offer her all his comfort and love until she recovered from the experience.

But Antonia had woken up unrefreshed after a night haunted by nightmares, and was in no mood to listen to reason. Her father's unaccustomed severity had also affected her badly, and she felt lost and bewildered. When James came she listened without interruption to his patient explanation, but it made not the slightest difference to her feelings. When he would have taken her hand she pulled it back.

'I'm sorry, but how can I marry you when I still feel I don't really know you at all?' she asked despairingly. 'I can't do it!'

This rebuff was the last straw, and James finally lost patience with her. Pale and grim, he said curtly, 'Then I see no point in prolonging this discussion. It's clear that you regard me as a villain, whatever I say. I am disappointed, Antonia. It is, of course, your choice whether we continue with our engagement, but after last night I have an obligation to you in the eyes of the world. I think you would be wise to wait a little before breaking it. To end it would provoke just the sort of gossip we have so far managed to avoid.'

Sir Henry intervened. 'Lord Aldhurst is right! What is more, I won't *allow* you to end it! You would be ruined, Antonia. Aldhurst, give me time to talk to my daughter. Surely you can see that she is still in a state of shock?'

James hesitated, then said, 'I'm in something of a state of shock myself. I would never have imagined that Antonia would lose her trust in me so completely. I had thought that what we had would survive any test.' He was silent for a moment. 'I think we would both be happy not to see each other for a while. I shall leave London tomorrow. Don't worry—I'll find some excuse that will keep the gossips quiet.' His tone was carefully neutral as he said to Antonia, 'Can I assume that the engagement can stand until we see each other again?'

Antonia nodded without speaking and he said, 'Good! Then I will take my leave of you both. I…I hope this break will help us both out of…out of a most unhappy situation. I never thought—' He stopped. 'It doesn't matter.' He gave each of them a brief bow. 'Miss Calverley, Sir Henry!' And he left.

After he had gone, Sir Henry said sternly, 'I only hope you don't live to rue this morning's work, Antonia! You've never done a worse one.'

Meanwhile, back in Brook Street, Lady Aldhurst sat in her chair by the window, a cashmere shawl draped over her arms and a glass of wine and a pile of papers on the table next to her. She was reading her copy of the *Gazette*, which contained the morning's announcement of Lord Aldhurst's engagement to Miss Antonia Calverley, with relief and the greatest pleasure. James had not only kept his word to choose a bride before the Season was over, he had found a girl with breeding, character and looks. Antonia Calverley was exactly what he needed.

Now that the future of the Aldhurst family was settled, the temptation to return to Hatherton was very strong. Her course of treatment had been successful and she was feeling much better. And she missed the place. The gardens would be looking particularly lovely at this time of year, and the thought of their peace and tranquillity attracted her more every day. What if she invited Antonia and her family to visit her there to celebrate the engagement?

She was astonished when James came in soon after to tell her that he was leaving London the next day.

'Nonsense! You can't possibly leave Antonia the day after your engagement is announced in the *Gazette*!'

'It's the only way the engagement will continue, ma'am! And there's no guarantee it will survive my return.'

'But *why*? You are ideally suited!'

'I would have thought so, too—but the lady is no longer so sure,' he said curtly. 'And perhaps I'm beginning to agree with her!'

'But you mustn't cry off! Think of the scandal!'

'I can't *force* the girl to marry me, ma'am!' He stopped and then said more calmly, 'That's why I'm going away for a while—to give Antonia time to think of the consequences.'

He refused to say any more on the subject, merely stating that he had an afternoon appointment in the city, which he would have to keep, but that he would leave the next day.

His grandmother looked at his set face and decided it was useless to argue. James was unreachable. He had been deeply hurt, and as usual had withdrawn into himself, rejecting any attempt to sympathise or advise. She would have to find another way to rescue the situation. So that afternoon she called on Miss Calverley in Upper Grosvenor Street to request a private interview. Antonia could not refuse to grant one.

Lady Aldhurst wasted no time in coming to the point. 'I don't think anyone could call me a doting grandmother, Miss Calverley, but I *am* very fond of James, and I'm worried about him. Is it true that you no longer wish to marry him?'

'Is that what he says?' Antonia asked.

'Yes, but I cannot believe it! I would have sworn you were as much in love with him as he was with you. You've hurt him very badly, Miss Calverley. James doesn't wear his heart on his sleeve, but his feelings run deep, all the same. What has gone wrong?'

'I...I can't tell you.'

'Of course you can, girl! In fact, at the moment you seem to be as miserable as he is!'

Antonia's expression was stony. 'Lady Aldhurst,' she said, 'if your grandson had loved me as much as you say, he would have told me about Hatherton as soon as he met me again. He must have known how desperately anxious I was to know what had happened in that lost week, but he said nothing. *Nothing!* And I can't forgive him for it.'

'But surely he has explained *why* he didn't tell you!'

'That it was for my own good? Yes, he tried to say that. It doesn't appear to have been very successful, does it? I've been *told* about Hatherton now, but I still can't visualise anything about my time there, not what I did, not what I felt... I can't even remember James himself! Croxton's desire to ruin me is understandable. It was James, whom I loved and trusted, who really betrayed me—' Antonia stopped and got up. Obviously struggling for calm, she said, 'Lady Aldhurst, I'm sure you wish to be helpful, but I don't see the point of this discussion.'

'Sit down, girl! Sit down!' Lady Aldhurst waited until Antonia was seated again, and then said slowly, 'I hadn't realised that you *still* don't remember Hatherton... Of course you won't feel secure until you do! James is a fool not to have seen that for himself. But the remedy is obvious. You must go back to Hatherton, and *I* shall take you. It will give you something to do while he is away.'

Antonia was doubtful, but Lady Aldhurst could be very persuasive. Sir Henry's permission was soon obtained, and it was settled that Lady Aldhurst would take her grandson's betrothed with her when she returned to Hatherton. Sir Henry made one condition—Lawson should accompany Antonia at all times until they knew for certain that Croxton had left England.

When James returned to Brook Street that evening he sought his grandmother out. 'Is it true that you are taking Antonia to Hatherton, ma'am?' he demanded.

'She *must* go back! I'm surprised you hadn't already thought of it yourself! After I had spoken to her it was obvious what the situation was.'

'I *had* thought of it, had even planned it, but after last night I decided I couldn't do it.'

'Why not?'

'You probably wouldn't understand.'

'You never know, James,' said Lady Aldhurst drily. 'Old as I am, I may have a few ideas. Try to explain.'

'The girl I called "Anne" was so…so vulnerable. She gave me her complete trust throughout her stay with me at Hatherton. And now… now I seem to have lost it. I don't believe that taking Antonia there will help, and… To tell the truth, ma'am, I can't bear the thought of seeing her look at me there as she looked at me last night and this morning—with such rejection, such condemnation in her eyes.'

'I see… Well, James, I think I *can* understand,' said Lady Aldhurst after a while, 'but I'm not sure *you* do. Consider for a moment. That girl was under enormous stress from the moment she arrived in London. She can't have stopped wondering where she had been and what she had been doing during that forgotten week, waiting for someone to say something, dreading the moment when the axe would fall. And when it did fall it was cruelly delivered. Croxton revealed the truth brutally and without warning in front of every-one at the Furnesses' party. That shock was bad enough, but Antonia could have survived it. It was infinitely worse when she learnt at the same time that *you* had known the truth all along. You could have eased her mind, prepared her for the shock, and you had chosen not to. You may have meant well, James, but in the event you failed her. I can understand her feelings of resentment towards you, even if I think she's wrong.'

'That is all very well, ma'am, but I'm not sure what I can do about it now.'

'It's obvious what must be done! She needs to be reminded of what Hatherton meant to you both. The sense of security you gave her must be restored before she can forgive you. And in my opinion Hatherton is where she will find it.'

'Will she ever forgive me? From what you have said, she has every reason not to.'

'She'll forgive you, James. She loves you. Listen to me. I am taking Miss Calverley to Hatherton, and have invited Sir Henry and Lady Pendell to follow a few days later. I don't know what you are planning to do, but you might think of seeing how Roade's restoration is getting on.' She smiled. 'From what I've heard, you can't have spent much time on it when you were last there.'

James said thoughtfully, 'I could stay at Roade...'

'An excellent idea! Have faith, James! I haven't the slightest doubt that Antonia Calverley loves you! Go down to Roade and prepare it for occupation. Then join us when you're ready to face her again.'

James left London the next day, and Lady Aldhurst sent an announcement to the *Gazette* to the effect that she was taking Miss Calverley with her to Hathcrton. Lord Aldhurst was to join them there as soon as his business affairs permitted. Sir Henry Calverley and Lady Pendell would also join her in the near future for a family celebration.

'That should silence the gossips!' she said to herself when she read it through. 'Now for Antonia!'

The weather was kind to Lady Aldhurst and Antonia on the journey, and though it was early evening by the time they arrived at Hatherton the house was bathed in sunshine. Lady Aldhurst put her hand on Antonia's arm and said, 'The servants have been told to treat you simply as a guest of mine. Hatherton is a lovely spot. Enjoy it for its own sake, without feeling obliged to remember anything at all.'

'When do you think James will join us?'

'I've really no idea how long his business will take.' She gave Antonia a quizzical look. 'Do you think you'll miss him?'

'No! That is to say—'

'Good! We shall forget him for the moment. Now here we are! You must meet my house-keeper, Mrs Culver.'

So this was the redoubtable Mrs Culver, Antonia thought. She looked just as Lady Barbara had described her. Respectable, severe, unbending, showing no sign of knowing her.

'Miss Calverley,' she said with a slightly stiff inclination of the head. 'I expect you would like to be shown your room. Would you follow me, please?'

Once inside the room Antonia walked over to the window and looked out.

'Miss?' The voice came from behind her. One

of the maids was waiting. 'Mrs Culver has asked me to help you change.'

Antonia slowly turned round. 'Thank you,' she said absently. 'I'll wear the green muslin, Rose.'

'Oh, Miss Anne! Mrs Culver said you wouldn't remember us—but you do!'

'Do I?' Antonia looked at the girl more closely. 'I called you Rose, didn't I? I remember...I think you helped me.' She added uncertainly, 'You want to be a lady's maid? Is that right?'

Rose laughed in delight, but then grew serious. 'Yes. I do, Miss...Miss Calverley. It's so lovely to have you back. And to know that you're safe, too!'

'Safe?' said Antonia, looking round the room. 'Safe? Yes, I do feel safe here... This was my room, wasn't it?'

'Yes, miss,' said Rose, busy with the dresses. 'You spent most of your time in this room when you first came. You were so ill that first night.'

'Was I?'

'His lordship sat with you most of the night.'

'I remember being very thirsty...' Antonia could feel it now. Hot, dry, raging thirst... A calm voice, a man's arm supporting her while she drank...

* * *

The hall clock was chiming six as Antonia came downstairs. Lady Aldhurst had not yet appeared and the dining room was empty. She wandered round the room and stopped in front of a portrait of a young lady in an old-fashioned striped dress. She had seen herself in that dress in the mirror in London, looking like a girl about to meet the man she loved. And the man she had met that same evening in London had been James. But the man, here at Hatherton, had been James, too.

'Do you like it, Antonia?' Lady Aldhurst came into the room. 'It was painted shortly after I was married. The pearls were a wedding gift from James.' She added with a smile, '*My* James. I still wear them quite often.'

'They're…they're beautiful. So is the…the dress.'

'Yes. It's in a clothes press upstairs. I could never bring myself to give it away. James always loved it.' For a moment she looked sad, then she straightened her shoulders and said, 'Don't stand about, girl! Sit down, sit down! Culver is waiting to serve!'

They had a lively conversation over dinner in which neither James nor Antonia's recent experiences were mentioned, and by the time the meal was over Antonia was exhausted. Her hostess took one look at her heavy eyes and gave a crack of laughter. 'Go to bed, child!' she said. 'I think you'll sleep tonight. I enjoyed our conversation and would like to continue it tomorrow. But for now, go to bed before you fall asleep in that chair!'

Antonia was only too glad to obey. The combination of so many recent sleepless nights, the journey, the odd sensation of knowing and yet not knowing this house and the people in it...all these combined to produce a desire for nothing so much as sleep. Rose dealt with her almost in silence, and Antonia was soon in bed.

The room was in darkness except for the embers in the hearth. Her own voice came out of the dark. 'Your name is James Aldhurst,' she heard herself say. 'This is your grandmother's house.' And full of warmth and comfort, she slid into sleep.

When Antonia woke the next morning Rose was opening the curtains and sunlight was streaming in through the windows. 'Good morning, miss!' she said as she came over to the bed. 'Your breakfast is here.' She busied herself about the room while Antonia ate her breakfast. 'I expect Mrs Culver was pleased to see you,' she said as she put Antonia's dresses away. 'She was that worried about you, especially after his lordship gave her such a roasting. To tell you the truth I was quite sorry for her. I've never seen him as angry as he was after you left here. She tried to tell him you'd be safe, but he wouldn't listen. And then he was off like the wind after you. Of course, we could all tell even then how fond of you he was…' She paused and her cheeks were pink as she added, 'We're all so happy that you're going to marry him.'

After breakfast Antonia went along to Lady Aldhurst's room. She found her hostess sitting up in bed propped up against a pile of pillows.

'Goodness gracious, child! What are you doing up and about so early? I expected you to be in bed till noon. Did you sleep well?'

'Very well, ma'am, thank you,' Antonia replied.

'Hmm,' said Lady Aldhurst, eyeing her. 'Well, you needn't expect me to entertain you much before midday! What will you do till then?'

'I'd like…I'd like to go for a walk in the garden. May I?'

'Of course! You'll be perfectly safe in my garden.' Lady Aldhurst settled back more comfortably against her pillows. 'I don't think you'll get lost—you might even find someone,' she added with a smile.

Antonia went downstairs, stood for a moment in the hall, and then followed a corridor that led to the back of the house and out into a herb garden. Here she stopped to enjoy the dry herby sharpness in the air and saw a stone-flagged path leading towards a gate at the far end. The gate was open, but when she went through to the garden beyond the spring flowers she had half-expected to see had gone, and it all looked so different that she felt obscurely disappointed. But the grey stone walls were familiar, though roses were rioting over them now. There had been pots of lavender... Yes, here they were! And honeysuckle... She knelt down to inspect some tiny leaves half-hidden under a bank of lilies. These had been violets, purple violets. The flowers had gone, but the memory of their delicate fragrance remained. She gazed at the leaves, lost in thought. Was that why James had sent her violets in London? Had he hoped she would remember these violets in this garden? She had felt comforted by them... As she wandered on she could remember the feel of a man's strong hand holding hers; she could hear a voice full of warmth, of assurance... The hand must have been James's hand, the voice James's voice... She had needed his comfort. 'You cannot imagine what it feels like to live with only half a mind,' she had cried in despair. 'I'm in limbo!'

She remembered the warmth of his body as he drew her back against him. 'You're not in limbo, you're in the garden at Hatherton,' he had replied. 'And you're living with me, not half a mind. I'm better than that.' Antonia smiled. It had been so like James—the care, the warmth, the humour. She grinned as she remembered the expression of outrage on his face when he found she had tricked him over the game of chess that same evening... He had kissed her—for punishment, he said, but she had not felt it a punishment. Then they had laughed together.

She saw a bench at the end of the path and stood for a while looking at it. This was the bench she had seen in her dreams, though she had not recognised the figure sitting on it. Now she knew it had been James. Could the locked doors in her mind be opening? She sat down in the sunshine, surrounded by the scents and colours of Lady

Aldhurst's garden, and let her mind wander. She and James had ridden up to Roade the day after the chess game. She had seen it in her mind's eye in London without knowing where it was, but now she knew. A house of creamy-grey stone, more beautiful than any she had seen in Richmond. But for James it had held only memories of a bleak and neglected childhood... She had wanted to change it for him, make it live once again, to be the happy place it could and should have been. And for a few minutes they had managed it, as they danced in an empty room, and filled it with music and enchantment. And love. Passionate love. James had loved her. With welling happiness she realised what it meant to her that she, and no other, had been 'the girl in green'. James had loved her, and loved her still. He had looked after her, cared for her in London in the same way he had cared for her at Hatherton. And she had repaid him with anger, accusing him of betraying her, refusing to marry him. How deeply hurt he must have been!

Antonia jumped up and ran to the gate. She must find out where James was, go to him, tell him how much she loved him, and beg him to forgive her.

* * *

She ran back through the herb garden to the house. A stocky figure of a man had just arrived at the door. He looked worried. 'Good morning, ma'am,' he called, touching his hat. 'I'd like to speak to his lordship, if you please. My name is Holford.'

'His lordship isn't here. And I'm afraid I must—'

Holford shifted uncomfortably. 'Are you sure he isn't, ma'am? I don't wish to offend, but I could have sworn I saw him passing the end of the lane just a few days ago. It's important.'

Antonia saw that Lawson, ever watchful, was coming to join them. 'Mr Holford wants to talk to Lord Aldhurst. Do you know where he is?'

'Not here,' said Lawson. 'Nor is Sam Trott.'

The mention of the groom seemed to reassure Holford. 'If Sam Trott is with him I don't suppose there's much danger. I just thought it might be better if his lordship knew...'

Lady Aldhurst's voice came from behind. 'Good morning, Holford! Knew what?'

Holford shifted uneasily. 'It's like this. We had a couple of villains in the neighbourhood a while back. They wrecked a coach on my land, but we never caught them.' Antonia let out a cry. Holford stopped, but when she stayed silent he went on, 'I saw them last night at the Rose and Crown. They were asking questions about his lordship's whereabouts, so I kept quiet and listened. They had someone else with them—a gentleman, but he was in the private parlour. I heard Norris call him "my lord".'

Antonia looked at Lawson. 'Briggs and his friend with a lord? That's Croxton! But what is he doing here?'

Holford glanced at Lady Aldhurst. 'Nothing good, I'll swear. If his lordship was here I'd warn him to be on his guard. They're three very ugly customers, and from what I heard they don't mean him well.'

'That's very likely! They're almost certainly out for revenge,' said Antonia. She turned to Lady Aldhurst who, in spite of her brave words, was looking pale. 'He's safe, ma'am. They won't find him here.'

Lady Aldhurst shook her head. 'James isn't safe at all! He's up at Roade.'

'Roade? But I thought...' Antonia drew a breath. 'They *will* find him!' she said blankly. 'He's in danger, and he doesn't know!' She turned and ran into the house, but Lady Aldhurst was too preoccupied to notice.

Turning to Holford, she said, 'Holford, you must round up some of the men, and go up to Roade House at once. Hurry!'

'I'll do my best, your ladyship. But it'll take more than a minute or two—they're all working over in the seven-acre field today.'

'Go as quickly as you can. Go on, man! Lawson, how many men are there in the stable block?'

'I didn't see that many. Sam Trott is with his lordship, of course, and two of the others went off this morning to the market.'

'Why the devil are these people never there when you need them? Go back and see if anyone is back!' In spite of her brave words Lady Aldhurst was worried. 'Antonia!' She looked round. 'Where has *she* gone now? Rose! Find Miss Calverley!'

When Lawson came back from the stables he was shaking his head. 'No one back yet.'

Lady Aldhurst drew in a breath and said, 'Then we shall have to hope Holford finds his men sooner than he thought!'

Lawson said, 'I'll go to warn his lordship, my lady.'

'It's hardly enough. What *are* we to do? Antonia will have to take the chaise to Guildford to let the magistrate know we need him. Where *is* she? Ah! There you are, Antonia! Good girl! You're ready!'

Antonia had changed her muslin and sandals for a riding habit and boots. 'Fetch the horses, Lawson,' she said briskly. 'I'm going to Roade. Holford's men won't be here for a good half-hour, and it's more urgent than that.'

She ignored Lady Aldhurst's objections, calling over her shoulder as she made for the stables. 'I'm sorry, ma'am, I haven't time to argue. I have to reach James before those others do. I know Croxton. James has to be warned. Lawson, are you coming?'

Lady Aldhurst could only stare as, after a moment or two, Antonia and Lawson galloped past on their way to the bridle path that led up to Roade. She turned into the house and called for Mrs Culver. Someone else would have to go to Guildford with a note requesting the presence of the law.

Chapter Eighteen

James frowned as he drew up outside Roade. When he had driven over the bridge he could have sworn he had seen movement in the big saloon… yet he had left his agent behind in Guildford, and the builders were working only in the outbuildings at the back of the house. That room should have been absolutely empty, even of furniture. He strode through the hall, throwing his whip and gloves aside as he went—but came to a sudden stop at the big doors that led through into the room. Croxton was waiting for him over by the window.

'Ah, there you are!' he said.

'What the devil are you doing here?' James demanded without moving.

'I should have thought that was obvious. I've come to see you. We have some unfinished business.'

'Well, I'm afraid *I* don't want to see *you*! Get out!' James started towards his unwelcome visitor, but he was attacked without warning by two men who had been waiting unseen behind the door. He fought fiercely, but was hopelessly outnumbered and before long he was held with his hands pinned behind his back, facing Croxton. The men had been rough and their hold was tight and painful, but James ignored the discomfort and looked with contempt at the man standing a few feet away.

Croxton was thinner and paler and his former air of sleek self-satisfaction had been replaced by a look of feverish malevolence. He regarded James with triumph.

'Look at you now!' he said. 'It's a different story now, isn't it? No admiring public to applaud you, no smug hypocrites to foist their daughters on you.' He looked round at the empty room. 'Is this where you brought her? It's a poor place to bring your doxy, I must say. I'm disappointed in you, Aldhurst, I thought you had style.'

'Hold your foul tongue, Croxton! Try to remember you were once a gentleman! Miss Calverley is no concern of yours.'

'You're the one to hold your tongue,' said

Croxton viciously. 'Miss Calverley, our virtuous Antonia, is very much my concern. She and her meddling father have ruined me! And now *you* can pay for that along with all the rest.' Croxton pulled out a pistol.

James braced himself. It was unlikely that anyone would come to his rescue. Though the outbuildings at the back were overrun with workmen, the rest of the house was deserted. He had dropped Sam Trott off at the lodge gates. But he must try something.

'I suppose you think you can get away with murdering me, Croxton. You're off to the West Indies. But what about these two? Are you taking them with you? Briggs is known. He won't be safe in England after this.'

Briggs started to say something, but Croxton interrupted. 'Don't listen to him! You're being paid enough to take care of yourself!'

'But I'd like to know…' James felt Briggs relax his grip. There might be hope yet.

'There's no time for argument! Mind you don't get in the way of this!' Croxton snarled. He lifted the pistol and pointed it at James. There was a click as he cocked it…

* * *

Antonia had pushed her horse as hard as she dared, full of the need to reach Roade. She had no doubt that Croxton was out to kill James. James had humiliated him in front of the very people who had formerly revered him most. And his last act before leaving England for good would be to take his revenge.

There was no sign of anyone outside the house, though they could hear sounds of hammering and sawing at the back. The front looked deserted. Antonia came to a halt in front of the porch and leapt down. She threw her reins to Lawson and ran inside. Without a second thought she went straight through to the big saloon.

As she reached the doors, she felt as if her heart had stopped. It was too late to warn James. He was being held fast by the two men who had abducted her. She heard him say, 'I suppose you think you can get away with murdering me, Croxton. You're on your way to the West Indies. But what about these two? Are you taking them with you? Briggs is known. He won't be safe in England after this...'

Not sure what she could do, she looked round frantically for something—anything—she could use for a weapon, and saw the whip James had put down on his way in. She snatched it up and went back to the doorway.

Briggs was now arguing with Croxton, and she thought for a moment there was a chance they would fall out. But then Croxton lifted the pistol and pointed it straight at James. She heard a click as he cocked it…

James mustn't die! Not when she had just found out what he meant to her! Frantically she leapt forwards and let fly with the whip. The leather thong flew out in a tall arc and wrapped itself in a vicious loop round Croxton's wrist. He let out a howl and the weapon exploded harmlessly into the air. With a roar like a wild beast Croxton grabbed the end of the whip and dragged Antonia towards him. Before she could stop him his claw-like hands were tight round her throat, choking the life out of her… Confusion and noise broke out as James threw his captors off and was on to Croxton, dragging those murderous hands away from her throat. Croxton thrust her aside and turned on James like a madman.

Antonia lay where she had fallen, dimly aware that others had come into the saloon. Croxton and James were fighting, but Lawson was there, and so was Sam Trott. They were dealing with a demoralised Briggs and his friend, and, as she watched, she saw Croxton drop like a stone as James's fist met his jaw. She was still trying to get up when James came back to her. He lifted her in his arms and held her tightly to him. 'Are you all right?' he asked urgently.

Her throat felt too sore to speak, but she nodded.

'Thank God!' Holding her close, he looked round. Lawson was trussing Croxton up like a chicken. His two accomplices were already out of action.

'Sam, go to the workers' foreman and get him to bring one of his carts round to the entrance. We'll send these three down to Hatherton and lock them in the cellars until they can be picked up. If Miss Calverley is happy to be left here, Lawson and I will take them to the door and they can be picked up there. Will you be all right here for minute or two, Antonia?'

Once again Antonia nodded, and he set her gently on the floor. 'I won't be long,' he said with a smile.

She tried to use the moments before his return to decide what she could say. But she saw James

coming back into the saloon and was over-
whelmed with an impossible mixture of love, remorse and fear. She couldn't say anything. He
stood and looked at her. 'Well?' he asked.

Antonia gave a sob and ran to him, finding
her voice on the way. 'Oh, James, I love you so
much!' she cried.

He held her off. 'Is this Antonia talking? Or is
it Anne?'

'It's both. I've remembered all of it. And James,
please, please, I know I don't deserve it, but you
must forgive me! I...I couldn't live without you.'

By way of answer James wrapped his arms
round her holding her so tightly that she could
hardly breathe. 'I'd forgive you anything as long
as you love me, Anne-Antonia. Darling Anne-
Antonia.' He kissed her again and again, and she
clung to him, responding with all her being.

Then gradually he began to waltz with her round
the empty room. 'Here at Roade we Aldhursts
always dance the waltz wearing riding boots, you
know,' he said gravely when she protested. 'It's
an old family tradition.'

But the waltz they danced was interspersed
with kisses and murmurs of love, with hardly an

inch between them as they danced. It would have shocked the chaperons of Europe to the core.

At the end James swept Antonia up into his arms and held her there. Kissing her, he said, 'Will you live here at Roade with me? Will you join me in making a home where our children will be happy? Will you love me almost as much as I love you?'

'Yes, yes and more than!'

James began to laugh. 'Impossible! For I love you even when you look as you do now!'

'What do you mean? What do you mean "as you do now"?'

He took her to one of the mirrors. 'You may not have a squint, my darling, but you have a very fine black eye!' He laughed out loud at her wail of dismay. 'And I still love you to distraction!' he went on as he kissed her again.

They were still wrapped in each other's arms when Lady Aldhurst came in. 'I had to see for myself that you were both safe,' she said. 'But I must say I'm glad I didn't bring Lawson with me. I'm not sure *what* he would have told your father! I take it you've decided to marry after all? I certainly hope so—from the look of it, the wedding can't take place a moment too soon!

Good gracious, Antonia, what *have* you done to your eye? Never mind, child! Come and kiss me. Roade has been waiting for you for twenty years or more. And the Aldhursts are delighted to welcome you at last.'

* * * * *